All the Right Answers

All the Right Answers

by

Robert Noah

HARCOURT BRACE JOVANOVICH, PUBLISHERS

San Diego   New York   London

Library of Congress Cataloging-in-Publication Data

Noah, Robert, 1926–
    All the right answers: a novel/by Robert Noah.—1st ed.
      p. cm.
   ISBN 0-15-104779-0
   I. Title.
  PS3564.023A78 1988
  813'.54—dc19 88-14767

Designed by G.B.D. Smith

Printed in the United States of America

First edition

A B C D E

For Marian

All the Right Answers

1

THE NEWSPAPER INTERVIEWS WITH MIKE ALWAYS REFERRED TO the office as his penthouse suite, high above Madison Avenue. Even the story that ran in *Time*. Stu howled at that one. He had the clipping blown up and framed, and it hung on the wall right over his head. Afterward, he used it as exhibit A in his famous rationale. Who are they, he'd ask, to talk about us for misleading? Everybody builds illusions. I mean, look at this place. Is this what you'd call a penthouse suite?

He was right about that. It was a penthouse, it was a suite, and it was on Madison Avenue. But when you added it all up, the whole came to less than the sum of its parts.

The building was in the Sixties, up where Madison had started to show its age, even then. There were two glass-doored, brass-caged elevators that had recently been converted to self-service, and that clattered and lurched their way to the top, on days when they were running at all. Only the one on the left went all the way to the penthouse, so naturally that was the one that kept breaking down.

At the top, a massive steel door that had once led out to the roof now opened on an afterthought of offices that an enterprising management had hammered together right after World War II. The reception room was fluorescent, with the kind of muddy blonde furniture that looked as if it had started life on sale. The offices were faded brown walls and chipped wooden desks. Even the fresh coat of paint that Stu finally sprang for after the show was renewed didn't cover very much. I don't know whether Stu refused to move because he thought the place was lucky, or because deep down he knew his empire was built on fragile supports and one day had to come crashing down. But when things were going great, and that was for a couple of years, he could have afforded any suite in town.

The newspaper guys saw the same place we saw when they came up to interview Mike. But they all automatically called it his penthouse offices high above Madison Avenue because that was the groove the story seemed to want to slip into. Mike Prince was a glamorous figure then; a television star. They knew what people wanted to hear.

In the years after all of it collapsed, I had lots of time to think about truth and lies and illusion, and whether or not the last two are really the same. I don't think they are. I never took the comfort some of the others did from the notion that at least some of the time everybody builds illusions. What we were involved in was not simply an illusion; it was a lie that had grown in enormity until it towered over us all. And it was clearly wrong. I'd known that from the beginning.

It was ten after six and my appointment had been for five-thirty. For a while there'd been a parade of people saying goodnight, but for the past few minutes things had been quiet and I'd been alone with the receptionist and a loudly ticking brass alarm clock that sat on top of the switchboard. Then the door to the inner office opened again and a short, trim, efficient package of a woman bustled into the room. She ignored me and spoke to the receptionist.

"How late are you staying?"

The receptionist shrugged. "He's still on the phone. This gentleman had a five-thirty."

She nodded and turned to me. "Can anyone else help you?"

"Not really," I said. "I'm supposed to see Mr. Leonard about a job."

She smiled suddenly and stuck out her hand. "I'm Astrid Knudsen," she said. "He should be with you soon." She turned back to the receptionist. "How long's he been on this call?"

"Almost an hour."

Astrid smiled at me again. "Then I'm sure he won't be long."

I shook my head. "Just the opposite," I said. "The longer a phone call's gone on, the longer it's likely to continue."

She looked at me for a moment. "Why is that?"

"Beats me. That's just the rule."

"I see," she said.

A buzzer sounded on the switchboard, and the receptionist pulled the cord. "He's off," she said.

Astrid laughed. "Better luck with the rest of your rules." And she left.

The switchboard buzzed again, and the receptionist plugged in. "Yes, Mr. Leonard," she said. There was a long pause, then another "Yes, Mr. Leonard." She looked up at me. "He has to make one more call. He says it will only be a minute."

I nodded and sat down again and picked up a copy of *Variety* on the theory that if I got this job I might as well start learning a little something about the business. The receptionist placed the call, then pulled out a mirror on a stand and started doing things to her face. After a few minutes, she leaned back and sighed.

"Toby has beautiful hair, doesn't she?"

I looked up from the Weekly Grosses. "Who's Toby?"

"Oh, that's right. She introduced herself as Astrid."

"Astrid is Toby?"

"Astrid's her real name, but everybody calls her Toby. You see, she has this thing on her desk she keeps her pencils in. It's shaped like a pirate's head, and the first day she was here Perry—he's the office boy—asked her what it was, and she said it was a Toby jug. That's what it's called. Perry told Stu, and he—" She stopped suddenly. "I shouldn't really be telling you this. I mean, it's a little personal."

"Make believe we're old friends."

She shrugged. "I mean, it's just silly, but I don't know how you'll take it."

"I'm sure it's something I can handle."

"Well, anyway," she went on, enjoying it, "Stu thought he said 'You ought to see Toby's jugs.' " She laughed. "So she's been Toby ever since."

I smiled politely.

"I knew you wouldn't be offended," she said. She went back to her eye makeup and managed to keep herself busy for the ten minutes before Stu Leonard finished his phone call and buzzed her again.

"He's ready to see you," she said, and I went in.

The job was writing for a puppet show Stu Leonard Productions did on Saturday mornings. I'd never seen it, being several years past the upper limit of its viewing audience, but I'd had it described to me on the phone by a gentleman named Frank Dean, about whom you'll be hearing more later. At this point I hadn't yet met Frank Dean, but I learned about the job from him through a chain of interrelated girlfriends, wives, and brothers that's too complicated to go into. Everybody I knew was aware I was getting desperate about work with the newspaper strike heading into its ninth week. Here I'd finally managed to land a job as a reporter with the *New York Journal-American* after five years on the paper in Waterbury, Connecticut; and not a month after I'd started, the International Typographers Union had pulled its members out and shut every paper in town up tight. Now, almost nine weeks later, my life's savings, some six hundred and fifty dollars, had just about disappeared and I was getting desperate for a job. Just something to tide me over, you understand. Just something temporary.

Temporary, indeed. The French, I've been told, have a proverb that goes, "Nothing is so permanent as the temporary." If the French really do have such a proverb, my hat's off to them. If not, I can only recommend that they jot this one down. As proverbs go, it's dynamite.

The dim light from one lamp was all that relieved the darkness in Stu Leonard's office, but he was large enough so there was no trouble finding him. He must have been six five and weighed I couldn't begin to guess how many pounds. He had long, shaggy hair and a full beard that came to a devil's point. He was leaning over his desk writing something and without looking up he signaled me to a chair. He finished writing, put the cap back on the black fountain pen he always kept on his desk, and creaked his chair back to what seemed to be a dangerous angle.

"Frank Dean tells me you're a reporter."

"I was," I nodded.

"What happens when the strike is over?"

I was ready for this one. It was like applying for a summer job and telling the boss you weren't going back to college. Either you lied or you didn't get it.

"If this works out, it's exactly what I want. I won't be going back."

He shook his head. "That's not what I'm worried about. This job's only for a few weeks, anyway." Frank Dean hadn't told me that. "I'll tell you what I'm nervous about."

He stopped and stared at me, and I had the feeling that unless I asked the question he wasn't going on.

"What's that?" I asked.

"You work here for a while, you'll find out a lot about us.

5

This may not be General Motors, but we have our own trade secrets. Six months from now, I wouldn't want to be reading them with my morning coffee."

"The *Journal-American*'s an afternoon paper."

He smiled. "You see, you take it lightly. I don't." He leaned forward again and shoved the piece of paper he'd been working on toward me. "Read that," he said.

It was in the form of a letter addressed to him. It was dated February 8, 1956, and it read: "I hereby agree that both while I am an employee of Stuart Leonard Productions, and after such employment terminates, I will fully respect the privacy and confidentiality of anything I might have learned here." There was a place at the bottom for me to sign. It seemed pretty inclusive, but I nodded anyway and started reaching for a pen. I wanted this job.

"Hold it," he said. "Let's talk for a minute. Maybe there won't be any point."

So we talked. Or rather, he did. It was something he was good at. But, of course, he had the upper hand. He had me hanging on every word because I was trying to figure out what I had to say to nail this down. He asked me a couple of questions about myself, but mostly he held forth about Stuart Leonard Productions, "Corky's Gang" (that was the puppet show), and whether or not Adlai Stevenson was likely to try again for the Democratic nomination. Yes, said Stu. Even though he can't win in November, no matter how sick Ike is. Stu was very into politics. One of these days, he was going to chuck all this and get in with both feet. That's where the real excitement was.

"Okay," he said finally. "The job pays two and a quarter, maybe two fifty. That sound all right?"

"I'd need two fifty," I said quickly. Why should I pick the lower figure?

"Okay," he said, having been fully prepared to go to three hundred. "Now you can sign, if you're still willing to." I nodded and started to pick up the fountain pen on the desk, but he stopped me. "No, please," he said quickly. "Everybody's touch is different. That point's worn in just right for me." He shoved a ballpoint toward me and I signed. He picked up the paper.

"I doubt that it's very legal," he said. "But it might some day be a good reminder for both of us that it's something we talked about."

"When do I start?" I asked.

"Tomorrow. The office opens at nine-thirty." We shook hands, and as I started out he was putting the piece of paper into a folder in the file drawer in his desk. I was to see that paper again.

The drugstore downstairs had condoms in the window. Frank Dean pointed them out to me as we went in for lunch. Sol Block, one of the two brothers who owned the place, waved to him.

"What's good today?" Frank asked.

"The chopped sirloin at Barney's, up the street. Delicious."

Frank laughed and introduced me to him. Then we went to one of the small marble tables in the back.

"I usually sit at the counter," Frank said. "But this seems more sociable."

The trick was to get there before twelve-fifteen. After that, it started to fill up and pretty much stay that way till two o'clock. We ordered hamburgers, which came on slices of rye, and I had a chocolate malted. Weight was no problem back then.

"I told Nicole where we'd be," Frank said. Nicole was the girl at the switchboard. "Don't forget to do that when you go out. He gets crazy when he doesn't know. Actually, he gets crazy when you go to lunch. He always has to talk to you right about twelve o'clock."

"Doesn't he go out to lunch?"

Frank shook his head. "Never eats lunch. He weighs twelve billion pounds and he never has a meal. Of course, if you're walking crosstown with him, he'll stop at an umbrella stand and shove down two hot dogs before the light changes. But restaurants are out. They're not on his diet."

Frank waved at two people I'd met upstairs as they sat at the counter; Perry, the office boy, and Alma, the bookkeeper.

"It seems to be the commissary," I said.

"It's handy. And Stu doesn't like people out very long. He's still got Toby eating at her desk."

There were maybe a dozen people in the office altogether. Frank had taken me around to meet them this morning. There were the basic office people: Alma, Perry, Nicole, and Doris, who did everybody's typing. And there were the people who worked directly on the two shows Stu Leonard Productions had on the air: "Corky's Gang," and "Help Wanted," a kind of advice-to-the-lovelorn panel show with Mike Prince as host. I was replacing Frank for a few weeks on "Corky" while he worked on getting together a run-through of some new game idea he'd come up with.

"I guess this could be pretty good for you," I said.

He nodded. "It's not what I want to do, but I guess it could," he said. It was an old story. Nobody in New York was doing what he wanted to do. But it seems that Frank had come close. He'd had a comedy he'd written open on Broadway two years ago. The reviews had been somewhere in between, but not good enough to keep it running more than a month. Still, though, an honorable failure, and he was working on another one.

"But it's slow," he said. He was married, with a two-year-old daughter and a baby coming and there was no way he could take the chance of writing full-time. It was something that had to be squeezed in evenings and weekends, and there wasn't always a lot of time then. Stu had this habit of calling meetings for six o'clock and Saturday mornings and just about any time his own social life was flagging. It was always something important because around here he was the one who defined important.

"He who hath wife and children, hath given hostages to fortune," Frank said. "Francis Bacon. You're not married, are

8

you." He knew because it had been his wife's brother's girlfriend who had told Margo, my girlfriend, about the job.

"Not even close," I said. That was what Margo and I always told people. Everyone was anxious to get you married back in those days; especially so in our case because we'd been going together, except for a two-year hiatus, since I'd met her in Waterbury, right after I'd started there. She'd made it to New York, to the *Times* in fact, before I did. Hence the two-year hiatus. But now we were back together again. Not living together. People didn't. But we managed to spend most nights together, with one of us sneaking back to his or her own place early in the morning. It might have been complicated, but it seemed to suit us both just fine.

Sol Block was at our table looking at Frank. "He just called," Sol said. "He wanted to know if you were finished, and I told him you just got your hamburger."

"Thanks, Sol," Frank said.

"That buys you five minutes."

"Is that how fast I eat?"

"It's really four, but if you don't know, neither will he. He wants to see you as soon as you get upstairs."

Frank nodded. "What kills me," he said to me, "is I don't even hate it. I try to act like I do, but I know I don't. You know what I'd hate? I'd hate it if he'd said he wanted to talk to *you* and then left me alone all afternoon. Now that's insanity."

But it isn't. I began to find that out as slowly Stu brought me into his inner circle. At first, I thought it was because I was the new boy. That's what I told Frank Dean. But he said it was more than that. There was some way in which Stu wanted my approval; that's why he started including me in meetings that had nothing to do with what was supposed to be my job, and then kept turning to me to see if I agreed with him. It was flattering, I can tell you that. Especially at the beginning.

"I don't know," Frank said one day after a meeting on the quiz format he'd been working on. "You've got his number. He doesn't want to start till you get there. Then if he thinks you don't like what he's saying, he doesn't want to go on till he can get you to change your mind."

"But notice he doesn't change his."

Frank laughed. "He *never* changes his."

Which was true. It didn't take many sessions with Stu Leonard to learn that in addition to being quick and resourceful, he had one of those minds that, once it bites down on an idea, just digs in harder when someone tries to shake it loose. But it was true about his wanting me on his side. He seemed to want me to think well of him and everything he did. I was being courted and I rather liked it.

Margo, though, had the opposite reaction when it started to spill over into our personal life.

"I don't *want* to go to the concert with him."

I grinned at her. "You're stamping your foot."

"It's my foot and I can stamp it all I like."

She was sitting on the edge of the bed without any clothes on after what had been an absolutely delightful hour. We were still very good at this even after a series of couplings that had extended, on and off, over a period of some four years. It sometimes made me wonder why we weren't married. But only sometimes.

"Has it occurred to you that maybe *I'd* enjoy it?"

She snorted. "You haven't gone near a concert since you've been in New York."

"Maybe it's not just the concert. Maybe I think it would be a pleasant evening."

"Then you go. I have plenty to keep me busy."

Which was true enough. Since the newspaper strike she'd been hustling magazine assignments and she was in the middle of something for *Collier's* on women working at the UN.

"Let me explain about the world," I said. "It moves in pairs. Two by two. What do we do with the empty seat?"

She looked at me and smiled. "Don't ask me a second time."

She went, of course, and disliked Stu just as much as she'd thought she would. Stu's date was someone he'd never been out with before, a thirtyish divorcee with boarding-school lockjaw who worked in the bookshop at the Museum of Modern Art. Afterward, we had shashlik at the Russian Tea Room, and if I hadn't been aware of Margo's guard being up all evening, I might have had a terrific time.

"I hated him," she said back at her place.

"No kidding," I said, lighting a cigarette. I hadn't even bothered to take my coat off, anticipating a quick flare-up and an ugly good night.

She turned to me. "You know what his problem is?"

"No, but I have the feeling I'm about to find out."

"He wants it fifty different ways," she said. "That's what's wrong with him. He's a street fighter who wants to look like a class act. He's a self-centered taker who'd knock down old ladies on the way to the pot of gold, and then lecture the freshmen on loving your fellow man. If you want to see him, that's fine with me. But from now on, just put me down for a permanent headache."

"Starting now?"

"You guessed it," she said, and I crushed my cigarette out elaborately, a little annoyed at myself for having handed her the exit line.

The next day things were fine with Margo and me. We'd long since learned that the only unpleasantness worth extending was the kind that went to the heart of what we were stuck with calling our relationship. Little upsets like this were quickly gotten past. But notice I didn't say settled, or even forgotten. Margo made it clear that she didn't want to see Stu again, and when I saw him socially after that it was either alone or with another date. Oddly enough, Margo never minded that. Either she just wasn't jealous, or she really didn't care enough. I was never sure which.

I confess that I've always been a little in awe of Margo. I suppose it's because right from the start I was aware of the difference in the ways we approached our jobs. Put at its simplest, she burned and I didn't. I was stuck with the kind of mind that always presented the other guy's point of view. I liked to think of it as understanding, but whatever it was, it got in the way. While I was busy understanding why some handcuffed child molester might be reluctant to talk to reporters, Margo got the story. She wasn't hung up on such things as a subject's right to privacy; at least, not while she was working. It was her strength, the thing that made her valuable in everything she did. It took her past every kind of no and through doors that, in her place, I might have allowed to remain shut. In the Waterbury days, I tried to make not wanting to compete with her look like a matter of gentlemanly concern, but no one was fooled. Don't get me wrong; I did everything well. But sometimes I'd let people off the hook. Margo never did.

I'd forgotten the difference after she'd gone to New York, but then there we were together again. This time it was easier to live with because we worked on different papers. But still I was aware of something in the way she did her job that simply wasn't in me.

I had become a reporter because I'd always had an idealized notion of what it was all about. And the high school and college taste of running around on press passes fed the fantasy. Reality turned out to be a ruder than necessary awakening when the only job I could find turned out to be in Waterbury, Connecticut, where instead of covering the intricacies of the Marshall Plan, it was fires and the tedium of local politics.

Tedium, I might add, for me. For Margo, everything was important. She joined the paper a few weeks after I did to work on the society page, but within a matter of days she was into everything. It was she who turned up the first stories about Municipal Stadium, the baseball diamond surrounded by a few scruffy bleachers that, it finally turned out, had cost more to build than the Yale Bowl. She'd gotten onto the story when the daughter of somebody social got engaged to a pitcher for the

Class D Waterbury Timers. The girl was invited to toss out the first ball that spring, and Margo went along to cover it for the society page. At the party afterward she started hearing things from some of the players. Being Margo, she dug in. Days of research at City Hall, still more days talking to the various construction companies, and then the first couple of stories and the violent reaction. When it was obvious how big the story was getting, they took it away from Margo, and for almost a year she fumed as revelations and denials chased each other across the front page while she was back on the pink-lemonade circuit. Every once in a while she managed to force her way back in with a human-interest story she'd dug up herself that was so good they had to run it, and when the grand jury investigation led to indictments and finally to a Pulitzer Prize for the paper, there was glory enough for all. The result was that Margo managed to parlay even her minimized share into an exit visa in the form of a job with the *New York Times*.

Margo had marked me as a friend as soon as she joined the paper. For one thing, we were both young and single, and for another, she was instantly aware that I was Jewish.

Jewishness meant a lot to Margo. She had been brought up in a largely Jewish suburb of Chicago, and her biggest concern in coming to Waterbury was that there wouldn't be a lot of Jews working on the paper. There weren't.

I'd never thought a lot about looking Jewish, but she had me spotted within ten seconds of hello.

"David Beach," she said, tensing her forehead as she considered it. "That doesn't sound like a Jewish name."

"Maybe it wasn't," I said. "But I guess it is now."

"Did you change it?"

"No," I said. "It's always been Beach." And it had. For me. My father had rescued the family name from the curse of foreignness long before I'd been born. He'd been brought up Meyer Lipschitz, Max to his friends, and had proudly weathered all the obvious hilarity such a name engenders. But when he opened the luggage shop, he'd finally been persuaded that Lip-schitz Leather was out of the question. Much as family and friends urged Lipton on him, he'd have none of it. If he was going to change his name, he wanted something whose anteced-ent could not be so easily traced. And staying with the letter *L* meant absolutely nothing to him, because, as he patiently ex-plained, he didn't own a thing that was monogrammed. So Beach it became, for no better reason than that he liked the sound of it. And if the neighborhood was at first confused into thinking that Beach Leather was some new line of luggage de-signed for sun and sand, they soon understood where the name came from, and explaining it to newcomers became a form of advertising that my father hadn't foreseen but was nonetheless grateful for.

I told Margo none of this until several weeks into our rela-tionship, which started at once and ripened fast. We were going steady by the end of the week, with dinner at my place every night until she finally found a decent apartment, and then it was back and forth. Both of us hated to cook, but cooking was cheaper than eating out; so we learned. On special occasions, which seemed to be every week, we downed a bottle of sparkling burgundy and smacked our lips over every drop because neither of us had yet learned enough to despise it. It was maybe the only time in my life when I knew things were terrific while they were happening, and I found myself biting into every minute knowing beforehand just how good it was going to taste.

Close as we became, she made it clear at once that she had no intention of getting married, and that suited me just fine. Or I thought it did, until the day she broke the news about the job in New York and I found myself fighting back an urge to tell her to forget it; to stay here and marry me and make it all forever. Fortunately for my fragile male ego I managed to keep my mouth shut, because I know what her answer would have been. She was ambitious, and this was her chance. I couldn't really blame her, but it did hurt that she could so easily walk away. For me the relationship had become incredibly important, and faced with the kind of decision she'd had to make, I don't think I could have broken it up. It did nothing for my self-image to see how easily she could.

Well, maybe not easily. Later, when I'd come down to New York and we were together again, she swore she hadn't been to bed with anyone in the year we'd been apart. She hadn't wanted to. That went a long way toward putting things right. Not that I'd have been upset if she had. We'd broken up, you understand. She was free to do as she pleased. But it was nice to know she hadn't found anyone else she'd wanted to share herself with.

So here I was, back with this terrific girl with whom I'd had fights and a long separation, but never a moment's strain, and for the first time there was a point of friction between us. It bothered me some, but mostly I shrugged it off because, for one thing, the job was only for a few weeks, and for another, even if we'd been married there wouldn't have been any great need for her to like Stu Leonard. He was my boss, not my best friend.

It was the day after Stu asked me to stay on permanently that I stumbled across the script for "Help Wanted."

To appreciate how astonished I was, you must understand about me that while I don't think I'm especially gullible, I do tend to accept things as being what they are represented to be. I do not have one of those Byzantine minds that automatically weaves simple facts into swirling tapestries of plot, deception, and conspiracy.

So I believed that "Help Wanted" was exactly what it had purported to be: an ad-lib panel show where guests came on and presented their romantic problems to a panel of always bright, sometimes amusing people, who then used the problem as the springboard for a series of irreverent comments that might or might not culminate in a suggested solution. It was all very light and frivolous, and had once been very successful, thanks largely to the popularity of Hilda Wragge, a sometime stage actress who was now better known for the kind of chic parties nobody I've ever known has ever gone to. The enthusiasm for Hilda's insouciant humor had long since peaked, but it was generally agreed that if you watched the show at all, you watched it for her.

It was a Friday afternoon and I had finished rewriting the script for "Corky." As I did every Friday after lunch, I brought it to Doris to be typed. She was flailing away at her machine as usual, but this time so totally absorbed that she didn't even look up. She just waved me away.

"But I need this for tomorrow," I said.

"Emergency," she said, without a break in her rhythm. "This we need for tonight." "Help Wanted" was on tonight.

I looked to the left of the typewriter at the work she'd already finished. I picked up the top page and started reading.

. . . with a man who's twenty years older and married.

HILDA: Twenty years older is nothing. Married is something else again.

MIKE: So you're really a moralist, Hilda.

HILDA: What moralist? The only time a girl should let herself get involved with a married man is if she's a masochist and he's a Mormon.
(HOLD FOR LAUGH)

MIKE: Then you'd advise her to give him up.

HILDA: Either that, or lay in a big supply of waterproof mascara.
(HOLD FOR LAUGH)

I put the page down again just as Doris pulled another one out of the typewriter.

"Go away," she said. "You're making me nervous. I'll send

up a rocket when I'm finished." She had another page in place and her fingers were flying again.

I stood alongside the desk for a moment, letting it all sink in. What we had here was a script for a show that claimed not to have one. These were the jokes that Hilda would think of tonight, right on the spot, right off the top of her head. Here they were, ready to be loaded into Hilda's fabulous sense of humor and fired off later, on cue. Ad-lib remarks, off-the-cuff badinage, spontaneous wit that Hilda's nimble mind would seem to invent for us later, but that Doris was typing out now as Doris must type it every week. Openly. No big deal. Right out here where it was nothing more than part of the office routine. Yes, there was a rush today because someone had made some last-minute changes, but basically this was just your typical office crisis; a typing problem being solved by someone who knew how to make it smoke.

Suddenly the typewriter stopped, creating a sonic void that startled me. Doris was looking up. "I'm beginning to make mistakes," she said. "It's going to take twice as long with you standing there."

I nodded and dropped the "Corky" script on her desk. "Leave it in my office when you're done. I'm going out for a little while." She shrugged and went back to her work, and I started for the reception room. Then I stopped and doubled back and headed for Stu's office. His door was open. It was his boast that it was always open.

He was on the phone, but he waved me in.

"I'll call Murray if you want me to," he said into the phone, "but you're the one who should see it. You're the one with the instincts." He winked at me, making me part of the action. "Okay, Donald," he said. Donald Scheer was president of Capricorn, the hand lotion that sponsored "Help Wanted." "That'd be terrific," Stu said. "And even better if you can move it up a week. Okay," he said again. "Just let me know." And he said good-bye and hung up.

"He'll come over with Murray. You know what that means?"

"Tell me in a minute." It had come out sharply, and it broke his mood.

"What's wrong?"

"I just saw a script for 'Help Wanted.' "

His brows came together. "What script?"

"The one Doris is typing."

He pursed his lips and started moving the lower one out and around while he thought it over. "Doris is typing a script?"

"You mean you don't know?"

"What kind of a script? Format? Lead-ins?"

I leaned forward. "A script script. A funny-stuff script. Jokes for Hilda Wragge."

He nodded slowly, as if he was thinking over a way to handle some new piece of information. He leaned forward and pressed down on the crude, kit-assembled intercom that sat near his telephone.

"Toby," he said in a firm monotone that barely covered his anger. He released the lever and waited for her to answer. When she did he snapped: "Get in here right away." He released the lever again and leaned back. "Let's just find out what's going on here," he said, and for an insane minute he had me believing he didn't know. Although why he bothered I can't imagine, because as soon as Toby was in the room he made no attempt to hide the fact that of course he knew.

He spoke to her in a low tone that seemed to have picked up a light vibrato from passing over the tightened muscles in his throat. "What's this about Doris typing a script?"

"She had to," Toby said. "I needed help. You threw everything out at lunchtime. I couldn't do it all myself."

"I told you I never wanted anyone in this office to type that script but you. Have you forgotten that?" His voice was rising.

"But Doris has done it before."

"Never!"

"She has," Toby insisted. "You knew about it. She helped

18

me the last time we got jammed up. You said it would be all right."

His hand came down hard on top of the desk. "Well, it's *not* all right. Not last time, not this time, not ever. Understand that?"

"All right, Stu," she said calmly. "I'll take it away from her."

Something about the calm way she was handling this seemed to drive him bananas. When she started for the door, he leaped out of his chair and cut her off.

"Don't tell me what you'll do. I know what you'll do!" He was shouting two inches from her face. "You'll do what I tell you to do. And if you can't keep that show together without pages flying all over this office, we'll put you back to answering the mail. Now pull that fucking script away from her and make sure she knows she never saw it."

"Move aside, please," she said quietly. And after a minute of staring at her with his eyes bulging and his breath coming in short, hard gulps, he did move aside. She left and he stared after her for a moment, letting the rage tremble its way out of him. Then he took a deep breath and moved back toward his desk.

"Smartest girl I ever knew," he said quietly. "Sometimes I just don't understand her."

He sat down again and exhaled loudly.

"Then all this is really routine," I said.

He turned to me. "All of what?"

I didn't answer, assuming that the only reason for his question had been to give himself time to consider exactly what he was going to tell me. He sat quietly for a moment, then leaned forward and opened his appointment book to make a note. He shut the book and looked up at me.

"I've got to be at the theater by nine for dress rehearsal." "Help Wanted" came from a converted theater on 58th Street. "Come to the house for dinner and then come over with me."

I nodded and left. When I called Margo to tell her I was working late, she took the news impassively. I wasn't quite sure what it was I'd wanted her to say, but I knew it wasn't, "Okay, fine."

"Things don't work, they're *made* to work." He said it right after swallowing an enormous bite of a sandwich he wasn't having. The table was set for one. Me. He wasn't having any dinner.

"Premise out whatever you want. When you try to make it happen there's something you didn't count on. Adjustments. That's what makes the difference. The man who knows how to work the adjustment screw, he's the winner. The idea's just the beginning. When it doesn't work, that's when you're just getting started." The rest of the sandwich went down, along with half my beer. "I don't care if you're inventing the light bulb or devising some new scheme for price supports. It never works in practice quite the way you thought it would. But that doesn't mean it isn't good. It has to be messed with. A couple of tucks in the right places, and suddenly it's flying. You want another sandwich?"

I nodded. "I must be hungrier than I thought I was."

He turned toward the hall and bellowed, "Abbie!" while I picked up the small slice of pickle that was all that was left on my plate and wondered which it was that would be flying, the light bulb or the price supports?

Abbie (for Abner) came into the kitchen; a tall, very proper, gray-haired black man to whom I'd been introduced when we'd arrived. He'd wanted to set the table in the dining room, but Stu had said we didn't have time.

"What else do we have to eat?" Stu asked him.

"You mean dessert?"

"I mean food. We're dealing with a very hungry man."

"I can make another sandwich." His voice was smooth, pleasant. This, obviously, was not his first job.

"Good. Another of the same."

"All right, Mr. Leonard," he said, and turned to do it.

"I hate this Mr. Leonard stuff," Stu said to me. "I tried to get him to call me Stu, but he wouldn't hear of it." He turned back to Abbie. "Right, Abbie?"

"Yes, sir, that's right," Abbie said, popping two slices of bread in the toaster.

Stu turned back to me. "I was supposed to call him Tompkins, but I told him not on his fucking life." Stu shrugged. What were you going to do with the servile attitude? You can't change people who won't be changed.

"Hilda got laughs on her own," Stu said. "But everybody wanted more, so we started to help her. She set the style. We just gave her the kind of things she'd have thought of herself, only more of them, that's all. It's a matter of tightening the adjustment screw; taking the idea and making it work."

I nodded again. The more I thought about all of this, the less difference it seemed to make. They did whatever they did. In a couple of weeks it would have nothing to do with me. I wouldn't be staying. There was no question about that. I'd just sit tight until the strike was over, the way I'd planned to all along.

"Who gets hurt?" he wanted to know.

"I guess nobody," I said obediently as the sandwich came down in front of me. It didn't seem worth any further discussion.

But in the cab on the way to the theater it started bugging me again. "What about the deception?" I asked.

He gave me a kind of half smile that twisted his beard to a funny angle. "People love to be fooled," he said. "That's why they go to magic shows." It wasn't much of an answer, but it served its purpose, which was simply to blunt the question. It wasn't that he wouldn't have been perfectly capable of doing twenty minutes of solid justification on that subject or any other. It was simply that he wasn't in the mood right now. We were heading for the theater.

2

WHILE IN LATER YEARS I DEVELOPED A CERTAIN MISTRUST OF people who could do what they had to do, at the time we're speaking of I still found such things impressive. And God knows, everyone else did.

"He has brass balls," Carla said. The waiter pretended not to hear as he set our drinks in front of us.

"He has, indeed," I said, not so much endorsing the metaphor as admitting that despite its familiarity, no other seemed quite as appropriate.

We were sitting at a tiny black-topped table in the bar of an Italian restaurant a few doors away from the theater, having the drink she'd suggested we have the week before. Carla worked for the small, house-owned agency that handled Capricorn, and she'd been the one to take me in hand my first night at "Help Wanted," introducing me to everyone and trying to explain how it all came together. When she'd offered to buy me a drink, I'd had to beg off because of plans with Margo, but I'd countered with an offer to buy her one next week. At the time, I'd wondered how I was going to explain being busy to Margo, but as it turned out that wasn't going to be necessary. It had been an eventful week. On Monday, Stu had raised again the issue of making my job there permanent, and when I seemed hesitant he sweetened the pot by about a hundred dollars more a week than I'd be getting back at the paper, and I felt my resolve slip a couple of notches. Margo, of course, was horrified. I pointed out that so far the career of journalism had been considerably more hospitable to her than it had to me and that I'd begun to have my doubts about whether my particular light would shine its brightest among the ink-stained wretches. Well, that set off a tirade from her about how the trouble with me was a lack of self-confidence, and before I knew it I found myself defending a position I hadn't quite taken and locking myself firmly into a job that till then I'd still been uncertain about. The discussion had ended with her slamming the bedroom door and my walking out of there wondering what to do with two tickets for *Tiger at the Gates.* The next day the newspaper strike ended abruptly and she called, said "Congratulations, chump," and let the receiver drop. I hadn't talked to her since.

"You realize," Carla said, "that he's never directed any-thing." Her face reflected the wonder with which she still re-garded it all.

As a matter of fact, I hadn't. He had slipped into the chair so quickly, so certainly, that I'd just assumed this was some old skill, not recently used, but firmly acquired some time in the past and still tucked away in a kind of capacity reserve that could be called on in just this kind of emergency.

"Never," Carla said firmly. "Not even once. That's what had Murray in shock. I mean, the incredible nerve of him."

What had happened is this: Vince Martoni, the director, after having been perfectly fine through the entire evening, including the dress rehearsal, had suddenly collapsed less than five min-utes before air. He had entered the control room, faltered for a moment, tried to make it to his chair, and then suddenly

23

slumped to the floor. Toby was the first one to him, loosening his tie and unbuttoning his coat. Someone went for water, and as people pressed around him, Vince sat up and tried to get to his feet.

"Stay there," Toby said.

Vince started to say he was all right, when suddenly he grimaced and clutched at his chest, and there wasn't a lot of doubt about what was happening.

Just then Stu walked into the control room. Toby looked up at him. "He collapsed," she said, as if to explain why he wasn't doing his job. Stu nodded and looked around. He saw me and told me to call an ambulance. Then he turned back to Toby and told her not to let him move. We were about ninety seconds away from air. Stu walked over and sat down in Vince's chair. He cleared away the papers and the empty coffee cup and touched the headset in front of him. "Does he wear this?" he asked the technical director.

The TD nodded.

"I won't," Stu said. "You talk to the cameras. I'll just call the shots. Give me the opening."

The TD nodded again and started lining things up while Stu got himself settled in what was for him an undersized chair. When the clock made its final lurch to zero he barked out, "Up on two," as if he'd been doing it all his life. He called every shot for the whole thirty minutes in just that way, crisply, totally sure of himself, while behind him Vince was moaning on the control room floor with Toby kneeling beside him, mopping his forehead with a damp cloth. And Stu kept his eyes fixed on the bank of monitors in front of him when the ambulance attendants bustled in with the stretcher and hauled Vince Martoni out of there. Right afterward, there was an eerie silence that seemed as if it would go on forever and was finally broken when the audio man leaned back from his console and quietly muttered, "Jesus."

Stu stood up and turned around. "Where did they take

him?" he asked, and when Toby told him he grabbed her elbow and led her out of there and into a cab to the hospital. When I bumped into Carla just outside the control room, I remembered our plan, and it suddenly seemed a little odd for the two of us to be going out, but I figured I'd leave it up to her.

"Are we still on for that drink?"

She looked at me for a moment, then smiled. "I'm not sure one will be enough."

And now she was draining that one, and as she put the glass down I asked if she was ready for another. She shook her head. "I'd better give that one time to settle. I drank it faster than I'd planned to." She shook her head again. "I really can't believe him," she said.

I couldn't either, but at the moment my attention was more drawn to the pleasant curve of abundance above the neckline of what was not really a low-cut dress as she leaned forward intently with her arms pressed against her bosom. It was more than I was used to. Margo had the lean build of a woman in a hurry. Carla had the look of soft luxury even with her body locked in an attitude she meant to be strictly business.

"Tell me about you," I said in a display of the dazzling technique that generally kept me several conquests behind my contemporaries.

She smiled and leaned back. "Well, first of all, I'm single."

"Okay. That's a good place to start." I had already picked up Stu's habit of prefixing thoughts with an okay.

She was a year older than I was and she'd mentioned being single because she'd already been through an early marriage. She wrote copy on the Capricorn account, and at twenty-eight she still didn't have the vaguest idea what she wanted to do with her life.

Either she was good company or the four-day separation from Margo had left me lonelier than I'd realized, but I found myself enjoying being with her and wondering how soon I could decently suggest we get out of there so that I could put myself in a better position to make a move toward that pleasantly ample figure. She did it for me.

"It's getting late," she said, "and I have to meet with Murray in the morning." She was frowning.

"Is that bad?"

"Tomorrow's Saturday. I'd rather be sleeping till noon."

"Does he do that to you often?"

She shook her head. "We have a session with Donald Scheer on Monday. He wants to be ready."

I got the check and we started out. I was about to ask her where she lived when she told me she had her car and offered to drive me home. Not many people I knew bothered with cars in Manhattan.

Hers turned out to be a green MG that she drove with the top down winter and summer. This, you'll remember, was winter.

She laughed as we pulled out of the garage across from the theater. "I should have warned you I didn't have a top. There's still time to change your mind."

"Drive on," I said with bravado. But by the first traffic light I had sunk as deeply as I could into what had been until that moment a perfectly adequate winter coat.

"I never feel the cold," she said.

"Neither do I," I answered, and she looked at me and laughed again.

She was sure I'd be interested in all these meetings she had coming up because the fact that they were going on indicated that Capricorn had some real interest in the new quiz we'd run through for them earlier in the week. In theory, of course, she was right. But what she didn't know was that up until now I hadn't taken the whole thing very seriously. It had been kind of fun going over the format with Stu and Frank Dean, and helping them take things apart and rearrange them. And as I've said, it was pleasant to have my opinions sought. But I'd always treated it lightly because it was really just one of the motions I was going through in this temporary job that would be over before I knew it.

"Donald Scheer called the office today and said he loves the new idea. And so does Murray." She smiled. "Of course, I can't imagine Murray not liking anything that Donald liked. Do you have a quarter?"

We were stopped at a red light and a pathetically dressed little black kid had started wiping the windshield with a rag that left more dirt than it removed. I dug down and found a quarter. He stopped as soon as she gave it to him and darted to another windshield.

"I really think it's going to happen," she said.

"Terrific," I said, still trying to remember what the new idea was.

My face was frozen into immobility when we finally pulled up in front of my apartment building after the longest twenty-minute ride I've ever been through. But the promise of warmer surroundings was only one of the reasons I was glad to be there.

"Why don't you come up for a drink," I suggested with the smallest leer I could manage.

She shook her head. "I told you. Early action tomorrow." But she reached out and turned the ignition off. Cold as I was, I took my gloves off and touched her.

"You don't have to stay very long."

She shook her head again. "Some other time."

"I hope so," I said, and pulled her toward me in what turned out to be a warmer than hoped for kiss. Even through all those clothes I could feel her press against me, and my hand left her shoulder and moved slowly over the thick fabric of her coat to the spot right over where her breast must be. Just knowing it was under there somehow had me excited, but when I started to unbutton her coat she pulled away.

"I have to go," she said.

"I'm sorry to hear that."

"I hope there really will be another time."

She was being sure to send out just the right signals. I promised to call her, and never meant anything more in my life. It's amazing how tantalizing small samples can sometimes be. A fact, I was sure, that Carla was well aware of.

The new idea was money. And I hadn't been able to remember it because I'd never heard it before.

"It's *there,*" he said. "That's the amazing part. It was just a matter of getting them to look at a budget in a whole different way. They'd spend more than that on a dramatic series. The fact is, they already do."

The pacing figure stopped, reached into the white paper bag, and downed a bagel so fast it looked like some kind of magic trick.

Stu Leonard had pounded his way into my apartment at a little after ten on Sunday morning, shoving several bags from Zabar's in front of him. No warning. No phone call ahead of time to see if I was alone, or even awake. Just heavy knocking and then a loud voice through the partly opened chained door telling me he'd brought me breakfast.

"Ten thousand a week," he said. "You know what that is?" Fortunately, he didn't wait for an answer, because I had no idea what he was talking about. "Just an attitude," he said. "A way of looking at things, that's all. Something to get used to." He stopped and looked at me. Another bagel went down so fast that not even the people in the first row could see how he was doing it.

He pointed to the paper bags. "Don't you like this stuff?" I nodded.

"Well then, why don't you spread it out before it dies from lack of appreciation. You got plates around here?"

I got a few out and put them on the table. When I started to open the bags, he shooed me away.

"Make some coffee," he said. "I'll take care of this." He

inhaled deeply as he opened the second bag and closed his eyes in pleasure. "You're in for some treat," he said.

I was used to the game by now, and by moving fast actually managed to salvage enough for a perfectly adequate breakfast, while he stood there unconsciously putting away enormous quantities of bagels, cream cheese, Nova Scotia salmon, and other assorted delicacies that sped past too quickly to be identified.

The ten thousand dollars, I was finally able to understand, was the prize budget he had added to the weekly price of the show he was pitching to Capricorn.

"They didn't bat an eye," he said. "You know why?"

I shook my head obediently.

"Because that brings the whole package up to twenty-five, which is still ten thousand less than they're paying for that mystery dreck on Sunday nights."

He was on fire with himself, blazing with an idea that had burst upon him with the force of the suddenly obvious and then had ignited in others the same spark it had touched off in him.

As I said, the new idea was money, and he hadn't so much thought of it as had it overtake him. On Thursday night he had been reading a follow-up piece in *Life* about a supermarket checkout clerk who'd won the Irish Sweepstakes. Here was this ordinary life, suddenly jolted by the impact of a ton of money. Why couldn't we do that? Who said the prizes had to be a hundred or two hundred dollars, the way they'd always been? Why not an amount that could really change their lives? Ten thousand dollars, say. Or even fifty thousand.

"I'm telling you," he said, "I actually broke out in a sweat. I mean, I was drenched. I had to take a shower."

Later, he'd done some playing with figures. If you took an average budget of ten thousand a week, and somehow stretched things out so you didn't spend it every week, it wouldn't take long to get the prizes up to where they'd knock your eye out. Then it was just a matter of convincing Donald Scheer that it made sense for Capricorn to add ten thousand dollars onto the weekly package price that had already been discussed.

"But in a *separate* budget," Stu emphasized. "That's what finally clinched it. We're responsible if we go over; they get their money back if we stay under. We can't make a dime on that part of it. That's why they finally went for it."

He plopped down on the ancient couch that in my two-room apartment wasn't that far from the kitchen table, and sent up a cloud of dust that he was too preoccupied to notice. "People like Donald Scheer don't care so much what something costs as long as they don't think someone else is getting rich. They don't care what they're spending; in fact, they're even proud if the number's big enough. The only time they gag on price is if they think too much of it is winding up in your pocket."

Most of this had happened on Friday. Stu hadn't been in the office at all. He'd spent the morning at the agency with Murray Cashin, and then the two of them had had lunch and a meeting that went all afternoon in the private dining room at Capricorn, where, as I was later to find out for myself, tiny wilted salads were served on gold-rimmed china.

"He had a million questions," Stu said. "We must have gone over the same stuff a hundred times." In the mathematics of Stu Leonard's rhetoric, a hundred equaled a million. "He kept saying this was new ground and we had to be careful. But then yesterday afternoon he called me at home and I'm telling you he fucking loves it. He's already got Murray working on ideas for new commercials."

He got up again, quickly, with that unexpected grace big men surprise us with. "What am I doing here, right? It's Sunday. Why don't I take my kid to the park?"

What kid? I didn't know about any kid. Or, now that I thought about it, even that he'd ever been married. Of course, it made sense that he would have been. But it wasn't something he normally spoke about. He tended to live in the present. It suddenly struck me that I had no idea how old he was. Later that week, I made it my business to find out. He was forty-two. About what he looked, I suppose.

"How's Vince Martoni?" I suddenly remembered to ask.

The question seemed to surprise him. He frowned, and for a moment it was almost as if he wasn't quite sure who that was. "Toby didn't call this morning," he said. But then he waved it off. "He'll be okay."

He pointed his finger at me. "Listen," he said. "I want you involved in this. Frank expects to be the producer and, okay, he's got it. He'll be fine. But I want you involved. I don't want you stuck on 'Corky.' "

I wasn't quite sure what that meant, but I nodded. Then I thought this might be the time to find out. "What does that mean, exactly?" I asked.

He shrugged. "We'll make it up as we go along. I want you working with me. I like bouncing ideas off you." It wasn't the most flattering way he might have put it, but it held out the promise of putting me where the action would be. And a chance to get off "Corky" was not something to be passed over lightly.

"Maybe Toby," he said, thinking about it. "Maybe she could do both." He picked up the plaid peaked cap that he always wore buttoned flat and flipped it into place on his head. "Okay," he said. "We'll talk about this more on Monday. There's a lot to do." And he was gone without saying good-bye.

Monday began my two years of permanent residence in Stu Leonard's office. Each morning I'd come in twenty minutes after he did (he was there by nine-fifteen) and then continue to show my independence by heading straight for my own shabby cubicle for the few minutes before the inevitable call that summoned me into The Presence for what always turned out to be the rest of the day.

The summoning call usually involved some second thought about something we'd talked about that he now realized wouldn't work, and here was why. Scrawled figures on the wall blackboard. Then a quick cover-up pull on the map of the world that came down like a window shade to cover what we'd been doing when someone came into the office. Then back up again with the protective screen as soon as the prying eyes had left. Why the passion for secrecy? No reason. Reflex, really. Chances are whatever we'd been talking about was no more sensitive than the right size for the scoreboard numbers. Two inches wasn't big enough, he'd say. They'd be readable in the studio, but in the three-shot they'd wind up too small on the screen. Most of the time he was right. When I thought he was wrong it took all day and all the strength I had to win maybe one argument out of four.

But I was enjoying it, there was no doubt of that. I was daily being pulled to the whirling center, and if I couldn't really control the spinning events, at least I was given the feeling that I could influence them. My nod of agreement was constantly sought, practically fought for. Its absence would bog us down for hours while argument was piled on argument in an effort to bring me into line. It didn't matter that it wore me out; I loved it.

Toby replaced me on "Corky's Gang," and even though that really meant two shows for her, with of course some extra money, she wasn't terribly happy about it. With all the office energy flowing toward the new show, it really meant she'd been pushed aside.

We were heading for a June start, a summer run with more ahead if we could get some numbers. There were run-throughs one or two evenings a week. On nights when things went well we were out of there early. Other nights we'd sit around for gloomy hours, for however long it took for Stu to finally agree that things might look brighter in the morning. Morning still started at nine-fifteen.

It was almost April before I called Margo, and as soon as I did I was sorry. There was a forced brightness in her voice that announced that someone else was in her apartment. I suppose I shouldn't have been as surprised as I was. Maybe I hadn't realized how deeply she disapproved of what I was doing. Or maybe I simply hadn't called her soon enough.

We talked for a minute or two and I said I'd call again next week, but of course I didn't. It was a long time before I spoke to Margo again, and when I did both of our lives had changed completely.

3

GINGER MALLOY MADE THE GRAND GESTURE OF WAVING OFF A ten-dollar tip.

"That kind of work," he said, "I do for a smile and the promise of a welcome neighbor."

What he'd done had not been all that burdensome because I didn't own that much. But he had helped me haul up several cartons of books, records, dishes, canned goods, rattling silverware, and more armloads of clothing than I'd realized I owned, including two sweaters that dated back to high school.

"You planning a trip to the Malt Shop?" Carla asked, holding one of them up.

"You're here to be helpful," I said. "Keep remembering that."

She dropped it back on the pile, scooped up as much as she could carry, and headed for the bedroom.

Ginger winked and dug his elbow into my side. "She's okay," he said.

"Okay isn't the half of it, Ginger, my man," I said, slipping into his rhythms.

He nodded appreciatively. "Get all you can while you're able," he said. "That's what my father told me, and I've spent all of my life respecting his memory."

Up to this point we hadn't had many conversations, but in the few words that had passed between us Ginger had already made it clear that all subjects led to only one. At our very first meeting, when he was showing me the apartment, he had set the tone.

"I'm not just the superintendent," he'd said. "I'm really the building manager. That's why they let me show the apartment. How old do you think I am?"

The pleasantly lined round face and the slicked-back silver hair that had once been flaming red didn't leave much room on the minus side, but I plunged as low as I dared. "Fifty-one?" I ventured.

The grin was instantaneous. "Sixty-two this coming August," he said proudly, and then he leaned in closer. "But I wake up every morning with a mop-handle that would credit a newlywed, and I consider the day wasted that doesn't take it to a friend."

I nodded soberly and asked if the building owner would consider painting. He shook his head, but said that if I supplied the paint he'd do the kitchen and the bathroom himself. He'd just done the same for the woman in the apartment above me, with whom he'd had a regular liaison for the two years since his wife had died. "She's not a handsome woman, you understand. But there's much to be said for the plain ones. Gratitude can be beautifully expressive."

Carla came back with a leather jacket and my overcoat. "These should go in the hall closet," she said, putting them there.

"Well, all right," Ginger said. "I think maybe you two can handle the rest." And he winked at me again and left.

It was mice in my other apartment that had started me looking. Not one or two, you understand, but what had finally become an infestation. I'd wanted another furnished place, but Stu said it was time I joined the adults, and if I couldn't furnish a place completely, empty rooms were still better than another furnished apartment.

Naturally, Stu was convinced that I had to find something on the east side even though I kept insisting I couldn't afford it. But miraculously, some cousin of his managed to turn up this place on East Sixty-sixth Street that was going for a song because there was no closet in the bedroom. It was only about a hundred a month more than I could afford, so naturally I took it. I bought a bed, a large, upright cardboard box that Gimbels called a wardrobe, a kitchen table and folding chairs, and gratefully paid Carla fifty dollars for the sofa she was replacing with a hide-a-bed, and now that I saw them spread around I decided that the place didn't really look so bad after all. That's ownership for you.

Carla and I had by this time become good friends; and the phrase is used here in its precise, as opposed to its euphemistic, sense. I had been trying for some time to take the relationship into something more advanced, but from the first unsuccessful struggle in her apartment Carla had made it clear that friendship was the best I could hope for. The announcement had come as something of a surprise, since I'd thought I'd read the signals the other way, but repeated attempts only confirmed her stand. Enthusiastic caressing was acceptable, even encouraged, but the limits were clearly drawn and when I tried to exceed them my up-to-then compliant partner would sit up quickly and start buttoning things.

"I cannot figure you out," I'd finally said one exasperating evening.

She turned on the lamp. "We work together."

"Not in the same office."

"No, but close enough."

"I can't believe that's it," I'd said, and I went through a long speech about how it didn't pay to worry too much about getting involved with people you had to come into contact with, and halfway through it she burst into tears. Not just mild crying, but the kind of heaving, throbbing, convulsive crying that can't be brought under control. While I was waiting for her to come out of it, even I managed to figure out what the real problem was.

"How long's it been going on?" I asked when she finally seemed able to handle questions.

She tried to answer, but still had trouble getting the words out. She held up one finger.

"A month?" I asked. She shook her head. "A year?" She nodded.

She'd been having an affair with a married man, and of course they were very much in love and he was going to leave his wife as soon as Jupiter and Uranus lined up exactly right, and meanwhile he saw her whenever he could, which was why she was free almost all of the time. But she loved him, which meant no fooling around with anyone else, although she was really very fond of me. The story was familiar enough so we could all whistle the chorus together. But being familiar didn't keep it from being painful.

Having broken her silence she was full of more information than I would normally have cared to hear. But it poured out of her so uncontrollably that it would have been cruel to do anything but listen and nod at what seemed the right places. She held my hand tightly through all of this and finally fell asleep on my shoulder. I left there at six in the morning, so rumpled and weary that I drew from the doorman a knowing smile at what he was sure had finally been my night of triumph.

We went on seeing each other maybe once a week, and I'm embarrassed to admit that I continued to attack her with the same unfounded optimism each time we were together, and each time allowed her initial pleasure to fool me into thinking that this would be the time when we would finally get to where it always seemed we were going. It never happened.

Why I kept coming back for more of this is beyond me, but every few days I seemed to forget the indignities involved and set myself up for another maddening bout with frustration.

On this particular Saturday morning, I was too aware of the

likely outcome to be willing to risk getting anything started. I had a one o'clock meeting at the office, and I wanted to arrive neatly pressed and free of pain.

"Come on," I said. "There's a place on the corner that sells pancakes to practically anybody."

She seemed surprised and, I like to think, a little disappointed, but she shrugged and came with me and in a few moments we were facing each other over plasticized menus.

She studied hers for a minute, then frowned and looked up at me. "He'd be perfect," she said.

I knew exactly what she meant and it gave me the chills.

"I mean Ginger," she said, thinking I needed the help.

I put my menu down and frowned back. "No, he wouldn't," I said.

"Why not?"

"Because for one thing, he's my superintendent, and for another if you so much as mention that idea to anyone, I'll kill you."

"That's a non sequitur."

"It's a threat, and if I were you I'd be terrified."

"He's just what Stu's been talking about."

"He couldn't do it."

"You don't know that."

"I definitely, absolutely know that," I said firmly. "Now, we have here your silver dollar pancakes, your buckwheats, or your plain old standard stack."

It turned out she didn't want pancakes at all, but I did, although not as much as I had a few minutes ago. I don't know why the thought of involving Ginger disturbed me so profoundly. Maybe I'd begun to have some sense of the way things were going. Not specifically, of course, but just enough to make me feel uneasy.

We'd made a key discovery the last couple of weeks: Real contestants couldn't handle the kind of questions we had in mind. Funny how nobody'd thought to try that up to now. You see, we'd had these run-throughs where everybody just kind of decided which questions people could answer and which ones they couldn't. The point had always been to see how well the format itself worked. It had never occurred to any of us that there might be some difficulty finding people who could stand there and rattle off the answers to what had always seemed perfectly reasonable questions.

So it had become apparent (for the time being, that is; later it all changed again) that the questions had to be made easier. And as long as we were making the questions easier, why not find earthier, more colorful contestants? The fact that lowering both standards at the same time might leave us with the original problem could not be made clear to Stu, who always refused to be overwhelmed by logic when some cherished notion was being protected. So more colorful people were being brought in, and easier questions were being written, and at some point in the near future the two would be brought together.

Yes, Ginger was exactly what Stu had in mind. The problem was that I didn't want even the outer edge of my personal life tangled up with the office. The more I was drawn to the center of our enterprise, the more I found myself checking the exits. On the surface, my commitment was pure Musketeer; all for one and one for all. But to myself I could justify my involvement only if I continued to think I could end it at any point in one quick, decisive move.

The waiter put down Carla's orange juice and my silver dollar pancakes, along with my choice of powdered sugar or pure Vermont maple syrup. Carla eyed my plate so longingly that I asked if she wanted to change her mind.

She shook her head.

"Saving yourself for a monster dinner?"

She shook her head again, and even though she didn't change her expression I was sorry I'd said it. She'd told me how she spent her Saturday nights. Home, alone. Waiting for him to steal five minutes and call her from some restaurant men's room and tell her how much he loved her. She had to stay home, you see, because he always called, no matter how tough it was to shake himself loose. I was supposed to think that was terrific.

She shifted in her seat. "What time is your meeting?" she asked.

"One o'clock."

She reached across and turned my watch toward her. "If you hurry, we'll have time for a walk."

I nodded and started eating.

The further he was from a solution the more long-winded Frank Dean became, and the less able to read the clear signs of Stu's impatience.

Stu's chair was tilted back and his eyes were on the ceiling. His fingers tapped silently against his thigh as Frank droned on. What he was saying was certainly correct, but he'd already made the point several times.

"Forgive me, Frank," Stu said, crashing his chair to its forward position. "I think I see what you're getting at."

Frank's face took on that wounded look I'd begun to see so much of. "All right, Stu," he said. "That's fine."

The affable, pleasant Frank Dean who'd gone out of his way to make me comfortable in the early days had, as we'd begun to work closely together, become pontifical, a little pompous, and so easily hurt that it was a rare meeting that didn't at some point find him stiffly covering his damaged feelings.

"What you're saying," Stu said, "is that we're losing more than we gain."

Frank nodded stiffly, unwilling to speak again now that he'd been interrupted. Frank didn't like being interrupted, and it seemed to happen to him several times an hour. I had once considered explaining the reason for this, but I had wisely decided to leave it alone.

The subject, as it always seemed to be these days, was format. With the current version built around easier questions,

Frank felt strongly that we were losing glamour. Unless the questions seemed difficult, there was nothing for an audience to admire, to marvel at.

"The problem is we've been there," Stu said. "We tried it. It doesn't work."

"Maybe we haven't really been there at all," Frank said. "Maybe we only think we have."

Frank was in love with the elliptical. For one thing, it always did its magic. I mean, who in the room had any idea what he was talking about? All of us turned toward him to wait for his explanation.

"All right," Frank said once he had our attention. "All we know so far is that the people we tried couldn't do it. That doesn't necessarily mean nobody can. If you gather up a hundred people and then start looking through them for people who speak Armenian, you probably won't find any. But that doesn't prove that nobody speaks Armenian."

Toby bristled. "What you're saying is I haven't looked hard enough."

"Not at all," Frank said benignly. "I am saying that it's hard to find Armenians. Even harder than we'd thought. But it's possible that we still might get results with an effort a lot larger than we thought we needed."

That didn't quite satisfy Toby. She leaned forward to continue her defense, but Stu held his hand up and she stopped and slumped back on the couch.

"Frank may be right," Stu said. "It may be that we underestimated the problem. But it can still be solved. Let's get a few more hustlers in here and go to work on it."

By hustlers, Stu meant part-time college kids who'd work their tails off for practically nothing. This was television, a chance to break in. We'd already hired a couple to write questions.

"Okay, Stu," Toby said. "We'll arrange to start seeing more people."

"Not just more. Five times as many," Stu said, leaping to

his feet. "Ten times as many. Whatever it takes. Keep them flowing through here all day, all night. Weekends, holidays." He stopped, trying to think when else we could keep the office open.

"I think that covers it," I said quietly.

Stu looked at me for a minute, and I wasn't sure he'd heard me. Then he turned back to Toby. "Whatever it takes," he said. He pointed his finger at her and sighted along it. "And I don't ever want to hear you say you didn't have enough help. Hire whatever you need. Do whatever it takes."

Toby nodded. Stu stared at her for another minute, until he finally decided he'd made his point, then he turned and walked back to his chair.

"What if we still don't find them?" I asked.

Stu waited till he was seated again and back at his usual tilt. "You're always negative, David," he said quietly. "Maybe that's good for us. Maybe we need the voice that points out the problems. But if we listen to you too carefully, we sometimes run the risk of having the reasons for failure block the road to success."

It sounded a little like a fortune cookie, but there wasn't much to argue with, and anyway, an argument would prolong things and I had some hope that, with the contestant issue temporarily decided, we might be allowed to call it an afternoon. But it was only a little after three and Stu had said the meeting would run until four, which meant that he had nothing else scheduled till then, so of course there was a lot of ground we had to cover.

We were back on format again. The format had begun as something rather simple; one contestant playing against the house, answering questions of increasing difficulty for increasing amounts of money. But it seemed that as we kept adding production elements there was a need for something more substantial to support them. We'd considered so many formats that now we'd sometimes find ourselves well into a discussion of something that seemed promising before someone would remember that we'd already tried it and thrown it out. But we were always looking.

Stu had this vision of something essentially simple, but still intriguing enough to justify a game played for huge sums of money, and for the next hour he kept us looking for it, reviewing everything we'd already tried and trying to remember the reasons none of it had worked.

At ten after four Stu shifted his weight forward and brought his chair in for a landing. "Has anyone anything new?" he asked. The three of us shook our heads. "Okay," he said. "We'll go back at it Monday."

The three of us got up to leave, but he gestured for Toby to stay. As Frank Dean and I walked out of the office and down the long corridor, I heard what he said to her even though he said it in what was meant to be his quiet voice. "You know I could never do this without you," he said.

If she answered him I couldn't hear it.

The subway shuddered to a stop at the open station above 183rd Street, and I stepped out into the warm, red eight o'clock of a late spring evening. I'd made this stop so many times that without having thought about it I had automatically positioned myself at the door that would off-load me right at the center staircase, and I trotted down it to Jerome Avenue, herringboned now by the lines of sunlight that slipped through the cracks in the overhead platform.

This was Uncle Joe's neighborhood, not far from where I'd done most of my growing up, and now the place I meant when I thought about going home.

Joe Klein was my mother's brother, and we'd started our special relationship when I was three years old and pushed a brass clothes tree through the plate glass front of his drugstore. "Anyone else he would have killed," my mother had been fond of saying. "But David he spends an hour comforting." Of course he had, because he'd been less horrified at the damage I'd wrought than at my terrified reaction to what had been the loudest, most frightening noise I'd ever heard. I'd been running across the floor when suddenly I tripped and fell into the clothes tree, and as I was falling I heard this monumental shattering as the clothes tree crashed against the window. I've been told I cried for over an hour, and my memory says it was at least that long. And for all of that time Uncle Joe held me on his lap and tried to calm me down.

"He'll be punished for this," my father had said later, when he came to pick me up.

Joe shook his head. "It was an accident."

"He's been told about running. He's not supposed to run inside."

"He's already had his punishment," Joe said. "That noise was punishment, believe me."

My father looked at the shattered storefront. "You have insurance for this?"

"For this? Of course not."

"You don't have vandalism?"

Joe smiled. "My nephew's not a vandal."

My father pursed his lips and waited a minute to give Joe a chance to see what he was driving at. But Joe was apparently not following him, so my father laid it out. "I know how it happened. But it's a store window. If you have vandalism, you could say . . . "

Uncle Joe held up his hand and stopped him. "It happened how it happened," Joe said. "And it's nothing to worry about. Nobody got hurt."

My father nodded slowly as he thought about that. "All right," he said. "If you won't put a claim in, I'll pay to have it fixed."

Joe smiled and put his arm around me. "Max, I may never have kids of my own. So let me have the pleasure of paying for something that was broken by someone I love."

Well, that did it for me. Not only was the nightmare over, but

Uncle Joe had let me know that there was in this world at least one adult whose loyalty didn't have to be earned.

Both my parents died while I was still in college, within six months of each other, and from then on coming home meant Uncle Joe's apartment on 182nd Street, just off the Aqueduct. Joe was ten years younger than my mother, which put him in his middle fifties. He'd never married because somehow long-term relationships with women were beyond him. "I love them too much," was the way he'd explained it to me when I was older. "I mean all of them. I could never promise there'd never be anyone else." But he had been faithful one at a time to a string of temporary aunts that seemed to stay approximately the same age even though he got older. The current one had been in office for close to two years and had only last Friday served notice that she wouldn't be seeing him anymore unless he cared to get married. He didn't. But he didn't like not having her around. It was the first time I'd ever seen him upset by one of these breakups. Maybe it was because it was the first one he hadn't engineered. But that was part of the reason I was coming to have dinner with him. He'd sounded as if he needed company.

I walked past the Aqueduct Pharmacy on 183rd, with his name in shaded gilt letters on the plate glass window that looked smaller than it used to, and stopped in at the liquor store next door to pick up a bottle of Lancers. He liked that. I used my key to let myself into the apartment. He was just coming out of the bathroom, putting a Band-Aid on his left index finger.

There was a large speaker cabinet, brand new, pulled out from the living-room wall, and on the floor beside it some partly skinned wire and an open penknife.

"The problem now," I said, "is, given the evidence at hand, to try to determine just how this little accident happened."

"Don't be smart," he said. "Smart guys we always got plenty of. What do you think of it?"

He meant the speaker. "Looks terrific," I said. "I assume it sounds the same."

"You won't believe it," he said, sitting down on the floor and picking up the knife again. "That enclosure is half again the size Bozak makes for that speaker panel. This was made custom by that *gonoph* on Third Avenue." All tradesmen were *gonophs;* crooks. Not that he really thought that. It was a kind of protective word that showed he knew he'd paid too much or bought something foolish. By now, of course, it was just a synonym.

His brows came together as he concentrated on stripping the second strand of speaker cord. This, obviously, was how the knife had slipped in the first place. It was an old story with Joe. Knives and screwdrivers did funny things in his hands. Fortunately, he never messed with the big stuff, like chain saws or power mowers.

He relaxed as the insulation slid off without further incident, and started making the final connection. "Wait till you hear this thing," he said, and a moment later we did and he was right. It sounded terrific.

"You hear those strings?" he shouted over the music. I smiled and nodded, and he looked pleased. I looked at the album. It was Mendelssohn's *Italian Symphony.* He let it play for a few more seconds, then lifted the tone arm.

"Before they pound on the ceiling," he said.

"They do that?"

He smiled. "Not really. They're pretty good about it. Some system, huh?"

I agreed that it was.

"Now you know what's coming? Now that I spent twenty billion dollars on all of this? They're talking stereo records. Everything's obsolete. You start again from scratch. Everything but the speaker, and you need two of those. A second box like that in this room, I'll have to move out. Should I put that on ice?"

He meant the Lancers. "I'll do it," I said, and I went into the kitchen with it. When I came back out, he had the tuner on. WQXR, at background level. A piano concerto.

"What is that?" I asked.

He listened for a moment. "It's Mozart," he said. "But I'm not sure what. I know it, but I can't think. That happens to me all the time. I spend so much time with this, you'd think I could keep it straight."

"I don't know that it matters."

He smiled and sat down on the couch. "Of course it doesn't, but it would be nice. I'll get you a drink in a minute."

I started back to the kitchen. "I'll take care of it," I said.

"Ginger ale for me," he called after me, as if I didn't know. "In the next life," he said while I was putting things together, "I want to do the kind of work where I'm not on my feet all day."

I came back in with his ginger ale and a martini for myself. "You found everything okay?"

I nodded and raised my glass. "Skoal," I said, and we drank.

"It's funny about the music," he said later on, over dinner. "I've been listening to classical music maybe fifteen, twenty years. But I didn't grow up with it, so I'm still an outsider. You ever watch somebody swim who didn't learn how when he was a kid? He may be able to get around, but it never looks convincing. That's me with this music. I don't really know what I'm doing, but I like being in the water. How's your steak?"

I nodded. "Perfect," I said. "You've got it down to a science."

"I should hope so," he said. "You live alone for thirty years, you're in trouble if you can't cook a steak."

He didn't get around to Alyse (accent on the second syllable) till after we'd finished the wine. "She really means it," he said.

"Why don't you marry her?"

His eyebrows rose as he looked up at me. "Whose side are you on?"

There were Dixie cups of ice cream for dessert, half chocolate and half vanilla, from the drugstore. "I'm too old to get married," he said. "I'm afraid to get married."

I was scraping the bottom of my cup, but I turned down the

offer of another. "I can't help you, Uncle Joe," I said. "I've got my own mess to make."

"I know, I know. I'm just complaining, that's all. Fourteen times yesterday I almost called her. I miss her." He put his ice-cream cup down and wiped his mouth. "The trouble is, I need to meet somebody new. People erase each other. When one walks out, you don't get over her till you find somebody else. Then it's over in a minute."

"I'll keep my eyes open for you," I said. "Of course, it's tougher these days. We're competing for the same age bracket."

He frowned. "Don't tease me, David. I don't go looking for younger women."

I stayed till midnight, just talking and sipping a little brandy. He never allowed me to help him with the dishes on these visits, so I'd long since stopped offering to tackle the mess.

Around eleven, he caught me with my mind a million miles away. "Where are you, exactly?" he asked.

At the office, was where I was. I apologized and took out a folded sheet of paper. "Just let me write this down," I said. I hadn't even been aware of thinking about the problem, but suddenly a solution had popped out of nowhere.

"Something for the office?" he asked.

I nodded and put the piece of paper away and put the idea out of my head for now. What remained of the evening belonged to Joe.

Later, on the subway home, I pulled out the slip of paper again and felt a chill of excitement. It still looked like an awfully good idea.

Somewhere in this world there's a man who looks as crooked as Lenny Basch and is really as honest as the day is long. I feel sorry for that man.

I suppose it's possible that my memory of that first impression may be colored by my knowledge of his later behavior, but

I don't really think so. Shifty eyes, slick black hair combed side-ways over baldness, heavy horn-rimmed glasses, blue-black shadow of a beard that could be shaved close enough to gleam, but not to disappear.

He was sitting on the couch in Stu's office when I came in on Monday morning.

"Heard a lot about you," Lenny said, looking just past my ear as we shook hands.

I muttered some inanity, and Stu got up quickly. Apparently this meeting had gone on as long as he wanted it to go. "All right, Len," Stu said. "I'll start reading all the columns."

Lenny laughed. "Give me a few days, okay?"

After he'd left, Stu motioned for me to shut the door behind him. "He's a creep," Stu said, "but he gets space."

So that's what he was; a creep who got space. He'd been doing PR for Mike Prince for a couple of years and Stu had suddenly decided the new show might be able to use a little of that. There was a smell about this show, Stu said. It was going to cause a stir. And he was determined to push it as far as it would go.

I had his attention as soon as I uttered the magic word, format. And when I told him what I'd come up with, I got just the reaction I'd hoped for; the thoughtful, steady nod, the slight frown, the lips pushed out, the fingertips tapping against each other, and then the one word, "Terrific."

It came as a relief because my confidence had been shattered earlier that morning when I'd outlined the idea to Frank Dean. It had been something of a courtesy call. The original format had really been his, so I had the feeling that I should mention the change to him before I gave it to Stu. I'm not really sure why.

He'd listened stiffly, as he always listened to me these days, and then dismissed it completely with a tumble of reasons for why it wouldn't work. And for a few nervous minutes he had me thinking maybe he was right. But Stu liked it. The man who made the decisions around here thought it was terrific.

And as it happens, it was terrific. In the next few weeks of run-throughs we changed it very little from the format that went on the air, and at the time I was rather proud of that.

It solved almost every problem we'd been wrestling with. It enabled us to start out with easy questions, then increase the difficulty so there'd be a feeling of admiration for the players who could stay with them. And it stretched the contest out so that the ten-thousand-dollar weekly budget could be made to mount.

So now we had a format. And all that was left was to find people who could play it.

4

WITHOUT MOVING MY HEAD, WITHOUT EVEN SHIFTING MY EYES, I strained sideways for a glimpse of Stu's reaction. Nothing. He was staring straight ahead at the bank of monitors in front of us. He'd heard, you could bet on that. But there was nothing to be done about it.

In his booth, Ginger Malloy furrowed his brow and pursed his lips as he struggled for the answer. There was perspiration on his forehead.

Mike Prince leaned toward the booth holding the question card. He repeated the question. "I must have your answer," he said.

Ginger moved close to the microphone. Too close. "Carl Sandburg," he rasped.

"You're right," Mike said crisply, and there was applause. "We'll be back to you in just a moment." And the lights went out in Ginger's booth.

Still no sign from Stu that he'd heard anything wrong at all as the lights came up in the other booth. Ginger's opponent was an attractive young WAC who was stationed on Governor's Island. Stu seemed to be paying attention, but I knew his mind was where mine was. The fact that Ginger had used the line wasn't really so bad. What mattered was that he'd probably use it again.

The category was poets, and Ginger's question had been: "This poet is perhaps best known for his multivolume biography of Abraham Lincoln. Who is he?" At which point Ginger had pondered for a moment, nodded, and said, "Oh, yes. That's that fella from Indiana." And then he'd furrowed his brow and thought long and hard before finally coming up with the answer.

Why had he said Indiana when Sandburg was from Illinois? Ah, that's where the problem lay. Not an immediate problem. The question had not required Ginger to come up with the poet's home state. No, the problem was down the line. There was a good chance we'd be hearing more about Indiana, because Ginger had gotten his wires crossed.

Two days ago, in Ginger's apartment at the back of the building where I lived, Stu Leonard had gone over all this very carefully with Ginger while I spent a couple of hours at the movies, having flatly refused to have anything to do with it. Later, despite my objections, Stu had filled me in on the details. To the Sandburg question, Ginger was supposed to nod quickly and say: "He's a favorite of mine. Carl Sandburg." His *next* question, the one Mike Prince was about to ask him, was to have elicited the response, "Oh, yes, that's that fella from Indiana." Then a moment or two of thinking, and finally the poet's name.

So here we were, heading straight for the problem, with no real way to keep it from happening. Control was all in Ginger's hands. A clever man, having realized his error, would now confine his next answer to something simple. Was Ginger that clever man? Or were we about to be treated to a reprise on the state of Indiana? The oddsmaker in my head was up to twenty-to-one with no takers in sight, and if I'd known which plug controlled what in this stifling control room, I'd have kicked something out of the wall. But on we went, an accident about to happen.

The WAC answered her question correctly to polite applause, and Ginger's booth came on again. "Are you ready, Ginger?" Mike Prince asked. Ginger nodded, and the lawn mower in my stomach started churning. Mike held the question card up high (it became something of a trademark) and read: "He wrote the dialect poems, 'Little Orphant Annie' and 'When the Frost Is on the Punkin.' Who is he?"

Stu Leonard's expression never changed as he waited for Ginger's answer. Ginger nodded slowly, thinking hard, and then said, as freshly as if the phrase had just occurred to him: "Oh, yes. That's that fellow from Indiana." He leaned close to the microphone. "James Whitcomb Riley," he said. "Right!" said Mike, and the place came apart. They liked Ginger.

Ginger hung in there for a question on e.e. cummings ("The guy who didn't like capital letters"), then identified T.S. Eliot as the bang-and-whimper man, and finally won his match when his opponent missed and he named Hart Crane as the metrical builder of *The Bridge.* Not bad for a janitor who never went past the fourth grade.

Afterward, it was twenty minutes before I could get Stu alone, that's how many people were dying to tell us how terrific everything had been. And if anyone had noticed the glaring problem with the spinning red light on its head, nobody said a word. Donald Scheer and Murray descended from the client's booth full of smiles and satisfaction. "Of course," Murray said, "we have some notes. But those can wait till morning."

"Well done," said Donald Scheer, extending a hand from the sleeve of the best-tailored suit I'd ever seen. And then the two of them were gone and so was Stu, and it took me several minutes before I finally found him again, alone in Mike Prince's dressing room. He'd just finished dialing a number.

"I told you he couldn't do it," I said.

Stu covered the mouthpiece. "He did it fine. He won, didn't

he? And nobody noticed a thing." Then, into the phone: "This is Stu Leonard. Can you handle four people in fifteen minutes?" He waited for an answer, then hung up. "Get Toby and Frank and we'll meet at Toots Schorr's."

"What about Mike Prince?"

Stu nodded. "Yeah, I suppose so. Tell Toby to call back and change it to five."

"Four's fine," I said. "I'm not hungry. What makes you think nobody noticed?"

"Nobody did. And if you don't want to eat, come anyway and have a drink."

"I'm tired. I want to get home."

Stu grinned. "Still sucking your thumb, is that it?"

"We've got a lot to talk about, but I don't think now's the time."

Stu looked at me for a moment, then turned away and shrugged. "My door's always open." He picked up the cap that he'd left on Mike's dressing table and popped it on his head. "Change your mind and join us," he said, starting out. "It'll do you good to change your mind about something." But he knew I wouldn't.

Outside, the thick, damp summer heat flung itself all over me as I stepped out of the revolving door. Yes, I nodded to the doorman in answer to did I want a cab, but before his whistle could summon results I was aware of the green MG across the street honking wildly in my direction.

"I know you're still mad," Carla said when I crossed over. "But at least let me drive you home."

I nodded and got in. She leaned over and kissed me quickly. More of an experiment than an act of affection. "For God's sake, take your jacket off," she said.

I did, and my tie, and she whipped us through the city streets in a record that still stands for four cylinders. In front of my place I started to get out without saying anything, but she shut the engine off. "I'm coming up," she said.

"You're parked in a bus stop."

She slammed the door. "I'll install a coin box."

"Suit yourself," I said.

I'd been avoiding her not out of pique, but because I'd never felt so betrayed. We'd had what had really become a special relationship. Unusual, but in its own way very close. Close enough, I'd thought, so there was nothing I couldn't trust her with. When Stu had finally told me he'd been talking to Ginger, I'd gone into shock. I couldn't believe she'd done it.

The air conditioner was in the bedroom, so we brought our gin and tonics in there and propped pillows against the head-board.

"I don't like it when you're not talking to me," she said after a long drink.

I took a long drink myself. "You're here, so I guess we're talking. But there's not a lot I feel like talking about."

"Will you let me say I'm sorry? I am, you know. I've tried to tell you that."

"Okay," I said. "Now you've told me."

She'd gotten trapped, she said. She'd never meant to say anything about Ginger, knowing the way I felt, but one day she'd been talking to Murray about the kind of people she knew we were looking for, and before she had a chance to stop herself she'd said there was someone who'd be just perfect. Murray kept pressing for the name and after he said he understood her position and wouldn't say anything to anyone, she finally told him who it was. She'd had no idea he'd passed it on to Stu until the first press release with the contestants' names. She'd had a terrible fight with Murray about it and the upshot had been he'd given her a raise. How about that for irony? But she really hadn't meant to do it.

I couldn't stay mad forever and now seemed as good a time as any to get past it.

She put her head on my shoulder and touched my arm.

"Now don't start that," I said quietly. "It's been a long night

55

and I'm tired, and I'd rather go to sleep than get myself all worked up just to get hung out to dry."

Her hand moved up my arm with a touch I'd never felt before. "Not this time," she said.

My arm tightened to keep her from moving closer, and a wave of anger came over me so suddenly it caught me by surprise. "What is this? One you figure you owe me?"

"Don't be a bastard," she said softly, and that really did it. I jumped up, knocking the drink off the nightstand, adrenalin pumping its way in several directions.

"Now look," I barked at her. "If there's one thing I don't believe in, it's fucking my troubles away. And you'll have to forgive me if I can't keep up with these sudden switches. If affection wasn't enough for you, don't expect me to settle for an act of contrition. You said you were sorry. Now why don't we drop it at that and just say good night."

By now she was crying and after a minute or two of letting the atmosphere settle I had to go over and calm her down, and the rest went pretty much the way you might imagine.

Afterward she held me tight even though we were both a little sweaty. The air conditioner hadn't quite had time to be fully effective.

"Oh, God, that was lovely," she said. I stroked her hair and kissed her forehead and said nothing, keeping my mouth shut being company policy at times like this.

"I don't know what to say," she said. "I mean, about . . . you know," she said.

I nodded, but it turned out I didn't know at all. I thought she meant what had happened with Ginger, but she was talking about her married friend.

"I mean, I still love him. I know I do. And then I let myself do this with you. I know I'm a big girl who can do as she pleases, but shouldn't I feel just a little bit sorry?"

"Give yourself a couple of hours."

She pulled her head back and looked at me. "You mean you think I'll hate myself in the morning?"

"I wouldn't be surprised."

"Will you?"

I smiled at her. "Of course not. But I'm not having an affair with a married woman."

"Man," she said. "Oh, woman, of course. I see." She put her face against mine and held on. "I'm not really always this stupid," she said, and then we were at it again and if anything it was even better.

"Stay the night," I said, considerably later. She shook her head and sat up.

"No, I have to get home."

"I thought you were a big girl who could do whatever she pleased."

She got out of bed and started putting her clothes on. "Maybe not as big as I think," she said. Then she looked at me and grinned. "Besides, I'm parked in a bus stop."

The next morning there was a hand-delivered note waiting for me at the office, marked personal. The envelope was typed, but there was something about it that made it look feminine and Nicole, the receptionist, smiled when she handed it to me. I waited till I got to my own office before I opened it. It wasn't at all what I'd expected. The note was from Margo.

"Have you really lost your mind?" it said. *"I can't wait till next week to hear more about all those guys from Indiana."*

I sat down quickly, thoroughly shaken. Someone had noticed all right.

I ripped the note into tinier pieces than could possibly have been necessary and threw the remains in the wastebasket. Then I went looking for Stu.

He wasn't in the office, which was surprising for almost quarter to ten, but when I checked with Nicole she told me he'd called in earlier to say he was taking his son to breakfast at the Plaza.

That took some of the steam out of the sense of purpose I'd

walked in with, but it also gave me a chance to shut my office door and put myself through another silent rehearsal. There was no question about what I was going to say; it was just a matter of getting the words exactly right.

We had to go on with Ginger. He was due to start next week against a new opponent. But there'd be no more answers. None. And don't try doing it without telling me, because I'll know and I won't even bother showing up the next morning. It's straight from now on, or count me out.

The phone startled me. It was Nicole. Murray Cashin was calling a second time for Stu. He wanted to know what time he'd be in. "How do I know?" I snapped. "He's never done his father act before."

"Well, what should I tell him?"

"Tell him you don't know," I said irritably, but in a minute she was back on the line.

"He wants to talk to you."

She put him on, and Murray sounded excited. "Jesus," he said, "some time he picked not to be in. You can't believe the reactions to Ginger Malloy. Everybody loves him. Donald's called here four times already. I think we really have something."

"I'll have Stu call you," I said, trying to make that the end of the conversation. But Murray wasn't finished.

"An eight-year-old to the Plaza? What kind of place is that to take an eight-year-old?"

"Maybe he didn't," I said.

"What do you mean?"

"Nothing," I said. "I mean I really don't know anything about that."

"What's he trying to do, make an impression? That's it, you know. His own kid and he's trying to impress him. Listen," Murray said, "be sure to have him call me." And he hung up.

One thing I'd learned by now was that the truth was not something for which Stu had unusual reverence. And while he might at this moment really be having that breakfast, the chances were no better than fifty-fifty. For most of us, the truth is at least what we tell when there's no reason to lie. Not so with Stu. For him the truth was simply one of several possibilities, so at any given moment the words that came out of his mouth were whatever words he wanted to hear himself say. Sometimes he'd invent things for no better reason than to try on an attitude, walk up to the three-way mirror, and see how he looked in it.

It was one of the things I'd allowed myself to get used to over the weeks we worked together; one of the many things that I'd have firmly disapproved of if I'd been sitting on the outside watching all of this develop, but that I managed to accept as part of the forward momentum of this project I'd somehow become a part of.

The problems had started with the pilot. Donald Scheer was committed to the show, but a pilot was in order just to shake things down. As it turned out that was the one thing that didn't happen. At least, not the things that mattered.

Stu was in love with the whole project and fastened all his attention on making this the slickest, best-dressed half hour of its kind that anyone had ever seen. *Important* was the word he kept using. He wanted the whole thing to look important; not like some schlocky giveaway.

And by the time we got on stage it really did look pretty good. Two impressive soundproof booths set boldly in the middle of lots of glass and polished metal. Reflections all over the place, but Stu didn't care about that. Let the technicians figure out some way to live with all that glare. He loved the way it sparkled.

As for the reality of the game itself, Stu quickly decided that wasn't really what this pilot was all about. For his purposes, it would be enough just to demonstrate how well the set photographed, how simply the rules could be clarified with just the right camera shots, how effectively the twenty-piece live orchestra could accent the drama with all that terrific original music.

It would be tricky getting all this exactly right in the little time we had, so when it came to the questions and answers the best thing would be simply to stage things. Cast the show with people who'd learn their lines and get things right or wrong as we told them to. It was just a pilot, after all. Nothing was at stake. Why not use it to find out how all the mechanical elements would come together?

Okay. And it came together great. Not right away, of course. It was chaos the first few hours. But by the time we got around to making the kinescope (no tape in those days), everything seemed somehow to fall into place.

It went over big with Murray Cashin, and the next day when Donald Scheer got back to town from company business in London we had an even bigger triumph in that private dining room at Capricorn.

"Well done, gentlemen," Donald Scheer said in the crisp, clipped rhythms that I later learned were much more British just after he'd been through customs. "Must that trim be black?" he asked Stu, and while I had trouble remembering what trim he was talking about, Stu seemed to know at once, and quickly agreed that a change could be made. Yellow was settled on, which meant it would photograph medium gray. A very big decision.

Lunch appeared as the result of Donald Scheer's having pressed a button under the table, and it was the first of many disappointments I was to have in that dining room over the next few months. Donald Scheer was as trim now as he'd been in his rowing days at Princeton, and the price he paid was a succession of thoroughly uninteresting salads that he seemed to relish but that left me with the lasting conviction that nothing that crunched could possibly taste any good.

There were fresh yellow pads at each of our places, but we never got to use them. Aside from his objection to that offending black trim, he liked it all. Every detail. We left there on a wave of euphoria, confident that if someone with the solid judgment and immaculate taste of Donald Scheer could show this kind of enthusiasm, the dimensions of our impending success would turn out to be difficult to measure.

But the glow failed to survive the night. By morning, Stu realized that most of what Donald Scheer had admired had had nothing to do with reality. What he had seen had been carefully manufactured. How could we now be sure we could deliver in the real world anything that could possibly measure up?

There was, of course, a way, and as the date of that first show approached it became obvious that Stu was drifting closer to it. Finally he mentioned the subject and I responded with a no that was firm enough to end the discussion, but not, as it turned out, to affect his decision. He shut himself behind his office door for two full days and then summoned me to announce that he'd worked out an arrangement with Ginger Malloy *(What!),* and that he wanted my help in talking to him. I'm not sure what I'd have said had somebody neutral been involved, but the shock of learning that he'd somehow plugged into Ginger sent me storming out of there in something close to shock and ready to kill just about everyone I knew.

That night he showed up at my apartment with the usual gift of food. Takeout cartons from a Chinese restaurant; nothing for him, of course. He wanted to be sure I understood that Ginger would be the only time, just to get things started, and I could stay completely out of it. He understood perfectly how I felt. He agreed with me that it was wrong to operate this way, and we never would again, but this was insurance he had to have, just for openers. It wasn't something he planned to keep on doing. By the time he got to the lichee nuts he was once again assuring me that I was his closest friend on earth, the brother he'd never had, and the only person in the universe he could not function without.

At quarter of twelve Stu finally called and asked me to meet him at an antique shop on Third Avenue.

When I got there he was looking impatient even though I

thought I'd made remarkable time. "How was breakfast?" I asked him.

"What are you talking about? You know I never eat breakfast."

"With your son," I reminded him. "You took him to the Plaza."

"Oh, that," he said. "He loved it. Come on," he said, shoving open the door. "I have to show you something."

It was a brass bookend in the figure of a Buddha. "What do you think?" he asked.

I wasn't sure what he had in mind. "You mean, do I like it?"

"They want a hundred and fifty for it."

I picked it up and examined it closely, with no real idea of what I was looking for. "I guess it's terrific," I said. "Where's the other one?"

"You don't like it," he said.

"I don't have any strong feelings one way or the other."

He took it out of my hand and set it down. "Come on, let's get out of here," he said impatiently, and a minute later we were seated in a pizza place because he knew I must be hungry.

He knew I had something on my mind and he kept me from it with a constant stream of notes for next week's show. The lighting was bad on the woman's face, one of the readouts was too bright, the cutting had to be crisper. Was Vince really good enough for this? He'd never done an important show. I let him check off the items until finally he seemed to wind down. Then I let him know that unless Ginger went on next week without being given answers, the entire enterprise could continue without me.

He waved me off airily. "Of course, of course. That goes without saying. That's not why I wanted to talk to you." Why he wanted to talk to me was that he'd been doing some thinking about how well and how quickly our business relationship had come along, and how important it had become to him, and how much he wanted to be sure it continued. That was why he wanted me to have a royalty on this show, and on anything new that came up in the office, regardless of whose idea it was. It would be a continuing percentage that would be mine regardless of whether or not we were still together, but of course he'd want some kind of commitment from me. Two years, say.

The money was fabulous, and the flattery had precisely the effect on me I'd seen it have on others. I mean, here was this at least moderately successful guy who thought what I'd done was important enough to want to make sure I'd hang around. If you're having trouble understanding that, you've never bathed in the sunshine of someone's approval. It feels terrific.

The next morning the contract was on my desk, and it read simply enough so that even a moron could understand it, so I just signed it and handed it back. If it was a mistake, and it very well may have been, there's no lawyer in the world who could have saved me from it.

Stu's office door was closed a lot the rest of the day, and the day after that, with what I gathered were mostly calls from Donald Scheer and Murray Cashin, but I welcomed the freedom because it gave me a chance to push ahead on material, and also to get out at a reasonable hour both nights.

Both nights were spent with Carla, who was suffused with guilt, but not sufficiently to keep us from continuing our newfound pleasant contact. Both nights she made it clear that although she loved me, she was really still in love with this other guy, who would remain the most important man in the world to her. Are you aware of the difference between loving and being *in* love? Well, Carla was, and apparently it was all the difference in the world. All of which was fine with me because for the first time it provided me with the delights of a warm relationship that wasn't expected to go anywhere.

On Thursday, when Stu called me into his office there was a tape recorder on his desk.

"I want you to hear this," he said. "Shut the door."

I did, and he started the tape, which began with the clumsy room noises all amateur recordings seem to start with.

"Okay," Stu's voice said, hollow and informal, "you understand these are just samples. These aren't the questions we'll be using Monday."

"Um hm," said the other voice. "Go ahead and ask them." It was Ginger.

"They're just random, jump-around questions," Stu said. "Let's see how you do."

Ginger knew that Babe Ruth had set his home run record in 1927, but could not name one member of Eisenhower's cabinet, except, for some reason, Oveta Culp Hobby, who'd been out of office for over a year.

He knew Hemingway was a writer, but was surprised to hear that he'd written *For Whom the Bell Tolls.* He named Shakespeare as the author of *Evangeline,* failed to come up with the country that shares the Iberian Peninsula with Portugal, and was fairly certain that Benjamin Franklin had been our second president.

Stu clicked it off. "You need to hear any more?" he asked. I shook my head.

"Okay," Stu said, pitching back in his chair. "So here we are on Thursday. On Monday, we go on with episode two of "Face to Face," wherein we pick up our janitor and our WAC in the middle of their second match. Only our janitor suddenly has trouble remembering his middle name."

"Can't we say he's sick?" *I* was, because I could see where this was heading.

"What about the girl?"

"What do you mean?"

"What makes you think she'll do any better?"

My stomach did one of those little flips that lets you know all your parts are connected, and I slumped deeper on the couch, nodding slowly as what should have been obvious right along finally sank in.

Of course she'd gotten help. Maybe not the detailed scenario that had been given to Ginger, but help enough to enable her to hold up her end of this exciting contest. You see, the way it worked there were seven questions in each category, starting out with something very easy and gradually getting tougher as the contestants alternated up the line. If one player missed, the other one had to answer correctly to win. If they managed to get up to number seven, they both got asked the same question. Whoever got it right won. If both or neither did, we had a tie.

It's not really necessary to understand every detail of this to see that things would be at their most exciting if both players did well until they got up to the higher numbers and then knocked off some fancy-sounding questions. Last Monday both players had, and I should have known that Stu would not have risked the possibility of any other outcome.

It was clear enough what had to be done. Ginger could not go out there unprepared without making it painfully obvious that he was not the same person he'd been the week before. Neither, Stu assured me, could the girl. So we'd have to go through one more week of total scripting. The girl would beat Ginger in a very close first match; then she'd continue without any further help against a player chosen for his or her ability to answer questions, and she'd undoubtedly get knocked off quickly.

And when Monday rolled around, the world may have been surprised by what happened on "Face to Face," but none of us had any reason to be. Ginger finally walked away with eight thousand dollars, every penny of which he had, in his own mind, come to richly deserve. The WAC left with twenty-five hundred and Mike Prince's thanks for helping us get our new show off to such a rousing start. She seemed very grateful.

For two weeks after that we played the game straight; the only time in its history that "Face to Face" was played that way. And the smartest people we could find got some right and missed a few, which really wasn't good enough, because in this format that I had helped to refine, if the players missed two questions in a row things didn't really work out too well. Yes, we could have made the material easier, but you'd be surprised how many times they missed the ones we hadn't thought were especially hard. And anyway, the questions had to sound challenging, didn't they?

So what it comes down to is that after two weeks of frustration, embarrassment, and panicky phone calls from Donald Scheer, we were all aware that something had to be done. Which made us perfect setups for the advent of Matthew Sklar.

5

ELAINE KRAKAUER'S PARENTS WERE FAR FROM WEALTHY, BUT THEY were realistic enough to know that the heavy young man with the close-set, steel-rimmed eyes who giggled joylessly at most of what was said represented about the best their large, formless, monosyllabic daughter could expect, and so they had promised that if, after the marriage, the young man successfully completed one year's employment in the cabdriving job Ben Krakauer's connections would get him, they would pay half of the thirteen thousand dollars it would take to buy the medallion he would need to put him in business as an independent owner.

He was halfway through that year, the driver explained to the fare he'd picked up in front of the Martin Beck. And that fare might not have paid any further attention, except that as the cab turned into the park at Sixth Avenue, the driver, inspired by the equestrian statue at the entrance to the park, reeled off a dazzling string of facts about the subject of that statue, who was, it seemed, José Martí, the poet of Cuban independence, who, having been exiled at the age of sixteen, took up residence in New

York, where he became a well-known journalist, the founder of the Cuban Revolutionary party, and a hero when he returned to Cuba in 1895, joined the insurgents, and met his death at Dos Rios.

This cascade of information might have numbed the average fare, but it made Lenny Basch sit up and start asking the driver a little more about himself. Two days later, after several private discussions and the signing of a bizarre personal-services contract that nobody was to hear about for several months, Lenny Basch brought Matthew Sklar in to meet the gang.

"Okay," Lenny said when everybody's hand had been properly shaken, "ask him anything."

There was a quiet moment as all of us waited deferentially for Stu to make the first move. He looked at Matthew as if trying to imagine what could possibly lie beneath that uninspiring exterior. Then, finally, he spoke. "First of all," he said, "may I call you Matthew?"

Matthew grinned and gave us that dry, nervous giggle, along with a nod.

"Okay, Matthew," Stu said. "Please tell me what 'ileitis' is."

We all knew we were gathered to put tough questions to this pheenom Lenny had found, but this first one wasn't really all that difficult. Just two weeks before, the president had gone through an operation to correct the damage wrought by his ileitis, so it was a disorder the whole country was suddenly familiar with.

"It's an inflammation of the ileum," Matthew answered.

"And where's the ileum?" asked Stu.

"It's part of the small intestine, along with the duodenum and the jejunum."

Lenny Basch leaned back and raised his eyebrows at Stu. "You hear this?" he asked.

Frank Dean cleared his throat. "I think we're all a lot more familiar with the small intestine than we used to be."

Lenny gestured to Frank and smiled. "Your witness," he said.

"Tell me, Matthew," Frank said. "Who won the pro football championship last year?"

Matthew didn't skip a beat. "The Cleveland Browns," he said. "They beat L.A., thirty-eight to fourteen."

"Is that right?" Stu asked Frank.

"I don't know," said Frank.

"It's right," said Matthew Sklar.

Toby leaned forward in her seat. She'd gone from not working on the show at all to helping out with contestants and finally to supervising all the questions. She never left the place. "What movie won the first Academy Award?" she asked.

"Wings," said Matthew.

Stu got up and went for a thoughtful stroll around his desk. Then he turned back to Matthew Sklar. "In the presidential election of 1876, what candidate got the most popular votes?"

"The Democrat," said Matthew. "Samuel J. Tilden. But he lost the electoral vote by one to Rutherford B. Hayes."

Stu nodded approvingly. It was a favorite topic of his; the foolishness of the electoral-college system and the need for a constitutional amendment that would put control of the presidency where it belonged, firmly in the hands of the people.

Frank asked Matthew the real name of the man who wrote as Stendhal, and Matthew came up with Marie-Henri Beyle. And he knew that it was sixty feet, six inches from the pitcher's rubber to home plate, and that Laocoön was a Trojan priest who offended the gods and was strangled by sea serpents. We kept lobbing them in to Matthew, and he kept banging them over the fence. It was a mighty impressive performance.

Especially to us. By now we'd been through an almost endless string of frustrations with the very bright. Smart though they may have been, there hadn't been one who'd been able to stand there and keep coming up with right answers. They knew what they knew, and often that was a lot, but even the smartest of the smart drew some amazing blanks. It had been true of everyone we'd ever seen.

Except Matthew.

We were dazzled, I can tell you. Here at last was someone who could really do what we'd only begun to appreciate as the nearly impossible. If we'd met him on day one, we'd have taken what he did for granted. But we'd seen a lot of people and there'd been nobody like Matthew.

It had all started for him, he told us, with "The Quiz Kids" blaring out of his living-room radio and astonishing his parents and their friends with their remarkable feats. If these little one-note prodigies could elicit such squeals of admiration by multiplying five-digit numbers or coming up with the names of obscure birds, how much greater might the adult world's appreciation be for him if he made it his business to learn, quite simply, everything.

To this end, he spent every afternoon in his local reference room, memorizing an encyclopedia called *The Wonderland of Knowledge.* He read it through (every volume, every entry) exactly a dozen times, and then started in a less organized but no less determined way to gnaw his way through the other loose-backed volumes on the reference shelves. Soon his skill with facts gave him a reputation among his friends that put him right up there with the heavy hitters, and if there was a piece of information someone needed for a homework assignment, or to win a small bet, every kid in his class knew just who to turn to. The more he was encouraged, the more it became his hobby, his passion, his mark of distinction. Ask Matthew, his friends all said. And the more they asked, the stronger his reason for learning more, and still more, so that no matter who asked about what, Matthew would never be stuck for an answer.

Stu couldn't keep the smile off his face. The creature he'd always imagined really existed. If not as one of an abundant species, at least as one of a kind. And the creature was here, in his office.

"All right, Matthew," Stu said quietly. "Why don't you just wait outside."

Matthew looked at Lenny Basch, and Lenny nodded. Matthew got up and Stu went to him and shook his hand. "That was a marvelous performance," he said with some feeling.

Matthew giggled. "I was just getting warmed up," he said.

Stu nodded. "Lenny will be with you in just a minute."

"Will I be on the show?"

"That's what we're going to talk about."

"I can beat anybody," Matthew said.

"Well, I don't know," said Stu. "We've got some pretty good people. But I'm sure you could hold your own."

The invitation arrived on Friday morning. Ginger brought the mail up, as he did every day he thought I might be home. He had sensed that I was less than thrilled with his having appeared on our little epic, and he was anxious to repair the breach. Something perverse in me was determined not to make it easy for him.

"It's in a lady's hand," he said, giving me the envelope, and indeed it was. I looked at the envelope and smiled a smug smile designed to communicate my total familiarity with the lovely body attached to that lady's hand.

"She's always so grateful," I said.

"Grateful, is it," said Ginger, shaking his head.

He stood there waiting for me to open it, but I pressed the door shut gently and left him imagining my successes. It served him right.

The invitation was from Mr. and Mrs. Harold Birnbaum to attend the wedding of their daughter, Alyse, to Mr. Joseph Klein. And in a life that has never been short of surprises, this one still ranks up there with the biggest.

A week from Saturday, there I was at the Concourse Plaza, having agreed in the meantime to serve as best man to a very uncertain Uncle Joe.

"Do I know what I'm doing?" he'd asked on the phone. "It's blackmail, you understand. Pure and simple."

"Why don't you have her arrested?"

"You know what I mean," Joe said. "She wouldn't see me otherwise."

"I think that's considered fair, Uncle Joe."

"In your circles, maybe. Should I get out of this?"

I cleared my throat. "About my suit. What would you think about blue?"

He stopped for a moment. "Okay," he said. "Another wise guy."

Champagne tumbled gently down the plastic waterfall that was set in the middle of the dozens of trays that bore the usual caterer's tidbits, and a quivering accordion forced all conversation up to the level of a shout. Joe nodded and smiled in all the right places, and through it all managed to look both reluctant and pleased. After the bride had danced with the groom, between the soup and the chicken tetrazzini, I excused myself and went to make a telephone call.

The booth was in the lobby, with a view straight down the hill of 161st Street toward Yankee Stadium, where the flags were flying. Joe and I had gone there only once when I was a kid, to see the second game of the 1941 World Series with the Dodgers. Usually if we went to a ball game it was across the river to the Polo Grounds, because Joe was a Giants fan. Maybe the only one in the Bronx. This World Series thing happened because Joe had been given the tickets by a salesman for some laxative. "He thinks this way I'll give him better counter space," Joe said with a wink. The Dodgers won it, three to two, and we were delighted because even though we spent the regular season rooting against them, the Dodgers were, after all, the National League.

"Stu Leonard Productions." It was Toby, on the second ring. Stiff and formal, even on a Saturday.

"Hi," I said.

"Oh, hi." Formal still. Not your friendly hi. I could see her

72

with all of them in Stu's office, answering the phone while everybody waited to see who it was.

I asked to talk to Stu.

"Hold on just a minute." Noncommittal. How was she to know Stu's pleasure? He might be dying to talk to me, or he might want her to say he'd left an hour ago. She'd given up trying to forecast his moods. I was on hold long enough so that I'd started searching for extra coins when he finally came on.

"Well, how's the bar mitzvah?" A light note there, to let me know he didn't hold a grudge.

"Inspiring." It was the best I could do. Besides, I wanted to get to what was on my mind. "What's been decided?"

"Well, I don't know." Then his mouth moved away from the phone to let me know he was talking to the others in the room. "Has anything been decided?" Unintelligible murmurs. Then Stu again. "Well, I guess something has. You should have been here, David, to represent your point of view."

I felt my heart head south. They'd decided to use him. "How soon?" I asked.

"This week. If it's right, what are we waiting for?"

"Not a thing," I answered dully.

"We'll talk on Monday," said Stu, and we hung up.

It wasn't anything as grand as a premonition. I don't have those. It was simply that I couldn't stand the sight of Matthew Sklar. Probably for reasons that didn't do me credit.

We'd been arguing about whether or not to use him ever since his appearance in the office, and as soon as I announced that there was a wedding I had to go to on Saturday, the meeting to make the final decision was scheduled on what Stu assured me was the only possible day. I should just do whatever I felt was more important. I did.

Or did I? I was here, as I knew I should be, and vaguely aware of Joe's pleasure in showing me off to his new wife's family.

"David!" he called to me across the room, and when I came

to him he put his arm around the man he was standing with. "David works in TV. Don't you, David."

I nodded.

"David, do you know who this is?"

I wasn't really sure.

Joe laughed. "This, David, is my new father-in-law." And both men laughed again, because the father-in-law was two years younger than the groom.

"What do you do in TV?" the father-in-law asked. And then he had to ask again, because even though I was here where I'd told myself I ought to be, not all of me was always in the room.

"David!" Uncle Joe said sharply. "Harold's asking what you do."

I told him, and he was impressed even though he hadn't seen the show. He made me write down on a pack of matches when it was on.

There'd been a phone call earlier that week from a doctor I'd been to a month ago about an ear infection. He'd called to ask if it was true that Matthew Sklar was going to appear on our television program. When I told him it was possible, he seemed surprised. He hadn't wanted to discuss the matter any further because Matthew had once been a patient, but I finally got him to tell me a little more, including the fact that Matthew habitually told grandiose lies and liked to linger in his office asking inappropriate questions about sex. Inappropriate, that is, to ask of an ear, nose, and throat man in a leering, giggling, wrong-note sort of way.

"Give me an example," I'd asked him, and he'd been reluctant to supply one but finally did.

"He asked me once," the doctor said, "if I thought there was anything wrong with a man who liked furburgers."

It had taken me a moment to be completely clear about that one, but when I was I agreed it was not the sort of question that had likely been asked in a search for medical information.

"I see," I think I'd said.

"Look," the doctor had continued. "It's none of my business, and please don't quote me, but I think you'd be wise not
to get involved with him."

That made sense to me, but it didn't to Stu when I reported
my conversation. In fact, he thought it was pretty funny.

But I hadn't been the only one with reservations. Toby had
found him crude; the kind of judgmental word she generally
disliked using, she explained, but the only one that expressed
her reaction. Frank Dean had been properly dazzled by his performance, but had been put off by something that Toby finally
helped him describe as Matthew's negative personality.

But Stu had remained convinced that Matthew Sklar could
do for us precisely what we'd always envisioned, and that far
from being negative, his personality would grow on an audience,
especially women. Toby had actually shuddered at that, but Stu
insisted he was dead serious. There was something about this
boy. And, of course, there were the continuing phone calls from
Murray Cashin, passing along the concerns of his boss, the impeccable Donald Scheer, who wanted to be sure Stu understood
that "Face to Face" had been envisioned only as something for
the summer, and that unless something radical happened
quickly to the ratings, we would not be around to see the leaves
turn. Not only would we not be renewed, Murray Cashin emphasized, but unless the quality level went back to where it had been
the first couple of weeks with Ginger Malloy, the well-tailored
Donald Scheer would be likely to lose considerable respect for
this office, and loss of respect was not good for business. It
would specifically not be good for the Capricorn business on any
other Stu Leonard Production, since faith in the competence of
this organization was in considerable danger of being undermined. So if Stu felt some pressure, I suppose it was understandable. Hey, everything's understandable, doesn't everyone know
that?

"I pronounce it 'Uh-*lees*'," Alyse was explaining to the

75

woman who'd interrupted our earnest conversation to wish her well.

"Of course. I should have known," the woman said. Her husband was a business friend of Harold's, and this was really a lovely affair, which was something she really wanted to say before she left, and she left.

Alyse's brows came together as she continued our important (her word) conversation. She understood the role I played in Joe's life, and I must understand that our relationship was to continue exactly as before. If she could become a part of it, so much the better, but she understood that was something she'd have to earn. She hoped I understood what she was trying to say. I got my eyebrows as close together as hers were and assured her I understood perfectly, which brought forth a smile of relief and the positive assurance that I would be their first dinner guest as soon as they got back from Bermuda. Did Bermuda, she wanted to know, make sense in the summer? I told her I'd heard it was lovely, because I didn't see much point in telling her I didn't have the faintest idea, and later, when Joe asked the same question, I was just as reassuring. But it wouldn't have much mattered what I'd said because several glasses of the sticky champagne had put a silly smile on Joe's face and a dimming glaze across his eyes. "I'm gonna be happy, David," he slurred. "Sheza wunnerful woman."

I nodded, but it wasn't enough.

"You think she's wunnerful, right?"

"The best," I agreed. "Like Bermuda in the summertime."

Joe pursed his lips and bobbed his head up and down. "I knew you'd like her. It means a lot for you to . . . "

He never finished the sentence because he was much too busy turning green and slumping to the floor so fast I barely managed to break his fall. I had a fair idea what was likely to be next, so I dragged him to the bathroom in the hall and held his head while he got rid of all that unfamiliar booze. There was a lot of knocking at the door by people who had no idea anything was going on in there, but simply wanted to use the bathroom for its more usual purpose. I managed to turn them all away with the calm assurance that I'd be right out.

When he finally came around his head was pounding, but he couldn't remember being sick and all he cared about was did anyone know. All of us in my family have always cared a lot about things like that.

6

HOW, AFTER ALL THE WARNINGS, DID I LET IT HAPPEN AGAIN?

If I was really as determined as I thought I was, how did I manage once again to find myself in the middle of an intrigue for which I had no taste, and against which I had argued endlessly? I can tell you the sequence of events, but it isn't enough of an explanation. I have no explanation.

Nor can I explain Stu's total fascination with Matthew Sklar. Having made the decision to use him, he spent endless hours alone with him. There were question-and-answer sessions to further test Matthew's encyclopedic capacities, conversational sessions to try to get under his skin, and later a shopping session to cover that skin with something more acceptable than the faded leather jacket that until now had been his uniform. Stu paid for the suit out of what he referred to as his own pocket, and Matthew was properly impressed with the gift, even though it was at least a size too large and hung on him as if it had been bought by careful parents for a teenager who would grow into it next year.

Matthew worshipped him, of course. And I suppose it's possible that this alone explains Stu's willingness to spend so much time in his company. The figure being worshipped rarely tires of the worshipper.

All this seems in memory to have taken longer to develop than in fact it did. The events that fell in the time between the decision to use Matthew Sklar and his first appearance on the program are so vivid and particular that it doesn't seem possible for them to have been crowded into so short a span as nine days. But nine days is all it took to forge bonds between Stu and Matthew Sklar that made one the total master and the other the eager slave whose better life ahead was clearly dependent on his doing exactly what he was told.

"He wants to see you," the soft, almost whining voice said. I looked up from the sheet of questions and saw that endlessly grinning, bespectacled face. Other people wore glasses. Why were his the only ones I ever noticed?

"All right," I said, and looked down again.

"He said right away," said Matthew. I nodded, and Matthew stood there, waiting for me to get up, or at least look up again. It became a contest.

"Aren't you going?"

I nodded and went on reading. The block of Matthew didn't move. "Good night, Matthew," I said, my eyes still on the sheet of paper. He didn't move, and I could feel the anger line moving up my neck. Silly things sometimes get to me. I went on reading.

"I really think you should go in there," Matthew said again.

I looked up at him so quickly he turned his eyes away. "I think I should, too," I said slowly. "And I will in just a moment." This time I kept staring at him and without saying anything else or even looking at me again, he finally turned and left. Some victory.

Stu's chair was tilted to its farthest-back position, where his bulk at that impossible angle presented a picture that looked like a frozen frame in a sequence that would end in disaster. His eyes were shut and his lips were thrust forward in an attitude of thought. I knew he'd heard me come in, so I just sat on the couch and waited for him to speak. The tilt forward came first. A dramatic move accomplished with the very slightest shifting of his weight; a practiced move that took him in slow motion from somewhere on Mars back to the planet Earth, with his eyes coming open just at the moment his wheels made contact with the ground.

When he spoke, his voice was low and soft. "Do you have dinner plans?" he asked.

"No," I said, not too happily. Not that I'd have minded having dinner with him, but I knew where his notion of dinner would lead. To some ethnic takeout spread where his planned role of voyeur would quickly be dropped in favor of something unadmitted but highly active.

"Let's get out of here," he said getting to his feet quickly, and a moment later we were.

The cab ride would do me good, was the way he justified the long trip down to Houston Street. Inside the door, the marvelous smells of Katz's Delicatessen put a wide grin on his face as he inhaled them slowly.

"Ahhh," he said in satisfaction. "No place like it in the world."

He ordered slowly, thoughtfully. Too much, of course, but with the relish of one who knows what's good.

"You're gonna love this," he assured me as he handed me one of the enormous paper bags. And, as he later put those same two bags gently in Abbie's care, commanded "The best china!"

The details were the same as always. The single table setting (he'd just watch), the suggested order of delectation, the enormous sampling gulps. The only difference was the huge pitcher of ice water that was replenished twice by Abbie during what he really thought was a meal for me alone.

"It curbs my appetite," he explained when Abbie brought it

back the third time. "I drink enough of this, I don't even feel like eating."

I nodded soberly. What a terrific idea.

Something was coming. That was obvious by the elaborate lengths he'd gone to in avoiding it. Finally we were sitting in the den and he'd lit an enormous cigar. ("Just sometimes. After dinner. But, Jesus, these are good!") He exhaled the ritual first puff and leaned back, cradling one of the big sofa pillows with his right arm.

"We were lucky last Monday."

The beginning of a train of thought if I'd ever heard one. "How so?" I responded obediently.

"We were lucky he didn't get on."

He, of course, was Matthew Sklar. You'll recall that the decision had been made to use him right away. That meant last Monday. But the match in progress had taken longer than usual, and Matthew hadn't appeared.

"He might have lost, you know."

I leaned forward and opened the cigar box and took the cigar I'd refused a moment ago. "I've never smoked one of these."

"You'll love it," Stu assured me, passing me the cutter. I snipped the end off the way I'd seen him do it, then brought it to my mouth so clumsily he saw that I needed instructions.

"Don't hold it like a cigarette," he said. "Put it right in the middle of your mouth." I did and he lit it for me. The heavy smoke felt strange and unpleasant, but at least I had sense enough not to inhale it.

"Nice, huh?"

It wasn't, but I nodded, planning to put it down and leave it down as soon as the focus moved somewhere else.

"He's the best we're ever going to find, but I tell you, he might have lost. Nobody knows it all."

Apparently not all the questions he'd put to Matthew during their endless hours together this week had been fielded as flawlessly as the ones he'd handled his first day in the office. I was curious about the specifics, but I had the feeling that Stu was shaping this story in his own way, and I was about to hear them without having to do any prompting.

"Do you know who Samuel Gompers was?"

I nodded.

"Why doesn't he? Wouldn't you have guessed he would?"

"Yes."

"He knows that the first presidential candidate of the Republican party in 1856 was John C. Fremont, but he couldn't remember who Samuel Gompers was. How do you explain that?"

I was tempted to say that it meant he'd spent more time in the F's than in the G's, but that wasn't the tone of the conversation. This, however, was the perfect time to get rid of my cigar. I set it gently in the ashtray and he didn't notice.

"We'd be able to predict what Matthew knows better than we could anyone else we've seen. But even with Matthew, we couldn't be sure."

I leaned back comfortably, even though I could now see clearly where this conversation was going. Having unloaded the enormous prop that had made me feel ridiculous, I felt more in charge of myself.

Stu turned to me. "What if he misses a question at just the wrong moment?"

I shrugged. "He loses."

Stu smiled a patronizing little smile. "That's easy for you to say. Capricorn isn't holding you responsible for everything that happens."

Stu stared at me as if expecting an answer, but there didn't seem to be anything sensible to say. When he continued, it was in that quiet voice he used when he was being earnest. A baritone purr at a level so low it put pressure on the listener just to hear what he was saying.

"If this show is done well and fails, I've got no problem. All

I have to do is deliver what I said I would and nobody's going to be too upset, no matter what happens. It's better to succeed, but there's such a thing as honorable failure—that's the business.

"But if I don't deliver what I promised, that's something else again. I'm finished."

He waited a minute to let that sink in, but he didn't really have to. All there was left to wonder about were the details.

"You do understand what I'm saying?"

Oh, yes, I told him. I understood just fine.

"Now," he went on. "We come to you."

I started to say something, but he held up a large, imperious hand. "You want out. I know that. You warned me what you'd do."

"What about Matthew? What if he won't go along?"

"Matthew? We've already had our talk. He'd rather play it on his own—surprisingly competitive, that boy—but he'll do anything I say."

I really don't know why I asked.

"So we come back to you. Technically, we have a deal. I have your services for two years, and you have a royalty on "Face to Face" and anything else that comes along. If you pull out, that puts you in breach and I don't really owe you a dime. But I don't want to play it that way. You've done a lot to make all this happen. And the only reason you want to leave is because you don't really approve of the way things are going to be handled. I think you're wrong, but that's beside the point.

"The point is, I accept your decision. Leave whenever you want to. You still get your royalty, and we're still friends. Not only friends, but we still talk new shows once in a while. You keep your hands clean, but you're still available for conversation."

I wasn't quite sure how to take all this, but I knew what was expected of me.

"That's very generous," I said.

He nodded absently and looked away, and for a minute there it seemed as if, by choosing the noble course, he'd moved himself to tears. But then he smiled and looked back in my direction. "You didn't like your cigar."

I followed his eyes to the ashtray. "To tell the truth, I forgot about it."

He leaned back and laughed hard, and I had the feeling then that our relationship would not be coming to an end so fast.

Men lie to women and then wind up believing their lies. That was the tearful conclusion Carla came to after her second drink at the little bar halfway between her place and mine. My place was out, she'd told me on the telephone. And I couldn't come to her place because Stan was staying there. Why *all* men were being indicted wasn't really clear to me, but that may have been because I had troubles of my own that kept me from giving Carla anything like my full attention. This had not been one of my finest days. Mostly because I'd known as I was living it that it was a day I'd long remember as a turning point, and I wasn't really happy with the way it was turning.

Stan, as the more astute of you may have guessed, was the married man who'd so far brought her ecstasy but not a moment's happiness.

The lie? Nothing very original, really. In fact, the kind of pathetic little lie that could only trouble someone terribly involved. It was what he'd said to his wife when he'd been placed in the difficult position of having to say something. It seems that his wife had been told by a friend that she'd seen Stanley having a much-too-cozy drink with some woman (Carla), and the wife had then jealously shadowed Stanley early one evening to Carla's apartment house. In the confrontation that followed, Stanley had told the lie. He had told his wife that she, his wife, was the only woman he'd ever loved. She'd tossed him out anyway, but that wasn't the point. The point was that now, living

at Carla's, the one place in the world he'd always thought he'd
wanted to be, he had come to the realization, he told Carla, that
what he'd said had been true. His wife was the only woman in
the world he'd ever loved, and he wanted her to take him back.

"Are you listening to me?"

I was, but probably not as carefully as I should have been.

"He wants her to take him back!" The exclamation point was
hers. I was listening now.

"He'll get over it," I said lamely.

"That's all he ever talks about."

"Does he expect you to help?"

She looked up at me. "Don't be such a bastard."

"Honest to God, you really had me wondering."

She put her head down again. What I wasn't seeing, she said,
was the whole point. Having lied, he now believed it. Couldn't
I see that?

The path of her logic was not entirely clear to me, but this
didn't seem the time to check it out. Or even to ask why she was
dwelling on this. At some other time I might honestly have felt
the sympathy she so plainly expected, but just now the precise
direction of Stan's emotional flow had trouble holding my attention. I had blown it this afternoon. And badly. And I didn't know
why.

She looked up at me again. "Do you have a handkerchief?"

I looked in my back pocket and when I failed to find one
volunteered to undertake a Kleenex search. But she stopped me
and started mopping up with a cocktail napkin.

Getting herself cleaned up seemed to have a calming effect.
"It's *me* that I'm unhappy about. I don't like the way I've been
living."

For a second there it seemed as if she might lose control
again, but she managed to hang on. She looked at me. "Do you
realize that I've been sleeping with two men?" It wasn't the sort
of question that seemed to call for an answer. "I mean, if anything had happened . . . if I'd gotten pregnant . . ."

I nodded. "Yeah, I realize."

But she had to finish the thought. "I wouldn't have known who the father was? I can't stand that."

"Carla, I don't think this is a good time to trot out all the problems. I mean, why not get the Stanley business under control, then you can think about everything else."

"Stan," she said.

I looked at her, uncomprehending.

"Nobody calls him Stanley."

"Silly me," I said. "Maybe it has something to do with the fact that I've never heard his name before today." It came out with a bit of an edge, and she seemed surprised.

"What are you upset about?"

There were argumentative answers to that, but this wasn't the time. I must have been staring at her because she asked if her makeup was all right, and then went off to the ladies' room without waiting for an answer. I looked at my watch to see if I'd have time for a phone call, but then decided that, time or not, it would be better to wait till tomorrow. If I was going to change my mind again, it had better be for the last time.

"Are we having dinner, or what?"

She sat down again and looked around. "Here?"

"Or wherever you say."

"I don't want to eat here."

"Then let's go someplace else."

"I'm not hungry. What makes you think I'm hungry?"

"I don't think anything. It was just a suggestion."

"Are you hungry?"

"A little, but I'll live."

She shook her head in distaste. "I couldn't look at food."

Stu Leonard had reminded me last night before I left of the promise I'd made some time ago, the piece of paper I'd signed. He was sure I'd remembered, but he wanted to emphasize how important it had now become. He just wanted to be sure. We'd talk tomorrow. We did, and I heard myself saying things I hadn't realized I'd been thinking; things that in all my rehearsals of this conversation I had never planned to say. I couldn't pull out and keep collecting royalties, I said. That would be letting someone else do the dirty work while I kept my hands clean and collected. And quitting didn't really solve any problems for me because I was already involved. I went on telling him precisely what he wanted to hear, concluding with a promise to stay if I had his word that we'd change the format as quickly as we could to something that could be played straight, and he gave me his pledge on that one.

"You don't have any idea what I've been trying to tell you, do you?"

I looked at her and really tried to think. "What is it I'm missing?"

She sighed to underscore my denseness.

"I don't think we should see each other for a while."

No, I hadn't realized that was what this conversation was all about. But maybe I should have. "Okay," I said.

She smiled. "You don't seem to have a lot of trouble agreeing to that."

Suddenly all the annoyance I'd been feeling with myself found a perfect target. "Which side do you want me to come down on?" I asked in a voice much louder than I'd meant it to be. She looked around to see how much attention I'd attracted.

"What's your problem, exactly?"

"I guess I'm having trouble understanding," I said, really getting into it now. I mean, here was someone I could really handle. "If this guy's driving you crazy, why don't you throw him out? He's staying at your apartment, eating your food and God knows what else, and telling you how nuts he is about his wife. Why don't you throw him out?"

She shook her head, but I kept at it. "Tell him to take a hotel room."

"He can't afford that. I mean, whatever he has is tied up in joint accounts he can't get at right now."

I shrugged. "Just throw him out. It might make him re-sourceful."

She shook her head. "I can't do that."

"Want me to?" I stood up quickly and grabbed her arm. "Come on, let's go. I'll tell him I'm your outraged brother. Or better yet, I'll tell him I'm one of the two possible fathers of the child you're not having, and I'm pissed at having to share this phantom responsibility with a man who's still madly in love with the woman he's lawfully married to. That'll get him."

I was angrier than I'd meant to be and she looked around before suggesting quietly that it might be a good idea to keep it down. There are other times when that probably would have seemed very sensible, but at the moment it wasn't cutting any ice. I pulled her to her feet quickly and dragged her outside, and if it hadn't been raining hard enough to make cabs impossible to find, I probably would have stayed angry long enough to do something really stupid. As it was, when I finally flagged a cab and rode with it back to the doorway where she was standing, some sense had been drenched back into me, and I put her in the cab with a five-dollar bill and sent her home alone, still thinking she was the one I was unhappy with.

7

BY THE TIME THE MISTAKE HAPPENED, I HAD ALREADY TRIED TO contact Margo several times. The first attempts, around the middle of April, had failed because she'd been in Monaco covering the fairy-tale wedding. Then when I'd tried again, after her note about Ginger, I'd missed her again because she'd gone back to the same place for an exclusive interview she'd managed to set up with the new princess, to chase down rumors about her possible pregnancy. The world was more than ordinarily interested in the matter because it had become well known in the flood of ink that surrounded the wedding that, under the terms of a 1918 treaty with France, the Grimaldis had to deliver an heir or Monaco would revert to France, a prospect horrifying to the twenty thousand Monagasques, who would then have to pay French taxes and be subject to the French draft.

Margo could not have gotten back, because after the mistake I'd have heard from her if she'd been in town.

Mistakes had occurred in several of the early shows. Errors that should never have happened, but did because none of us had ever done any of this before and had not yet learned the importance of checking facts. Typical, I suppose, was the question that had given Eisenhower's birthplace as Abilene, Kansas, because that's what the writer had thought he'd remembered. But Ike had been born in Denison, Texas, and while the few infant months he spent there might not have had much effect on *his* life, they had a profound effect on the life of the young man who'd written the question. He was gone, not so much for having made the mistake as for having later failed to see the importance of all of this. That was the unforgivable crime.

There were other mistakes, and each time Stu threatened to sever other heads, but despite his stormy outbursts, everyone else survived. The irony was that when it came to the biggest mistake of all, Stu was the one who made it.

Like all such mistakes, once it's revealed it's impossible to believe it could have happened. And it wouldn't have if Stu had been either ignorant enough to have had to look it up, or wise enough to have wanted to. As it was, the same cockiness that most of the time made him an overachiever this time brought him down.

The preparation of Matthew Sklar had been taken on as a personal project by Stu, in an atmosphere of total secrecy. Frank Dean and I knew very well what was happening behind those closed doors, but Stu must have repeated a hundred times that no one else was to have the least idea. Not wives or girlfriends, or confidantes of any kind. Once the secret left this tiny circle it would be floating around somewhere, and that could not be allowed to happen. No one else was to know. And to emphasize the point as clearly as possible, he concluded by saying *not even Toby.*

But won't she guess?

She'll guess nothing if we insist it isn't happening. She'll think she's so close to this operation that it couldn't be happening without her knowing it. And that's what Frank's wife would think. And anyone *I* was close to.

And of all his pronouncements about how all of this would go, this was the one that turned out to be dead on. The most thoroughly fooled were the people we were closest to. And for just the reason he gave. They were insiders. If anything funny had been happening, they'd have been sure to know. Especially Toby.

Carbons of all the questions were carefully gathered by Frank and delivered to Stu in manila envelopes that found their way into the sturdy safe to the left of Stu's desk that had been bought for the purpose. ("Too many burglaries in this building," Stu had announced to the world at large in a sly bit of misdirection. And then, to emphasize his point, he had put his checkbook in it the moment it was delivered, with Toby standing there watching, and had then told her that if there was anything valuable she had to leave around the office, he'd be happy to store it for her.)

If there was one thing Stu prided himself on above all others, it was his considerable ability as an editor. I was then new enough to all of this not to have yet learned that this is what *everybody* thinks of himself. ("I may not be able to write, but I tell you something, I can find the problems and tell you how to fix them." Attribute that to any producer you can think of, and it's a hundred to one he's said it with no more than one or two words of variation.)

And editing was all Stu thought he was doing. The original question in the category of classical music had read: "Who wrote the play upon which Mozart's opera, *The Marriage of Figaro*, was based?" The answer, Beaumarchais. But because he loved to fiddle with questions and had long since convinced himself that his rewrites made all the difference, he changed it to read: "Mozart wrote the music for the opera, *The Marriage of Figaro*; who wrote the libretto?" The answer, Beaumarchais.

Except it wasn't.

Beaumarchais was the answer Matthew Sklar gave that Monday night at the end of his long think in that stifling soundproof booth, where the air-conditioning had been turned off because it was too noisy and because perspiration photographed so dramatically. "That was the Frenchman who caused all the fuss with his radical ideas," Matthew had ruminated. And then he'd said Beaumarchais. And Beaumarchais was the answer Mike Prince accepted as right, after he'd paused for a dramatic moment, as Stu had taught him to do, with the question card raised very high. Beaumarchais! That's right! Thunderous applause.

But it wasn't right. "How could they make a mistake like that?" Uncle Joe had asked me the following day. "It's right on the album cover." I told Uncle Joe I had no idea. These things happen.

Of course, Uncle Joe had not thought to ask the more penetrating question. And what was surprising was how few people did. And then how easily those few were satisfied with an answer that Margo never would have bought.

Mozart's librettist, as no shortage of people were quick to inform us, was Lorenzo Da Ponte. Stu was all smiles acknowledging that fact in the impromptu telephone press conference that Lenny Basch set up right after the show. "I don't know," Stu pleasantly told a reporter from the *Newark News*, "I suppose Beaumarchais was busy with the screenplay for *The Barber of Seville*." Appreciative laughs around the room. Taking it like a really good sport.

But later that night at my apartment, Stu wasn't smiling with Frank Dean and me. He was well aware of how lucky we'd been; at least, so far. For one thing, the scoring problem could be easily solved by replaying the match, because Matthew's opponent had been so far behind that even calling Matthew wrong at that point would not be enough to beat him. But more to the point, nobody had yet thought to ask that one embarrassing question: How come both Matthew and Mike Prince had the *same* wrong answer? Funny little coincidence there. Several hours of serious thought finally produced the conclusion that coincidence was our only defense, and the next day, when a handful of curious reporters did indeed call with just that question, they seemed to accept as fact that it had been coincidence.

Margo never would have.

I'd been calling Margo's apartment a couple of times a week, tentatively at first, almost hoping she wouldn't answer; and then when she didn't, with a sense of urgency. But after the mistake, I stopped calling. It would be wiser to stay away from Margo because she would be one of the ones I'd have to lie to, and I wasn't sure I could do it. For one thing, I never had, and for another, I knew I'd never get away with it.

Getting away with it had become the name of the game, and every minute of every day I was astonished that we seemed to be, and totally convinced it couldn't last, especially in view of the unexpected rush of publicity that had started to come our way. Lenny Basch had been hired to get us ink, but by now all he had to do was manage its flow. The press was coming to us, intrigued by the amounts of money involved and fascinated by the taxi driver who seemed to know everything. Instead of having to hustle interviews, Lenny's function was now to stand in the middle of the ringing phones at the end of each show, and get each reporter his minute or two with our budding star. So here we were, standing in a spotlight that each week seemed to broaden, and it was hard for me to imagine that one day it wouldn't reveal more than we'd like it to. No such thoughts, however, cast their shadow on Stu's clear enthusiasm for what was starting to become a tidy little hit.

Lunch at Capricorn. Sardines on brown-edged lettuce. Of course, says Donald Scheer, I could have called you with these, but I thought a little celebration was in order. And out comes a bottle of champagne as the ratings sheet is passed around. The bottle opens undramatically and tastes as flat as it sounds, but nobody pays any attention because all that's important is that our ratings have taken a considerable jump this week. I guess they like him, says Murray Cashin, and Stu agrees. Donald raises his glass. To the fall season, he says, and while it was far from a commitment, anyone could see what he was thinking.

The brass Buddha came into the office wrapped like the Maltese Falcon, cradled in the left arm of its proud new owner.

I was standing at the reception desk, looking at my morning mail. "You'll want to see this," he said, indicating the package, and a moment later I walked into his office to take a look. Stu was tilted way back in his seat, proud and grinning, and the Buddha was sitting on his desk.

"You won't believe what I had to do to get this," he said. Apparently, a lot. I hadn't seen him since our awkward little celebration a day and a half ago, and Stu rarely stayed out of the office.

"They'd sold it?"

His eyebrows came together as he wondered how I knew. And then he smiled as he realized it hadn't been that hard to figure out. If the figure had still been in the store, he wouldn't have had much of a problem.

"To a black woman who gave it to her son as a graduation present. He didn't want to part with it."

"What made you decide you had to have it?"

Stu stared at me for a moment very soberly. "Do you know anything about Gautama?"

Gautama, was it? Ah. Whatever I knew was not likely to measure up to what he'd learned in the last several hours. I shook my head.

That quiet tone. Low. Earnest. "Gautama became The Enlightened One—that's what Buddha means. He believed that the origin of suffering is desire." He took a dramatic pause to let that much sink in. "Could it be more simply put?"

Something was expected of me here, but I didn't want to give him more to work with than I absolutely had to. "No, I suppose not."

"There is no suffering without desire." Stu said it slowly, giving each word the kind of equal emphasis that was meant to suggest divine mystery. "Suffering ends when desire ends."

Whatever it meant seemed terribly clear to him. I nodded. "How did you get him to sell it?"

Stu looked at me as if I was missing the point. Then he shrugged. "Not easily, I can tell you."

There was no way I was going to get the short version of this story.

The young man had been graduated from law school in June and had just taken the bar exam. As an undergraduate at Columbia he'd shown an interest in Eastern religions, and when his mother saw the Buddha in the shop window, she'd bought it for him, planning to give it to him after the announcement of the bar results, but then she'd been too excited to wait.

Enter Stu. At his insistence, the shop had given him the mother's name, and when he called her she referred him to her son. Stu offered the son two hundred dollars, but the statue meant too much. Stu kept coming up, and when an offer of five hundred was refused, Stu told the son to do this: Call your mother. Tell her the offer you turned down. Then let's talk again.

That night (last night), Stu took him out to dinner. His mother had told him that if Stu was crazy enough to offer that much money, then he'd be crazy not to sell. But still he was reluctant. Stu offered him a thousand, and that took care of that.

"Marvelous young man," said Stu. "Bright, articulate."

"And a thousand dollars richer."

Stu looked at me steadily for a moment, then suddenly clicked his face into a crisper attitude, lurched his chair forward, and reached for the intercom.

"Toby!"

And after she responded: "Get Frank Dean and come in here right away."

He clicked it off and turned to me. "There's going to be a

whole new way of doing things. One thing there isn't going to be is any more mistakes."

And there weren't. Ever. The approach was two-pronged, worked out by Stu in that day and a half out of the office. The pursuit of the Buddha had occupied only part of his time. The rest had been spent on seeing to it that we were never embarrassed again. He explained the details when Toby and Frank Dean came in.

First, we had a deal with the *Encyclopaedia Britannica.* Lenny Basch had put him in touch with another PR guy who handled that kind of thing. In return for a plug at the end of the show, *Britannica* would assign someone to check out every fact in every question. The first packet was to be mailed to Chicago today.

Second, he'd talked to some friends at Time, Inc., and we'd be setting up our own research department.

"What about *Britannica?*" Frank Dean wanted to know.

"They do what they do," Stu snapped. "I said there'd be no more mistakes. That means we check questions as if our lives depended on it. Then when we know they're right, we send them to Chicago. And if *they* find a mistake, I'm going to want to know why."

From now on every fact in every question had to have three printed sources, with those sources noted on the back of the question. He turned to Toby and told her it was her department. Hire two people right away. Toby nodded.

Toby. She was the one seated at the single clacking typewriter that had drawn me to the end of the corridor. Everyone else was gone. It was seven-thirty, and she was still here alone, pounding away. She stopped, picked up a pencil to fix something on the notes beside her, and then in the quiet, suddenly became aware that she was being watched. She looked up at me and blushed, as if she'd been caught at something.

I smiled at her. "I was wondering who it was back here."

"Trying to finish up a new category," she said. "I don't get much chance during the day."

I nodded to indicate that I knew how crowded her days were. "Well, don't make it too late," I said mechanically. "I'm sure you can use some relaxation."

She smiled. "Today's my birthday."

Nothing could have taken me more by surprise. Not the fact that today was her birthday. (Every day is somebody's birthday.) But that after all the time we'd spent together in various meetings, discussions, planning sessions, and what-have-you, those were the first words she'd ever spoken to me on a subject other than business.

It flustered me a little, and I found myself stuttering something about how that was even more reason for her to get out of here and relax.

"I'm forty-two today," she said, still smiling.

Well, that surprised me, too. I'd never thought a lot about it, but I suppose if anyone had asked me I'd have put her somewhere in those perpetual middle thirties that all bright, energetic, sunglasses-on-top-of-the-head New York women seemed to be in.

I could easily just have said something polite and left, but I wasn't exactly crazy about the quality of my own leisure hours these days, so I didn't. She laughed when I asked her. A light, girlish, appreciative laugh that seemed to acknowledge the fact that even though she might have worked a little for this invitation, it was warmly welcomed. Five minutes later we were seated in a quiet corner of the very expensive French restaurant that was just up the block, her face had gone back to its normal look of concern, and she was wondering if she was well-enough dressed for a fancy place like this. I provided the sought-for reassurance and raised my champagne glass in a standard birthday toast. We clicked glasses very formally and drank, and then she laughed.

97

"Tomorrow you're going to wonder how you got stuck with all of this."

"Not stuck at all," I said. More sought-for reassurance, but I really think I meant at least part of it.

It was awkward going the first few minutes, with Toby back behind her office mask. Not intentionally, I don't think, but simply because that's the only way she felt comfortable. I was surprised to see the waiter back so quickly, refilling her glass. Mine was still almost at the top.

"I seem to be ahead of you," she said.

"Happy birthday," I said again, raising my glass.

She stayed ahead of me, and nodded yes to the waiter's suggestion of a crisp Chablis to go with the Coquilles St. Jacques, and I found myself wondering if this place would take my personal check if, as it seemed, we were going to slide right past the suddenly pathetic thirty dollars cringing in my wallet.

By the time we got to the main course and a lovely red the waiter recommended, we were talking as easily as if that had always been our habit and I was learning more about her than I'd learned in the previous five months. Booze was working its wonders, and with Toby they were wonderful indeed. Not a slurred word or awkward phrase gave her away, but alcohol untied the knots that normally strangled her conversation, and now she was blabbing away just like the rest of the world.

There'd been a young marriage, not surprisingly, to a promising attorney, and then a long relationship with Stu that would probably never be completely over. They'd been really close two years ago, with promises of something permanent, but then he'd suddenly seemed cooler, less sure that they were right for each other, and when she'd found him on his couch one evening entangled with a new receptionist who was later fired, she'd done a little cooling herself. What it came down to was something very simple: Neither of them was really all that anxious for forever. So these days Stu did as he pleased in the social department and never asked her any questions. Once in a while they saw each other.

"But not on your birthday," I said, sorry as soon as I'd said it.

The waiter was filling her glass again. I put my hand over mine and shook my head slightly.

She smiled her thank-you at the waiter and then turned back to me. "He never remembered my birthday, even when we thought we were getting married. But if I'd ever forgotten his, he'd have pouted for a month."

That was simply the way he was. There was only one important person in his life, and you didn't have to know him long to figure out who that was. You either accepted that about him or moved on. Sometimes he'd make up for it with some giant gesture, like sending her mother a wreath big enough for a gangster's funeral when she had her appendix out. Try telling her mother that Stu Leonard was anything but marvelous. Or try telling the doorman at the theater where they did "Help Wanted," who got a check for five hundred dollars when Stu heard his wife had cancer, with a note that said, Somehow, I'm sure you can use this.

But if consistency was what you were looking for, forget it. That same doorman, for example, would have been shocked to learn that Stu didn't know who Toby was talking about when she told him the woman had died.

"Have we ordered coffee yet?"

We hadn't, but it only took a minute to remedy that. The captain poured the last of the red before he left. "But I'm still around, right? If I don't really approve, what am I still doing there?"

There were several glib answers to that, but I kept my mouth shut and waited for hers.

She looked down. "I don't know; that's what I'm doing there. Buying time, I guess, till I can figure out what to do with my life."

In the cab she took my hand and held it tight, and put her

head on my shoulder and cried a little. When we got to her place there were no awkward questions or invitations; we both just knew that I was coming up.

I never fooled myself about that night. It had nothing to do with me. I'd been wandering along the shore, that's all, and happened to find the note in the bottle.

8

I FORGET THE NAME OF THE MOVIE, BUT IT WAS SOMETHING ABOUT barnstorming pilots in the twenties, all white scarves and leather jackets. This cocky young daredevil is constantly setting his crippled plane down in hay fields and barnyards, tearing up the airplane but managing each time to step out of it alive. And each time it's with the grinning observation that any landing you can walk away from is a good one.

By that standard, the fire didn't really amount to much.

Carter Boyd, the stage manager, had pulled me out of the control room to show me what was happening. He'd already shown it to Frank Dean, but Frank had pointed upstairs, and Carter had mistakenly assumed he'd meant to check with me. He'd meant Stu, of course, but Carter was new on the job and made the logical mistake of imagining that since I carried the heavy title of executive producer I might swing a little weight around here.

I followed Carter down the aisle as Mike Prince was turning back to Matthew for his next question. We were about halfway through the show and nobody in the audience noticed us as we passed through. All eyes were on Matthew.

In a corner to the right of the set, Carter pointed to the thin wisps of smoke, hardly noticeable, curling out of the gray metal box that controlled the scoring devices. "What do you want to do?" he asked, and for a heady moment I really thought I had the authority to make the decision. "Pull the plug," I said grandly.

Ten seconds later, a fuming Stu Leonard came storming down the aisle, demanding to know why the scoreboards weren't working. My explanation got only as far as the fact that they'd been turned off. Without waiting to hear why, Stu reached across and flipped them back on, producing alarm on the face of the electrician who ran them, more because of the union grievance than the possible hazard. I tried to explain again, but Stu wouldn't let me finish. He held his hand up. "They stay on," he said. That seemed to settle it for Carter Boyd and for the nodding electrician. I started to say something, but Stu cut me off quickly. "I want them on," he said firmly, staring at me in some surprise that he'd had to say it twice. Then he turned and made his way back upstairs through the audience as Mike Prince began to read the next question.

Instead of following him back to the booth I stayed where I was and kept one eye on the box. In another minute the same gray smoke began seeping out again. Carter looked at me and then quickly turned and walked a few steps away, clearly not wanting any further discussion. I kept staring at the box. Two minutes later the escaping smoke was denser and blacker, and after watching it worsen for a moment, I reached out and flipped the switch off again.

Carter was there in less than a second, snapping at the electrician to turn it back on. "Are you nuts?" I asked him.

"You heard what he said. It stays on," said Carter, and the electrician looked at me and shrugged, the decision clearly out of his hands.

Carter stayed posted between me and the box, physically blocking me out as we watched the last few minutes of the show. Or rather, he watched. At this point I couldn't take my eyes off that square foot of gray metal that I was sure was about to explode.

In another few seconds the smoke started to thicken again, uglier now than before, and several people in the first few audience rows were pointing the problem out to their neighbors and expressing precisely the kind of concern the situation seemed to call for.

Suddenly, the show was over, the cadenced performance sounds ending with a sudden "Clear!" followed by a jumble of unfocused conversation. I hadn't seen or heard the last few minutes. I'd been staring at the box. And now, as if on cue, it burst into flames.

Three stagehands dove for the fire extinguishers while the pages kept the terrified audience from jamming the exits. It was all under control in a minute or two and Stu had me by the arm and was firmly pushing me into an empty dressing room.

"You know what I'd have said if that had been someone else?"

It was as if there hadn't been any fire. That was over. That was nothing. It hadn't been important enough to turn his mind from the evening's one significant event. He was leaning against the door pointing a finger at me and apparently making every effort to control his rage. I was too astonished to be able to answer.

"If it had been someone else, I'd have torn his fucking head off," he went on. "But not you. I can't do that to you."

He let his arm drop and took a couple of those deep breaths I'd seen before. This wasn't an act. He was doing his best to stay controlled.

"Don't ever do that to me again," he said quietly.

"Do what?"

He raised his eyes and stared at me for a moment. Could I really be that dense?

"This is my show," he said. "My studio. My ass if things go wrong. That makes every decision mine. Every decision."

I watched him take a couple more of those deep breaths with the corners of his mouth curled down, and I suddenly felt an anger surge of my own, so strong it took a major effort to keep myself from doing things I don't usually even think about. I growled at him to get away from the door.

My reaction surprised him and he moved aside. I was out of there in nothing flat, down the fire stairs, and on the main floor walking toward the Plaza entrance, madder than I've ever been before or since. Outside, I was just setting foot in the cab when his hand was on my arm.

"Wait," he said. "No, I tell you what, move over." And he pushed me to the far side of the cab and climbed in after me. "Just drive around," he said to the cabbie.

And we did while I got this long, nonstop apology about how he should have realized he'd undermined my individuality, but he wanted me to understand the strain he was under with all of this, the importance of every detail being just right, and the fact that his authority must go unquestioned in front of the office staff and crew, because otherwise he'd be surrendering his badge of leadership, although he realized that he couldn't put me in a position where I seemed to have importance but wasn't allowed to exercise any authority at all, but I had to accept the fact that the lines of command had to be carefully defined. Finally he stopped and turned to me and said, "I'm sorry."

It was carefully crafted to sound as if a child had said it. He looked at me, waiting for an answer. This was his best stuff. It had always worked before. We were stopped at a light on Central Park South. The cab driver turned around.

"Still just drive?" he asked.

"Back where we came from," Stu said, and the driver nodded.

Stu settled back in his seat and folded his hands on top of that enormous stomach. "Let me tell you what I've been thinking," he said, taking my silence as the forgiveness he'd been asking for. And he started telling me that America had had enough of Matthew Sklar.

In the press room it didn't seem that way. Far from it. Lenny Basch had lined up telephone interviews with a dozen TV writers, including two of the biggest here in New York, but the problem was that no one was getting through because every available line started ringing again the second the receiver went down, with calls from all over the country. The front-page coverage had started a couple of weeks ago, here and everywhere. Last week, Matthew had gone over fifty thousand dollars, and headlines trumpeting the landmark had blared atop every clipping Lenny's clipping service had sent to us. From every major city, Lenny had pointed out, and if there was one that was missing I'd have had trouble naming it. And now tonight the response seemed bigger still. Twice as big. Explosive. And the very size of it seemed to stimulate something in Matthew, who never tired of giving the same responses to the telephone questions and tonight seemed to do it with renewed relish. Yes, facts had always been kind of a hobby with him. And, yes, it was wonderful to be able to win money for just standing there and spouting what he knew.

Stu stood around and watched for a while, then grabbed my elbow again and steered me to the back and into somebody's private office. "Now's the time," he said, slumping into a seat and putting his feet up on somebody's private desk. "Shut that door, okay?"

I did and leaned against it. He pulled out a cigar and looked at it for a second, then used it to push back the brim of his cap. "Right now, before they get sick of him."

"*Sick* of him? Didn't you see what's going on in there? He's some kind of national hero."

Stu looked at me and smiled. "They get sick of everything. It's time to give them something else. Besides, we're just looking at big when we could be looking at very much bigger."

That seemed to be hard to argue with.

He put his feet down quickly and sat up straight. "What are we doing here? Why aren't we on a plane to Chicago?"

The Democratic National Convention had opened in Chicago tonight.

"Lenny says he can get us tickets that will put us right on the floor. Press passes. What do you say?"

"What do we do on the floor?"

He stared at me for a moment, then leaned back again and put his feet back up on the desk. I had the feeling that once again he was disappointed in me. It seemed to happen whenever my imagination failed to measure up to his. In other words, often.

"Did you talk to Toby this afternoon?"

I tried to remember. "About what?"

"Some guy she has she thinks is terrific. I asked her to talk to you."

I shook my head.

He stared straight ahead for a moment, and then when he spoke it was softly. "Donald Scheer decided he doesn't like Matthew."

So that was what was behind all this. It wasn't America who was about to get sick of Matthew Sklar. It was Donald Scheer who already had.

One part of this had me a little confused. "Does the president of Capricorn know that Matthew Sklar's been getting answers?"

Stu shook his head.

"Then what makes him think you can just get rid of him?"

Stu looked up at me and smiled. "He doesn't think about it at all. That's the nice thing about being president. He just tells us what he wants."

Elliott Cross was a pediatrician with rumpled good looks and a way with young mothers that made his medical skills with their offspring almost beside the point. Toby had met him when she'd gone with her sister and two-year-old nephew to his perfectly located office on Seventy-ninth Street, a little east of Third. It seemed that every young East Side matron sooner or later fluttered her way into the growing practice of Elliott Cross. Elliott Cross was more than a medical man. He was a presence; a force in the life of the smart young set that went to all the right plays, thought all the right thoughts, and sneered at each week's new issue of *Time*. Elliott Cross was quoted at gallery openings, surrounded at East Hampton lawn parties, and constantly fussed over by a reverent clientele that sought his advice on matters from mumps to sexual boredom. Theirs, not their children's.

At the moment, his lips were pursed thoughtfully as he considered Stu's question. We were all gathered in Stu's office for another of those charming auditions. "Yes, I think he can," he said. "This time, I think the country's ready for him."

Stu nodded soberly. The question had been about Adlai Stevenson. If he won the nomination tomorrow night, as he seemed likely to, could he win the election?

"Is that just a hunch? Or do you know something we'd all be happy to hear?" Stu asked him.

Elliott laughed. That light, understanding, enthusiastic laugh that became so familiar, with his head thrown back like Franklin Roosevelt's. "It's completely scientific," he said. "Based on the only poll I pay attention to: Taxi drivers. They still like Ike, but they're afraid he won't live. And they have no use for Nixon."

"So there's hope," said Stu.

"Oh, I really think so," said Elliott Cross in a tone so persuasive that I had to remind myself that we were getting our forecast from a pediatrician. "It isn't just concern with Ike's health. It's deeper than that. The voters were nervous about Stevenson in '52. His intellectuality; his brand of humor—what they perceived as a flip approach to world affairs. They see now what the man really stands for."

The conversation stayed on "the governor," as Elliott Cross now started to call him, and then moved around to touch all the chic bases. And when we'd finished, it was obvious that Stu had been enchanted. It was Stu who walked him to the door, and when he came back he didn't waste time polling the room to see what the rest of us thought. He turned to Toby and said, "I want to use him."

The possibility that anyone Stu wanted as a contestant might refuse to go along had never occurred to him. And the fact was that nobody ever did. But among the several who started out saying flatly no, Elliott Cross was the one whose initial refusal had seemed the most likely to stick.

Stu was sure Frank Dean had bungled the approach.

"I did it just as you suggested," Frank Dean said coolly, annoyed both at being in the subordinate position and at having his performance doubted.

"You told him it would be for just a week?"

Frank nodded.

"And that nobody else would know? Not me. Not David. Nobody but you and him?"

Frank shifted in his seat. "I suggest we find someone else."

Stu shook his head. "I want *him.*"

"Maybe you'd like to try him yourself?"

Stu shook his head again. "Too late for that. The whole point here is that he's safe because nobody knows. Just two people. Him and you. He'll never agree if he thinks it's more than that."

"What you won't accept," Frank went on, still in that maddeningly smug tone he seemed to need for his self-respect, "is that he won't agree under any conditions."

Stu was standing at the window, looking out at nothing in particular. He turned back. "Take him out to lunch. Call him and say it's important you talk. Don't take him anyplace fancy. A delicatessen; someplace comfortable. Be sure he understands if it isn't him, it's somebody else. Why shouldn't he make an extra thousand dollars?" He turned to me. "He ties once, then loses. That wins him a thousand dollars."

I nodded. I didn't really imagine that Stu was having trouble with the arithmetic. He just wanted me in the conversation.

Stu turned back to Frank Dean. "Why shouldn't he have the money? It's no big deal. That's what you have to make him understand. A few extra dollars, and nobody will ever know. Who's going to say anything? Not you, because if I found out what you'd done, you'd lose your job. And certainly *he's* not going to talk. And aside from the two of you, there's no one else in the world who knows."

This was the approach Stu had carefully detailed when he'd told Frank Dean that from now on Frank would be working with contestants. "Working with" had quickly become the standard euphemism. Working with Matthew Sklar had taken up too much of his time, Stu explained. Did Frank think he could handle it? Frank had nodded confidently, and now seemed to wish to make it clear that he was still confident he could do the job, but not with Elliott Cross.

"More details this time," Stu persisted. "Tell him you've got to find someone to give Matthew some real competition. If you can't come up with someone, it's your job. And if he won't do it, it'll just be somebody else. That's the point, you see. This isn't anything special. He comes on, he plays, he goes off. The whole thing's over before he knows it."

Frank sighed. "I said all that."

"Say it again. Be persuasive. Give him a chance to let himself be talked into it. That may be what he's waiting for."

Frank smiled in spite of himself. "You make it sound like a seduction."

Stu shrugged. "Okay, whatever you want to call it. But remember, he's the one I want."

We got him, of course, and I've never really known why. Everyone always assumed it was the promise of fame and winnings of $125,000. But it was nothing like that. He'd have run hard the other way if things of that magnitude had ever been suggested. No, he did it, this young doctor with the growing practice, for the promise of a thousand dollars; for the few extra bucks that come in handy when you've only been at it a few years and your office rent's too high. For those few extra bucks, and the promise that no one would ever know.

That was the part that mattered.

If you weren't careful around Mike Prince, you found yourself doing all sorts of little favors; especially ones that saved him money. When I'd agreed to help him move a few things into the office Stu had let him have, I hadn't realized what I'd let myself in for.

The space had been a large storeroom up to now, and after considerable urging, Stu had finally agreed that if Mike would arrange to clean it out, the office was his, rent free. The cleaning-out part had been taken care of on Saturday by three researchers Mike had double-talked into service, and on Monday morning at eight I was standing in front of the building ready to give him a hand.

He pulled up in a panel truck driven by his sister and immediately started apologizing for what he insisted had turned out to be a lot more stuff than he'd ever imagined he owned. Meanwhile, his sister was double-parked and cars were screeching around us, drivers honking and swearing, and it was clearly time to get at it.

The first few trips were just small things, but then we worked our way toward the back of the truck to the heaviest desk in the western hemisphere. His brother-in-law had made it out of oak, and there wasn't a nail or a screw in it anywhere. Under other circumstances I might have found it an object of considerable beauty, but as it was, its weight was all that impressed me. We pushed, tugged, wrestled, urged, angled, and finally shoved it into the elevator, and then, still puffing from the ground floor exertions, had to reverse the process at the penthouse.

Ultimately, we struggled it into his office, and I tried to be gracious when he thanked me.

In my own tiny office I collapsed around a glass of water and promised myself to enroll in a health club as soon as I caught my breath.

"A friend of yours?" It was Mike's sister, standing in my doorway and pointing to something on my desk. My eye followed her finger to the folded newspaper with the red grease pencil circle around a picture of Margo.

"Yes," I said. "It seems to be." I was surprised I hadn't noticed it before. I angled the paper toward me. It was the entertainment section of today's *Times*. Stu must have left it on my desk. Margo, it said, was leaving to take a job with a morning network news show. "She seems to be moving up in the world."

"So's Mike," his sister said. And then she grinned. "You planning to help with her furniture?"

I shook my head soberly. "Nobody. Ever again. What did you do with the truck?"

"Somebody pulled away from the hydrant. I left it there with my fingers crossed. I wanted to get a look at Mike's new office."

"What do you think?"

"Nice. Well, I mean, pretty nice." She grinned again. "He said this was a penthouse."

That made it my turn to grin.

"Well," she said pulling out her keys, "I hope you didn't strain anything important."

"Most of the major organs seem to be back in place."

"If you ever need to borrow a truck, feel free to give me a call."

I nodded. "It comes up all the time."

She nodded back and seemed to hesitate for just a moment. "My name's Rebecca," she said and turned and left.

It was only then that I was aware of how good she'd looked in her too-large sweater and khaki pants. And I wished I'd said something to detain her.

Having moved into his new headquarters, Mike Prince was now convinced he had a lot to keep him busy. He was in at nine-thirty every morning, shuffling papers and making phone calls, and by ten-fifteen he was up and wandering around the place, trying to be part of its life.

Now a meeting would be interrupted by a suddenly opened door and a smiling Mike asking what's going on. A trip to the drugstore for lunch would be suddenly plus one. An encounter in the hall is an opportunity for Mike to explain some new way to improve the show. So is a chance meeting at adjoining urinals. Shut doors are ignored. So is a telephone in use. He sits patiently beside the desk waiting for the call to end, reading anything you were foolish enough to leave exposed. He is everywhere. There is nowhere to be that he is not.

At first, none of this seemed to bother Stu, but that was simply because it hadn't affected him. His had been the one office Mike stayed away from. But the day of the closed-door meeting on what to do about the Committee, Mike Prince was foolish enough to barge in.

"What's going on?" he asked, standing halfway in the room.

"This is private, Mike," Stu said, his eyebrows drawn together.

"I don't need to be protected," Mike said. He came all the way into the room and shut the door behind him. "I know what this is about."

No one doubted that he did.

"I want you to know what I think."

"If I'd wanted you here, I'd have asked you to this meeting," Stu said carefully. "There are some important decisions to be made. And we are the ones who will make them."

He meant himself, Frank Dean, Murray Cashin, and me. This was the first time Murray Cashin had been in our office.

"I know it's your decision, but I'm the man whose face they look at. I think that gives me the right to express an opinion."

And without waiting to have that right confirmed, he went on to give it in no uncertain terms. Regardless of what Vince Martoni decided to do in his forced appearance before the House Un-American Activities Committee, Mike wanted him off the show. Now. At once. The viewing public had to be assured that such people would not be tolerated. There could be no possible compromise. Not if we were to retain our integrity.

"Is that all?" Stu asked quietly, when Mike seemed to finish.

He nodded.

Stu looked at him, and those of us who knew the signs knew very well the effort Stu was making to keep himself in check. "Please wait outside," Stu said in that low, measured, and to those who knew it menacing tone. "I don't know how long we'll be, but I want you to wait. You and I have some talking to do as soon as this meeting is over."

And Mike Prince smiled, because that giant ego heard it the way he wanted to. Stu, he was certain, had asked him to wait because he wanted all the details on exactly what he thought at the earliest possible opportunity. Okay, Mike said, he'd wait. Take your time. He'll be in his office. And he nodded to us all with that inappropriate, self-satisfied grin. He'd be happy to wait. And he shut the door.

When he was gone, Stu turned back to the matter at hand, somehow keeping that seething anger bottled up. How could he manage to do that? How could he transfer not just his mind, but his passions, so quickly and completely from one level of intensity to another? Was that the special gift he'd been given in some secret compact with the devil?

"Tell me about this lawyer." Stu's request was addressed to Murray Cashin.

Murray shifted in his seat in the corner of the couch nearest Stu's desk. "Well, I don't really know if he can help. And he certainly can't do anything unless Vince is willing to cooperate."

"But if he is?"

Murray shrugged. "This guy's gotten a lot of people cleared."

Stu had been unsure before. For a few bad moments it had actually seemed as if our valiant leader had been ready to dump Vince Martoni for all the practical reasons other men in his position had been coming up with for the last few years. But Mike Prince's little speech had now made that impossible. There was this other way that Murray Cashin had brought up. And even though it would mean some bad publicity for the show, maybe it was still the better way to go.

"You want me to talk to Vince?" Murray Cashin asked.

Stu shook his head. "No, I'll do it."

"He'll have to name names, you understand."

Stu nodded.

"I mean lots of them. They won't accept 'I can't remember.' "

Stu nodded again and Murray went on persistently. "What I'm saying is, he can't hold anything back. He has to convince them he's really cooperating. He has to be forthcoming. That's the word they use. Then he gets his letter."

Stu picked up his pen. "What's this guy's name?"

"I have it in the office. I'll have my girl call you."

Stu put the pen down and stood up, suddenly all smiles. He walked over and put his arm around Murray Cashin. "Tell Donald we have somebody coming on who might give Matthew a contest."

Murray smiled back. "He'll be glad to hear that. Any chance he could beat him?"

"I doubt it," Stu said. "Matthew's pretty smart."

"There must be somebody somewhere," Murray said, and he shook hands and left. As soon as the door shut behind him, Stu's smile turned off and he reached for the intercom. "Mike!" He let go of the switch and looked at me. "We'll meet again in fifteen minutes." I nodded and Frank Dean and I started out as Mike Prince's voice came over the intercom. "We can talk now," Stu said sharply, and two minutes later, from behind Stu Leonard's carefully shut office door, there came the loudest, ugliest sounds I've ever heard in an uninterrupted solo performance that nobody clocked, but must have gone on for at least a couple of hours. Mike Prince came in less frequently after that, and when he did there were fewer problems.

Vince Martoni's letter worked its magic. He was, it said, a patriotic American who had cooperated in the work of the Committee. He had testified fully and openly, and was hereby commended for his candor. The network was satisfied, Donald Scheer was satisfied, and even Vince himself, after having spent the better part of a week tearing himself apart over whether or not to do this, seemed finally convinced he'd done the right thing. The letter came to Vince on official Committee stationery, signed by the chairman himself. Vince was clean. His youthful sins were expiated. He was free to lead a full and happy life. Oh, magic sheet of paper, dearly bought, but cheap at any price.

9

LENNY BASCH GLANCED TOWARD ME, THEN BACK IN STU'S
direction, those narrow eyes never quite touching anything they
looked at. "I think this should be private," he said.

"It's private enough," Stu said from his tilted-back position.
"David's private as far as I'm concerned."

Lenny looked back at me, still not happy with my presence,
but finally he shrugged and slumped deeper in his chair. He
waited a moment, focusing our attention. Then he said, "Matthew doesn't want to do it."

Stu's expression didn't change, but I felt my heart plunge to
somewhere just above my shoetops. It hadn't occurred to me
that Matthew might demand a vote in any of this.

"Do what?" Stu asked.

Lenny Basch smiled a knowing smile and shook his head.
"Save the bullshit, Stu. I'm telling you, he won't do it."

Stu's lips curled out as he thought about that. Then he
turned to me. "Do you know what he's talking about?"

I shook my head. "I don't have any idea."

Lenny looked back and forth between us, then smiled and shook his head again. "That's a cute little act you two have. You ought to take it on the Sullivan show."

There was a pause, and I waited for Stu to do his famous forward tilt. Pause. Still not a word. Everything on hold. Then the move began, that bulky body slowly arcing forward, accelerating to a crashing climax as both arms firmly thundered on the desk. Another pause as a startled Lenny Basch waited for him to speak. Then, "This meeting isn't going to last very long unless you tell us what it's all about."

Lenny looked at Stu, trying to see how serious he was. Very, he decided. "Okay," he said. "Let's lay it out. Matthew doesn't want to lose. He won't lay down for this doctor you have."

Stu's face remained expressionless. "I don't have the vaguest idea what you're talking about," he said. "But forget that for a minute. First there's something I want to know."

"What I'm talking about is what I'm telling you he doesn't want to do," Lenny went on, but he stopped abruptly when Stu suddenly slammed his open hand down hard on top of the desk. The sound had the effect it was designed to have.

"Now," said Stu quietly, now that he had his attention. "Let's take things one at a time."

"Whatever you say," said Lenny, trying to keep him calm.

Stu made him wait another moment, just to demonstrate who was controlling this conversation. Lenny had the idea by now. He'd have waited six months if he'd had to.

"What does any of this have to do with you?"

Lenny looked at him a little surprised. "Don't you know?"

"If I knew I wouldn't ask."

"I don't believe it," Lenny said. "I mean," he added quickly, "I believe it, but I thought he would have told you. He really didn't say anything? I'm surprised."

Stu stared at him patiently, not about to prompt him any further.

"Matthew's a client," Lenny said. "He signed a personal management contract with me."

Stu stared at him in disbelief. "He signed *what?*"

Lenny looked down and mumbled. "I figured he'd tell you about it."

Stu rose out of his chair and brought that six feet five around the desk. He reached down and grabbed Lenny's rumpled jacket and pulled him to his feet. It was a scene from a gangster movie, with Lenny curved back like a parenthesis and a raging Stu Leonard shouting down into his face.

"You're on a retainer from this office and you had the gall to sign someone *we're* using to a management contract with *you.* I don't know what to do with you."

"Calm down," Lenny said, thereby producing the opposite effect.

Stu's grip on Lenny tightened as his voice roared to still more threatening heights. "Calm down! I ought to jam you through the wall!"

For a minute there I thought he might. And so did Lenny Basch. But all Stu did was glare at him murderously and shake him so hard his eyeballs seemed to rattle.

Finally, Lenny summoned up courage enough to try to speak again. Quietly. Quiet seemed to be called for in his ridiculous position. "I'm sure you're strong enough to do anything you want," Lenny said. "But after you're finished, nothing changes. I've still got the contract. You have to talk to me."

Stu thought about that briefly, then relaxed his grip and shoved Lenny back into his chair. He stared at him for a moment with the kind of contempt that was wasted on this particular adversary. "Why am I getting upset?" a suddenly calm Stu Leonard asked the cosmic forces. "What do I care about your contract?"

Lenny allowed himself a little smile. "I knew you'd understand," he said.

Stu walked back around his desk. "It stinks. It's totally unethical. But what else do I expect in this filthy world?" He sat down again. "Okay, you have a contract. May I suggest a lovely place for you to keep it safe?"

Lenny shook his head again. "You're not getting the point, Stu. I'm telling you I talk for Matthew. And Matthew doesn't want to lose."

"Nobody wants to lose," Stu said. "But in every contest somebody wins and somebody loses. Whatever happens happens."

"Enough with the bullshit," said Lenny. "He doesn't want to lose, but if it means all that much to you, he'll do whatever you want him to do. Providing."

He left a hole for Stu to say, Providing what? But Stu kept quiet, and I found myself with a kind of grudging respect for Lenny Basch. Faced with the prospect of further arousing the anger of someone clearly capable of taking him apart, he'd held to the purpose of his visit. Admirable was too big a word for the little weasel, but I had to give him *nervy*.

"Providing," Lenny went on, "you help him get what he wants."

This time Stu responded to the cue. "And what does he want?"

"He wants to get into news. He wants you to help him."

"Help him do what—get a paper route?"

"He's not kidding, Stu, and neither am I. You know what I'm talking about. He wants to be on television. Doing news. Local maybe, to start. He'd be great."

There are times when keeping a straight face is a very good idea, and this, I decided, was one of those times.

"Well, that's terrific," said Stu. "But none of that has anything to do with me."

"We think it could have," Lenny said. "You know a lot of people. You could introduce him around. Matthew's made a good name for himself the last few weeks. People know who he is already. You help him get what he wants and he'll do anything you say."

Stu waited to let all of that settle. "Now hear this," he finally said. "And be sure you hear it right. There's nothing in this world I want from Matthew Sklar."

"You want him to lose," Lenny said.

Stu shook his head in disbelief. "Lenny, there's a real problem with the way you pay attention. Now let's just try again, and this time be sure you take it all in. There's nothing I want from Matthew. Understand that?"

Lenny nodded tentatively. "Go on. I'm listening."

"That's good, because if I ever hear from anyone that you're going around telling people that I asked Matthew to lose, I will hit you with a slander suit you'll spend the rest of your life defending. And you'll be lucky if that's all I hit you with."

Lenny thought about that for a moment. "Okay," he said. "Now what about this newscaster business?"

Amazing. He was going right on.

"Were you listening, Lenny?"

"Yeah, yeah, of course. We're friends here, right? I don't talk about my friends. That goes without saying. Now what about Matthew?"

Stu folded his hands on his stomach. "Matthew and I have become very close," he said. "No matter what happens, I would always do my best to help him achieve any goal he sets his sights on."

Lenny turned to me. "You heard what he said?"

I nodded, and Lenny turned back to Stu.

"That's terrific," Lenny said. "I knew we could count on you."

It wasn't really a date. Not by any normal standard. I didn't even pay for her ticket.

Mike Prince had stuck his head into my office that morning. "You're not going to believe this," he said. "But after waiting four months, now I can't even go."

The event he'd been waiting for was *My Fair Lady,* which had opened in March to hosannahs and squeals of delight. Why hadn't he been able to see it up to now? Because he was Mike and Mike didn't deal with brokers.

Mike had the tickets in his hand. He'd been planning to take his sister and he didn't want to disappoint her. Would I consider going? You bet I would.

"I'll pay for her ticket, of course," Mike said. "I mean, there's no reason why you should. So you owe me . . . " He looked at the ticket to mask the fact that he'd memorized the price, and I paid him whatever it was.

Afterward, we stepped out of the air-conditioned theater into the shock of damp heat that had seemed to grow more intense with darkness. I tried to get her to go with me for something cold to drink, but she said she'd promised the baby-sitter it would be an early evening. She stuck out her hand awkwardly to say good night.

"I'm getting a cab," I said. "Can I drop you somewhere?"

She shook her head. "I have the car."

"Okay," I said. "I'll walk you to it."

We started east and I found myself so eager to get a conversation going that I couldn't get my tongue in motion.

"I suppose Mike told you I'm divorced," she said as we crossed the noise and litter of Seventh Avenue. He hadn't, but I'd assumed there was some reason why it had been okay for me to escort his sister tonight.

"I hope you don't think this was a setup," she said, turning to look at me.

Actually, I didn't, and I told her so. Didn't I want to take my jacket off? No, it was easier to wear it. She'd been divorced for six months, she said, and Mike had been very attentive, but the one thing she wouldn't want anyone to think was that she was using him to try to get her dates. I assured her that it had never crossed my mind. What I didn't say was that if Mike Prince had been trying to set me up with his sister, he'd have picked some way that wouldn't have cost him the price of a theater ticket.

"How many kids?" I asked her.

"Just one. A boy. He's six."

"How's he taking it?"

She shrugged. "Not great. He cries whenever he talks to his father on the phone. The books say it's because he thinks the whole thing's his fault."

"The boy's fault," I said.

"Yes, of course." She turned to me and laughed. "Yes, I see. *His* fault. It could have been either. No, of course I meant Josh. The child. He blames himself. I guess they always do. Or maybe they don't. How does anyone know what they think?"

"Sometimes by what they say."

She shook her head. "Josh doesn't talk about it. He's just not very happy. But he'll get over it. Or someone will say he did." She looked at me again. "What did you think of Julie Andrews?"

"I thought she was fat and ugly."

She laughed, and as the traffic light changed I realized we were crossing Fifth Avenue. "Where did you park?"

"It's just another block or two. Not terribly convenient, but a dollar cheaper." She laughed again. "I suppose that makes me sound like Mike, but these days I have to watch my pennies."

The parking lot was long and narrow, crammed between two buildings, and the car when the attendant finally dug it out turned out to be the panel truck I'd already met. She laughed as the attendant held the door open for her.

"Not exactly a scene out of *Harper's Bazaar.*"

"I assume you're holding it for ransom."

"You bet. He says he needs it in his business, but I say he's the one who walked out."

"You're tough," I said.

She looked at me for a moment, and then stuck out her hand again. "I'm whatever I have to be." She pulled her hand away and got into the truck. I creaked the door shut for her and leaned down to talk through the open window.

"Would you mind if I called you some time?"

She shook her head. "No. I mean, no, I wouldn't mind."

I asked her for the number, and she pointed to the side of the truck. There it was, painted on the side, right under her husband's name. I smiled as I wrote it down. "Doesn't that get you a lot of unwanted action?"

She laughed. "Not as much as you might think."

She started the engine, and as she pulled away it occurred to me that she could have offered to drop me at my apartment.

They tied the first week. Matthew breezed through his questions, and a nervous Elliott Cross had to struggle, but finally managed to come up with the answers he needed to hang in there.

There were seven questions in each category, with the first player starting with the very easy number one, the second player getting the slightly tougher number two, and so on, back and forth as the questions got more difficult. The players stood in separate glass isolation booths, wearing earphones so they couldn't hear each other, and they kept alternating questions up the line until somebody missed. As soon as one player missed, his opponent got a shot at that same question, and won the round if he could answer it. If the players got all the way to number seven, they both had to answer the same question. The match ended in a tie unless one player missed it and the other one got it right. There were a lot of ties.

In the beginning that had seemed to present a potential problem, but as it turned out those ties provided most of the excitement. After one tie, the stakes were doubled. If the players tied again, the stakes were tripled. It was anything but boring.

"He wants to know what happens next week," a worried Frank Dean said. We were standing in that same little office just off the buzz of the press room, where Matthew Sklar was holding forth in a telephone interview on how hard he'd been pressed this week.

"How can you tell him?" Stu asked. "You don't know how well Matthew's going to do."

"I told him that. He wants to be sure he loses. He wants out. He's sorry he ever agreed to come on."

"Did he leave the building?"

"Are you kidding? The second it was over."

"Maybe we should have brought him up here. We'll do it next week if he's still on."

"I thought he loses next week," Frank said with a worried look.

Stu ignored him and turned to me. "Can you imagine him on those phones, handling those questions? He'd be terrific."

"He'd never do it," Frank Dean said.

"Maybe, maybe not," said Stu.

Later that week, Stu explained to Frank that Elliott Cross would have to be briefed for two full matches.

"He'll have a fit," Frank said. "I told you he wants out. We promised him one tie and then he loses."

Stu's eyebrows went up. *"We* promised him?"

"Okay, I did. You know what I mean."

"Tell him you think he'll lose. He should. He misses the number-four question. Matthew should have no trouble getting it right. But Elliott needs to be prepared just in case there's another match."

Frank sighed and turned to me. "Do you understand what the problem is?"

I nodded. "But he needs to be prepared," I said. "He could look very foolish if he suddenly had to play another match and couldn't come up with any answers."

Frank looked back and forth at us. "Level with me, gentlemen. What do you have in mind?"

Stu walked over and put a hand on Frank Dean's shoulder. "Everything works better if nobody knows any more than he has to know."

Frank nodded and slumped visibly. "I'm the one who has to talk to him."

"That's the point," said Stu. "This way you tell him only what you really know."

Later, behind shut doors, I told Stu he was out of his mind. If he insisted on scripting two more ties, at least do it in a manner that would be consistent with Matthew's spectacular performance up to now. But, of course, Stu wouldn't listen.

Elliott Cross would miss the number-four question, something rather simple about the president who served between Grover Cleveland's two terms. He'd say William Henry Harrison instead of Benjamin. Then Matthew, with a chance to knock his opponent out of the match, would take a long time struggling with the same question, and finally say he'd drawn a blank.

"Nobody'll believe it," I said.

"Of course they'll believe it. It's so wildly unlikely, it has to be legit. If we were fixing things, we'd never do it that way."

"But that's the kind of question Matthew could answer in his sleep."

Stu nodded. "Good line. I'll tell him to use that afterward, when the reporters ask him why he missed."

And the night it happened, that's exactly what he said. "I don't know," Matthew said to his telephone interviewer. "That's usually the kind of question I can answer in my sleep. Some kind of mental block, I guess."

The room was alive with PR guys from the network, people from Capricorn, Murray Cashin's group, a handful of reporters who'd come down to see the show in person, the usual group from our office, and a surprisingly relaxed Elliott Cross. Stu had grabbed him right after we went off the air and made it seem the most natural thing in the world for him to join us in the press room. The reporters Lenny Basch had lined up for telephone interviews all wanted to talk to Matthew, but the reporters in the room had to settle for the interview at hand, and Elliott Cross handled their questions as if he'd been doing it all his life.

Yes, he laughed, he'd felt ridiculous when he'd gotten his Harrisons confused, and he was probably the most surprised man in America when Mike Prince told him that Matthew had missed the same question. Talk about reprieves from the governor! And his head went back in another laugh, enjoying it thoroughly, leading the reaction, not the least put out to have the joke on him.

Later, Donald Scheer elbowed his way into the room and pressed first my hand, then Stu's. The most exciting show we'd had so far, said the president of Capricorn. His heart had been in his mouth. And there was a handshake for Matthew Sklar, and warm congratulations for Elliott Cross. A marvelous night, said Donald Scheer, and he leaned over for a private word with Murray Cashin that elicited a thoughtful nod.

10

"All the influences were lined up waiting for me. I was born, and there they were to form me, which is why I tell you more of them than of myself."

Augie March says that of himself, and it's tempting for me to say the same. It's not really something I'm proud of, but it seems to explain as well as anything how I managed to let myself become so central a part of something that as an outsider I'd have loudly condemned. Here I was, not as I'd always thought of myself, at the narrow noble end of the bell curve of morality, but huddled in the bulging middle, crowded in with all the others who could be saints or sinners.

The influences were lined up waiting for me. And when I came along, they formed me. It's as good an excuse as any.

The maître d' at 21 looked at me suspiciously, then broke into his broadest grin when I told him Harvey Gold.

"Oh, yes, you're meeting Mr. Gold," he said in the accent of that comic-opera country that seems to be the breeding ground of maîtres d'. "He called to say he'd be a little late. Come, I seat you." And he did, at a table I later learned was reserved for Frank Sinatra whenever he was in town. Getting good tables was one of the things that Harvey Gold was good at.

"Something while you wait?" the captain asked me. No, I said, I'll just wait. And as soon as he left, I looked quickly around the dining room to reassure myself that, unlikely as it seemed, Stu Leonard wasn't seated somewhere here. He'd stopped me on the way out of the office to ask if I had any plans for dinner, and I'd found myself mumbling something vague. It hadn't seemed advisable to say I was meeting Harvey Gold.

Harvey Gold was only a few years older than I, but he was a comer at William Morris and might even have been as important as he tried to make the world believe. He'd been hanging around with us lately, staying close to Stu. The objective, of course, was to try to bring Stu into the agency. There'd be no commissions on what we had going already, he'd reassured Stu, but it wasn't the present that interested Harvey Gold. His plan was to get us branched out into every area of the entertainment business in that limitless future that glows so brightly in every agent's eyes. Stu had turned him down last week.

"Boychik, you're early!" It was Harvey, short and apple cheeked, tie-pinned, and just a touch too elegant in a sharkskin that hugged his stocky frame. Beside him was Conrad, his pale imitation, sandy haired and sallow, as slope shouldered as a Burgundy bottle, with his bulky tie uncentered in his too-big collar.

"You remember Conrad," Harvey said, and all of us shook hands. "What are you drinking?" Harvey wanted to know, still standing. "Good!" he bellowed when he saw I hadn't started. "Conrad, order some Dom Pérignon. I'm going to take a short leak." And he was gone.

He was back before the wine came, loudly explaining that he'd ordered Dom Pérignon because it was the only expensive wine he knew by name, and anyway, everyone liked champagne. "I brought Conrad," he went on, "because I like him to know everything I'm doing. Is that right, Conrad?" And Conrad nodded.

We were here because Harvey Gold, having been turned down by Stu, thought it might be a good idea to get better acquainted with me. He'd been hearing a lot about me, he'd explained when he called, and he wanted to talk about my future. Okay, I'd said, let's talk. And that's what we were here to do.

"Who am I looking at?" Harvey Gold suddenly asked, staring into my eyes more firmly than I found comfortable.

"Me," I answered obediently.

"You got that right," said Harvey Gold. "And do you know why I'm looking hard at you?"

"No," I said, because I didn't.

"I'm looking at you because I'm here to talk to you. The room is full of important people, but I'm not here to check out the room. I'm here to talk to *you.*" He turned to Conrad. "Is that the way I operate?" Conrad nodded.

I was a comer, Harvey said. He was convinced of that. He'd asked around and everywhere he'd heard that I was the man responsible. That's not really true, I tell him modestly and with genuine conviction, but he'll hear none of it. Here's what's going to happen if I sign with them, he tells me earnestly, his eyes, as advertised, never leaving mine. First, he makes a network deal for me. That should take ten seconds. We give them first refusal on everything new in exchange for eating money. Next, we come up with a knockoff of "Face to Face," which he can sell in twenty minutes. Then he puts me together with some other clients to get me branched out into variety, drama, whatever else I want. Why should I have just one string to my bow?

I'm flattered, of course, I tell him as we sip Dom Pérignon, but I have a deal with Stu.

"Of course you do," he says. He turns to Conrad. "What did I tell you? Didn't I say he'd be tied up a hundred ways?" And when Conrad nods as called for, Harvey turns back to me, earnest now, patient with the obvious. "You meet a girl at a party. She's gorgeous. You want to nail her to the wall. But the first thing she tells you is she came with someone else. She's married, or worse, she's going steady. You think she was just standing there waiting for you to show up? Not on your life, boychik. But if you give up every time the news is bad, you never get anything you want. When's the contract up?"

Almost two years, I told him, and he nodded thoughtfully as menus started being passed around. Harvey turned to the captain without opening his. "Conrad and I want shrimp cocktails, and then T-bones medium well. And bring us some ketchup in a dish," he said, handing the menu back.

"Two years isn't the end of the world," he said after I gave the captain my order. "Besides, contracts were made to be broken. The question is, what is it you want? That's what I have to know."

What is it I want? A reasonable question. We spent some time talking about that in one of those unreal conversations I seem to be having a lot of these days, where I'm looking in on this group of people, of whom I seem to be one, and they're talking about things that have nothing to do with me. I see myself nodding soberly and agreeing with Harvey as he says again that expanding into other things is the way to unlock my future. A wonderful future it can be, Harvey assures me. There are people he wants me to meet, and I nod as he tells me who some of them are. Then suddenly I feel myself click back into place as my insides do one of those little flips. The room is real again and someone has just walked in who in the half-light of inattention I'd hazily thought was Margo. But now as I watch her move past our table I can't imagine how I could have been so thoroughly mistaken.

The applause erupted with the intensity of a concert hall ovation. Elliott grinned and Matthew lowered his eyes. The applause continued through the music as both men were helped out of their booths and led toward the center and Mike Prince. There's no telling how long the approving uproar might have gone on if Mike had not finally held up his hands as a signal for it to subside.

Matthew's face slowly broadened into a self-conscious grin as Mike shook his hand and congratulated him on the marvelous champion he had been. And the crowd applauded again as Mike recapped his winnings and wished him well in whatever the future might have in store.

And now we had a new champion, and the crowd acknowledged that fact with still another round of enthusiastic applause. There was no doubt in anyone's mind that things had gone the way everyone watching had wanted them to go.

Gracious was the word that was used a lot for Elliott Cross. In the flood of clippings that quickly poured in from everywhere, that was the word that kept reappearing. Good losers, one columnist pointed out, were really a dime a dozen. It was good winners who were hard to find, and Elliott Cross was giving the country a lesson in how to be gracious in victory.

The grace of Elliott Cross was also noted by Capricorn. It was one of the many reasons they were pleased with this new champion, as Murray Cashin pointedly advised us in a telephone call that was followed not five minutes later by a similar call from Donald Scheer. The company president was a man who understood grace and sought it in his clothes, his home, the things he had around him. It pleased him, he said, to note it in someone the viewing public connected with his company's products.

And afterward, of course, the grace of Elliott Cross mellowed into charm as he settled into the comfort of his reign. By the third week, defeated opponents were thanking him for having had the chance to play against him, and mumbling inanities about their endless admiration for the man.

The victories were swift and one-sided the third and fourth weeks. His opponents seemed stunned by his superior skill and meekly put the cause for their failure squarely on their own inadequacies, totally unaware that they'd been sitting ducks who'd been picked off by an opponent who'd entered the contest at a considerable advantage.

It was starting to look too easy, Stu decided, and so he matched the invincible Elliott against a young accountant who was set up to play two ties and then lose a dramatic squeaker. When it happened the audience roared its approval, and Elliott turned to his vanquished opponent and said, "I really thought you were going to beat me. I feel lucky to still have my skin." For some reason, that line made every account that was written.

On the surface everything was fine. Ratings were climbing every week, word of mouth was phenomenal, and the newspaper stories were bigger, more frequent, and now sometimes even mildly approving. But underneath, the rumblings had begun. Inside and outside.

Outside was speculation. The kind of questioning that came from Alyse over an experimental pot roast served at Uncle Joe's.

"I hope you won't think I'm awful," said Alyse, carving the roast into misshapen chunks, "but Joe said you wouldn't mind if I asked."

"Go ahead," urged Joe.

She looked at me, still hesitant, then back at him again. He nodded. "It isn't me, really," she finally said. "It's some of the girls where I work. At the office." She worked in a small advertising agency that specialized in subway display cards. "They think the people on your show, especially Elliott Cross . . ." She hesitated delicately. "Well, they think he couldn't really be that smart. I mean, they say . . . some of them say . . . he must be getting the answers." She handed me my plate heaped with carrots and boiled potatoes.

I smiled and reassured her. Elliott Cross was so good that I could understand how it might look that way. But we'd be very foolish to take that kind of chance.

Joe turned to her. "You see? What did I tell you?"

Alyse leaned back in her chair, relieved. "Joe said it couldn't be true. And I didn't think it could. I mean, he's a professional man. They take an oath. And anyway, Joe said you could never be involved in anything like that."

Joe grinned at me. "Do I know my customers, or what?"

I grinned back at him. I'd made my mind up long ago that there would be only one way to handle this when the question came up, as I'd always known it would. I'd do the lying so he'd never have to. If I made the mistake of telling him the truth, I'd be pulling him into my conspiracy; putting him in a position where he'd have to protect me by passing along an agreed-upon story to anyone who questioned him. This way he'd be free to tell the truth. Or what he thought was the truth.

The inside rumblings were deeper and more disturbing. They came to me via Rebecca. We were parked one night on a dark street a block away from the ocean at Long Beach, stretched out in the back of her panel truck with a thin blanket over us and a shared cigarette going back and forth. We were here because she couldn't allow herself the time away from Josh to come all the way to the city and my place. Motels were out of the question because she'd grown up in this area and some-one might see her going in. And it had to be Long Beach be-cause she was afraid to be seen meeting me at the train station in Rockville Center. And, besides, if a cop shined his flashlight into the back of the truck in Long Beach, at least it wouldn't be a cop she'd grown up with.

The floor hadn't felt so hard while we'd been pleasantly occupied, but now I was shifting my body, trying to fit myself against the corrugations, when she told me Matthew Sklar had called her.

"Three times," she said. "Even though after the second time I asked him not to."

"Where did he get your number?"

"The side of the truck."

I turned on my side to face her. "You mean he saw you? Where?"

"Leaving Mike's one night." She smiled. "I guess he thought I was Mike's girl."

"What was he doing there?" Matthew made my skin crawl.

"He said he was passing by."

"He stopped you on the street?"

"No, no. He told me this on the phone. I never saw him there at all. He must have been lurking in the shadows."

I shook my head slowly, not happy with any of this. Lurking. Yes, that's something Matthew would do. He must have been parked up there, hanging around.

"He said he wanted to talk to Mike. I guess he hoped he'd bump into him. You know, by accident."

"But how did he know where Mike lives? How do people find out things like that?" And as soon as I asked, I knew the answer. Lenny Basch.

She sent two tiny smoke rings wobbling toward the front seat. She'd been trying to teach me how to do that, but so far I hadn't been close. "He wanted to talk to Mike, but Mike wouldn't answer his calls. So he wanted me to put in a word for him. And then when he found out I was Mike's sister, he asked me out to dinner."

I raised myself up on one elbow and took the cigarette from her. "He gives me the serious creeps."

"He said it was important that he talk to me."

"Why didn't you hang up on him?"

She looked at me and smiled. "I've never been able to do that."

"Well, learn. It's a lot easier the second time."

I gave her the cigarette to finish, and then was suddenly struck by the fact that she'd managed to find time to visit her brother, who also lived in Manhattan, on Central Park West. "How come that was okay?" I asked her.

She grinned. "I brought Josh with me. Mike's his uncle, remember? Should I bring him with me to your place?"

"I'll think about it," I mumbled.

She handed me the glowing stub of the cigarette.

"What do I do with this?" I asked, looking around a little helplessly.

"Flip it out the rear window."

"Won't I set most of the western hemisphere on fire?"

She shrugged. "Okay, be a good citizen. There's an ashtray up front."

"How do I get there?"

"Any way you like, as long as you leave me the blanket."

It's fortunate that no pictures exist of the twisting naked body that worked itself clumsily toward the front and then reached over the high seat to put that cigarette out. It is to Rebecca's credit that she kept her mirthful outbursts down to a few breathy snickers.

"No more smoking," I said, reclaiming my place back under the blanket. "It leads to muscle spasm."

She drew herself closer and moved against me slowly, warmly. "Yes," she said softly, "spasm. That's what I like, lots of spasm."

"Hold it," I said, pulling away just a bit. "Matthew. Why's he so anxious to talk to Mike? Did he tell you?"

She frowned at me, disappointed that I hadn't picked up her mood. Then she shook her head. "No. There's something he wants Mike to know. That's all he'd say."

I didn't like the sound of that at all.

Heaping plates of antipasto were bustled to our corner table and set in front of Frank Dean and me. Frank pushed the oil and vinegar my way, and I started with the oil. By now I'd been around.

"You know what his problem is?" Frank asked. "He's forgotten what natural is. He's had every word set for so long, he doesn't know what to do when I tell him just to be himself."

We were talking about Elliott Cross. Being himself used to

be the thing he was best at. "But now it throws him. It's as if he can't be himself because he's not sure who that is." He looked down at his plate. "Do we really have linguini coming?"

Not for at least five minutes, I told him.

"You don't want to hear any of this, do you?" Frank said as he doused his antipasto.

I wasn't sure what I was doing that had announced it, but it was true I didn't. It was one thing to be involved in the general outlines of what was going on, but for weeks now I'd been insulated from the details. Again, the theory was that there was no point in anybody's knowing any more than he had to. I liked that theory fine.

"The rules say I'm not supposed to."

Frank glared at me. "Not my rules," he said.

I nodded and said okay, and he stabbed a square of provolone. "The Henry James question," he said, gesturing with his fork. *I'll name the characters,* the question read, *and you tell me the books they come from.* "Isabel Archer he knew. The other two he didn't. 'Okay,' I told him. 'Knock off the easy one first.'

" 'But how?' he wanted to know, and I said do it simply; just say it.

" 'But no,' he said. 'That doesn't seem right. I think I should be relieved when that one comes easy. What do you think?'

"By now I could see he wanted to be led by the hand. 'Okay,' I said, 'How about this: You smile, but you stroke your chin because even though you know this one, you're thinking ahead and you know you're in trouble. Isabel Archer is *Portrait Of A Lady,* you say. But we can see your mind's on the other two.' "

Frank had put his fork down after the first bite, but I was heavily into the antipasto, trying to cover my sudden loss of appetite with enthusiastic moves. Besides, I had to be finished by the time the pasta came; I heard echoes of my father warning me against such restaurant disasters.

"Now here's what's strange," Frank said. "He couldn't decide what to do with the first one because it was real; he knew it. But the other two he can handle, because the other two are make-believe.

" 'Okay,' he says, his back really in it. 'We'll do it like this.' Notice the editorial *we;* he's got me standing in there with him. 'I'll tell Mike I'm not really sure about Morris Townsend. I know he's a suitor, but I'm not sure what the novel is. I'll take a few seconds and then say, Is it *Washington Square?* And he'll say, Is that your answer? And I'll tell him yes.' "

We'd done a lot of that with Elliott Cross. It was a little routine he had going with Mike Prince. *Is it Philip Nolan?* he'd ask. *Is that your answer?* Mike would reply. *Yes,* Elliott would say, and Mike would call him right. It was as much identified with Elliott Cross as the nervous laugh had been with Matthew Sklar.

"So that left us with the last one," Frank said. "Roderick Hudson. And he knew right away what he wanted to do. 'I ask Mike to give me a couple of seconds, and he does. Then I tell him Roderick Hudson is an artist, I remember that, but I'm having trouble with the book . . . I take maybe four seconds, five, and then it kicks in and I break into a smile. I tell him it's the same. The book's the same. He asks me to be more explicit, and I say the name of the character is the name of the book. *Roderick Hudson.* And he tells me I'm right.' "

I put my fork down, suddenly feeling as if another mouthful might not be such a good idea. "Very nice," I said.

"But there's more," Frank said. "He adds a kicker."

The waiter arrived with two bowls of steaming pasta. He cleared my empty plate and put mine in front of me as I wondered what I'd be doing with it. He started to set Frank's bowl down to one side, but Frank looked up and shook his head. "I don't want that," he said.

The waiter looked at him for a moment, as if considering some rude suggestion, but finally nodded and removed the bowl.

"Okay," Frank Dean went on. "The kicker. He says after the applause Mike should say, 'I suppose you could call Roderick

Hudson an artist, but my card says he was a sculptor.' And of course, there'll be a laugh. One of those tension-relievers. But do you see what he's doing? He doesn't want Mike just to say he was a sculptor. No, he wants him to say *my card says* he was a sculptor. Mike, you see, can't be on the same intellectual level as Elliott. Mike can only know what's written on his card."

Frank shook his head and looked down at his food, as if trying to decide whether to attack it again. Then he looked back at me.

"The part that throws me," he said, "is that things have gotten so backward. He's become so attuned to all this that if he's dealing with a question he doesn't know, when I give him the answer he can stage his own business. But if it's something he really knows, he can't figure out how to react. It's the truth that's become the problem. How does that make any sense?"

The cover of *Time* magazine blared out at me from everywhere. Piles of them stacked on sidewalks, just delivered. Borders of them clothes-pinned across the top of every newsstand. Dozens of them flopped open in front of subway faces. Single copies sitting unexpectedly on desks. Everywhere the face of Elliott Cross, the fingers of his left hand touching his earphone, pressing it tight against his head to help him think the valuable thoughts that had already made him the highest money winner who'd ever been on television. Cover story, p. 58.

Stu had sent out for fifty copies, just to have. "Have you read it?" he asked as I came in. I shook my head. "Jesus, I can't believe it. There's a terrific part in there about you. How you're responsible for the questions, which they think are terrific. I made sure I mentioned that when the guy came in to talk to me. Is this unbelievable, or what?"

I started to answer, but the phone rang.

"No calls," Stu said. "Nobody, unless it's Donald Scheer." He banged the receiver down happily. "I mean, this is *us* they're talking about. There isn't enough money in America to buy a spread like this, and they gave it to us because they think we're a phenomenon. Can you believe it?"

I slipped down onto the couch, in my own way as overwhelmed as he was. "Honest to God, I can't."

"If it weren't for my diet, I'd say lunch at the Colony. Champagne, beluga caviar, poached breast of chicken in a light cream sauce, wrapped in a paper-thin crepe. For dessert, a mille feuille alongside a sinful crème brûlée." He reached for the phone. "Let's do it. You do it, I'll just have coffee."

"No," I said quickly. "We'd better stay around here. You can shut off the phones for just so long."

He shrugged. "Okay. I suppose." But then his face lit up again. "Why don't we have them send up a picnic. Food for everyone. Something fantastic. I'll have Toby arrange it." And he did, and they sent up the kind of picnic you imagine the French aristocracy smacking their lips over in a shaded corner of the Bois de Boulogne. Food and champagne for everyone, and toasts to Stu and Mike Prince and every member of the staff, culminating in Stu's observation that if this company lived a thousand years, this would be its finest hour.

Afterward, back in his office, away from the pleasant debris, he started talking about what was next. Elliott Cross had been on for six weeks. Time for him to get involved in a series of ties and then get beaten. Everything had to end. The new champion would be nobody special. Just somebody who happened to get lucky. Whoever Toby had in the files. A little lull would be good for us; set us up for something major. And something major is what would happen afterward.

He walked over to his desk and picked up the brass Buddha. "Remember this?"

I nodded.

Stu smiled. "The Enlightened One. The origin of suffering is desire." He picked it up to show me. "Notice the way his hands are, on his stomach. Not smug and satisfied, one hand resting

on the other. They're spread apart, the fingertips not touching."
He set it down. "There are new desires all around us, and they
will surely lead to suffering. I remember often how I got this. I
don't think it was entirely accidental."

There was a point to this, of course, and with a sudden chill
I realized what it was.

"I think we have a chance to focus attention on something
very exciting," Stu said. "Big changes are coming. There's
going to be a Supreme Court decision soon, and I don't have
any doubt which way it will go."

The bus boycott in Montgomery, Alabama. In June, the U.S.
District Court had ruled the state bus laws unconstitutional, and
the State of Alabama had appealed. The decision was due in a
matter of weeks. The papers were filled with the black boycott.
Something major.

I had not been so appalled since all of this had started. The
Buddha, you'll remember, had been bought from a young black
lawyer. "Don't do it," I said quietly.

"Why not?" Stu smiled. "Don't you like black people?"

"You know what I'm talking about," I said in a tone meant
to convey the fact that I was very serious about this. "This is a
kid who's just starting out. His mother broke her back to put him
through law school."

Stu shrugged. "All the more reason he could use the
money."

I shook my head. "He doesn't need money. He needs the
career he's trained for."

Stu was serious now. He stared at me for a moment. "Just
take a minute and think what it could mean to the civil rights
movement if a young black man went on and became the focus
of this country's admiration. If he could demonstrate week after
week how much he knew, how capable he was."

I walked over to the door and shut it quietly, then turned
back to Stu. "And are you planning to have him do all this
without getting any help?"

Stu turned his head sideways, not sure what I was getting at. "I assumed he'd have the same assistance that others have had."

"And what if all of this ever blows up? He's ruined. Disbarred."

"How's it going to blow up? Who's going to do the talking? You? Me? Certainly not him."

"I don't know who. But I know it can happen."

Stu shook his head. "No chance. Everybody's interests are lined up in the same direction. Whoever talks is destroyed. Why would anybody do that?"

I had no answer. None, certainly, that would have won the argument. I took a deep breath, held it while I thought about my options, then slowly let it out. "Have you talked to him yet?"

Stu shook his head again. "I thought I'd wait a week and then invite him down to see the show. There'll be plenty of time after that." He smiled. "And besides, it's Frank who does the talking."

11

THE BOAT HAD BEEN HIS IDEA. ALL I'D SUGGESTED WAS THAT IT might be better if we met somewhere other than his office. It hadn't seemed wise for me to be seen walking into Capricorn for a private meeting with the president. When I'd called him, I'd expected the unusual request to put him on his guard, but instead he seemed to relish the touch of mystery. If it could wait till Saturday, why didn't I join him on the boat? Perfect place to meet. No one had to know a thing about it.

I paid the cab and looked around the basin while I waited for my change. This wasn't his usual mooring, but now that it was early October he was keeping it here at Seventy-ninth Street to extend the season. There were half a dozen boats tied up a hundred yards from shore, and without being able to see the nameplates I couldn't be sure which one was the *Cappy II*. But I should have known that finding it wouldn't be a problem. As I pocketed my change, somebody young and seaworthy was rolling toward me and asking if I was the gentleman Mr. Scheer expected. A moment later we were in a freshly painted dinghy heading briskly toward the biggest and whitest of the proud vessels parked out there.

"Welcome aboard!" beamed Donald Scheer as I stepped onto the deck and fought off the urge to salute. We shook hands instead.

"Beautiful boat," I said, and his smile spread even wider. He was perfectly dressed, of course, from his buff topsiders up through his white duck trousers and on to a yellow canvas shirt that was held together by a lacquered cord that wound through metal eyelets.

First, of course, he had to show me around, a tour in which we were joined by Sam, the gentleman who had ferried me from shore. Sam, it seemed, had been responsible for choosing all the furnishings on board and took enormous pride in showing off his handiwork. I was every bit as impressed as I was meant to be. My life up to that point hadn't presented me with much to compare it with, but quality has a way of announcing itself, and it was all around me, from the burgundy opera drapes in the enormous master stateroom down to the hand-carved wooden faucets on the washstand in the smallest head. After the tour we settled in lounge chairs on the fantail, where Sam reappeared a few moments later asking what I'd like to drink. Nothing, I thanked him, but Donald Scheer requested Perrier for both of us, and if my life had depended on it I couldn't have spelled the word. Perrier was news to me, and I was mildly disappointed when the little green bowling pins turned out to contain nothing more interesting than sparkling water.

"Marvelous flavor," Donald Scheer said, setting his glass back down. "Can't get the stuff in this country." He had cases imported privately from France.

There was some efficient bustling around us and in a moment we were moving, heading up the river toward Spuyten Duyvil. The chairs had been perfectly positioned to catch the morning sun, and as soon as we were under way Donald Scheer removed his shirt and lowered his lounge chair to a relaxing horizontal.

"Wonderful," he exhaled, leaning all the way back and shutting his eyes. "Everything disappears. Just the warmth of that lovely fall sun soaking through. Take your shirt off. It feels marvelous."

"Thanks, I'm comfortable this way," I said. It actually looked like a pleasant idea, but something perverse wouldn't let me follow suit.

He kept his eyes shut and his head tilted firmly back, straining to let those rays in. Uncomfortable as he looked, it seemed to be his form of relaxation. I decided to wait before bringing up the subject that had brought me here.

"Well," he said, his eyes still shut, "the cover of *Time.* That's quite an achievement. And the ratings keep getting better and better."

"Number five last week," I said.

"It'll be number one before much longer."

"Yes, I guess that's possible."

He smiled. "I'm counting on it."

Neither of us said anything then, while he just lay back, relaxing as hard as he could. After a minute or two he sat up quickly in a brisk athletic move, straddling the lounge chair.

"All right," he said. "Tell me what's all that important."

I hadn't expected it. From the pace he'd seemed to be setting it had looked as if there'd be small talk till after lunch. But suddenly, there was the starting gun and although I'd thought very carefully about what I was going to say, the abrupt timing jolted my paragraphs out of line. I did a little throat-clearing, something about how I knew it was unorthodox to jump out of channels this way, but he had no patience with that.

And I started telling him, uncomfortable with the tack I'd determined to take, but convinced there was no other way. What it boiled down to, I said, was that I thought we'd need to do some careful planning if we were really going ahead with Henry Cavanaugh.

He frowned at the name, trying to remember. "Am I supposed to know who that is?"

"You met him Monday. At the show. The young lawyer who was there with Stu."

He remembered now. "Oh, yes. The Negro. Well-dressed young man. Impressive."

Stu had introduced him to everyone. That was the reason he'd brought him to the studio. And everyone had been impressed with Henry Cavanaugh; with his starched, crisp appearance, his quick smile, his lively interest in everything around him. Even Donald Scheer had smiled warmly when Stu introduced him. "Keep him in mind if you need another lawyer," Stu had said, and Henry Cavanaugh had looked faintly embarrassed.

Donald Scheer picked up his bottle of Perrier and poured the last few drops into his empty glass, uncertain whether or not he was supposed to understand what I was talking about.

"And just what is it we have in mind for this Henry Cavanaugh?"

I looked surprised. "I thought you knew. A contestant, of course."

There was no response to that. Just some slow nodding as the idea took hold.

"I assumed . . . I mean, I thought Stu had told you." I took a sip of my own Perrier. "Anyway," I went on, "I was anxious to see you to be sure you'd thought about some of the things we really ought to do. Stu's convinced, and so am I, that the timing's perfect for this. Having been exposed to the way you think, I was sure you'd be in full agreement, but I thought you'd appreciate a chance to plan ahead."

He put his glass down and stared at me. "Plan ahead in what way?" he asked.

I leaned forward confidentially. "Well, I think there's some advance PR that's called for. First, there's the matter of dealing with the Southern stations. These aren't the Dark Ages; they're not going to drop the show. But it might be wise to give them some advance warning, so they can absorb the idea. The same with Capricorn's Southern distributors. What if this guy goes on and does really well? Are they going to take heat from their regular sales outlets? Probably not, but it might be safer to tell them what's coming."

Donald Sheer nodded thoughtfully at all of this. Then he turned and reset his chair to its near-upright position and leaned back comfortably.

"I imagine you're getting hungry."

I smiled. "A little, I suppose."

"There's something about being on the water that seems to sharpen the appetite. I don't know what Sam has planned for us, but I'm sure it will be appearing very soon. He'll be joining us for lunch, if you have nothing else that's private."

Nothing else, I assured him.

"I leave all the arrangements for everything on board to Sam. That's one of the reasons I find this so relaxing. He doesn't cook, of course, but he knows exactly what I like. Marvelous young man. I must talk to Stu about him. He's eager to get something in the television business."

I wasn't sure what I was supposed to say. "I'll mention it to him, if you like."

Donald Scheer gave me a tolerant smile. "That might not be wise, since you and I haven't really talked. Let's not forget, this is a meeting that's not taking place."

He shut his eyes again and tilted his head toward the sun, making it clear that he saw no reason for further conversation.

As promised, lunch appeared, and even on this incredible craft where everything was possible, lunch was the same little cut-up vegetables sitting sadly on brown-edged lettuce.

Suddenly, there she was. Not imagined this time, but certainly not real. A figure in another world; moving, speaking, live but not present. The man with her was the Reverend Dr. Ralph Abernathy, and she was asking questions.

I'd never watched the morning news, but the new little TV set had come the day before, a housewarming gift from Alyse and Joe to celebrate my finally getting my last piece of furniture bought and delivered. I'd forgotten all about it till I noticed it this morning, sitting in its new place on the kitchen counter. When I clicked it on to accompany my morning coffee, there she was.

There was no doubt in his mind, said Dr. Abernathy, that the Supreme Court would rule in their favor. And, asked Margo, if that failed to happen? Dr. Abernathy gave her a patient smile. "I cannot believe such a thing is possible," he said.

She turned to the camera. "From Montgomery, Alabama, this is Margo Harris reporting."

Commercial.

My hand shook as I turned the set off, and I had no success at all when I tried to focus on the morning paper. I had made several attempts to get in touch with Margo, but after her phone hadn't answered a couple of times and she'd failed to respond to the message I'd left at the *Times*, I'd run into the brick wall of a new home number that was now unlisted. If I'd been persistent there'd have been ways to make contact. But I was never completely sure I wanted to. Contact, yes. But the commitment of actively seeking it, not really so sure. I had no way of knowing what kind of reception I might get, and certainly no reason to expect it to be warm.

Now here was contact of a different kind. One-way, protected. Contact that only I was aware of.

I began to watch every morning. She appeared two or three times a week, sometimes in the studio, sometimes from different parts of the country. There was no schedule that I could figure out, which added to the sense of excitement. She might be there almost anytime.

I bought another little set for the bathroom, and between the two screens saw most of the show every morning. (Except, of course, for those rare occasions when Rebecca stayed over because Josh was spending the night with his father. Those mornings I didn't turn the set on. It would have seemed strange for the two of them to meet.)

I watched her talk to Don Larsen two weeks after he pitched his perfect World Series game, and to Estes Kefauver as he started his New England swing. To a survivor of the *Andrea Doria,* to Lotte Lenya, to Grace Metalious, to Miss America Sharon Kay Ritchie on the occasion of her marriage to the golfer Don Cherry, and to presidential Press Secretary James Hagerty about our country's attitude toward the revolution in Hungary. And once again I was in awe of Margo, as I'd been in the days when we worked together. What she did was perfection, total preparation and then effortless command of her facts. I imagined myself sitting across the V-shaped table from her, fielding those probing, pointed questions. Yes, I answered, I did remember the incident when the apartment house superintendent kept mentioning the fellow from Indiana, and, no, I didn't have any explanation for that. The Da Ponte thing? Now what was that again? I asked, trying to buy a few seconds. And when she reminded me in elaborate detail, I broke out in little beads of perspiration, almost as uncomfortable as if it had really been happening.

I made her my conscience and questioned myself in her voice. How could you have let this happen? You had standards. You stood for something once. You were as decent as sweet Joe Klein.

Hey, look, I heard myself saying, suddenly shifting to the attack. If we're talking about selling out, this is a pretty commercial thing you've got going here. You were the serious journalist bound for important stuff, but now it's three giddy minutes with Miss America. I mean, who has the right to be throwing stones? But even in my imagination the words were unconvincing.

She seemed older, more polished. Her hair and her clothes

were no longer casual things, but were carefully planned by people who had names. She was someone I'd once known very well, but as I watched her that was something I had to keep telling myself. What kind of encounter could I expect if I suddenly ran into her on the street? Would we be old friends still glad to see each other, or would I now be an awkward three pleasant questions and good-bye? And why would I be any more likely to run into her than into Ed Sullivan, say, or Arthur Godfrey?

I watched every morning, and each time I saw her the distance between us widened. So when the telephone call came one morning three weeks after all this began, nothing on earth could have caught me more by surprise.

"You're still in the book," she said. "I think that's terrific."

I mumbled something awkward about liking to be accessible, and her tone seemed to soften.

"Tell me right away, how are you?"

"Right now? So surprised my stomach's doing flips."

"Oh, shit, David," she said, "mine is too." That kind of broke the ice, and in a minute we were chattering away as if there'd been no in-between.

"Listen," she said. "I just broke up with somebody. That's really why I called. What about you? Are you seeing anyone?"

I told her I was.

"Of course you are. I mean, I probably shouldn't have asked, and it doesn't really matter. What I was going to say is, let's meet somewhere and talk. Nothing elaborate. Just maybe coffee or a drink."

"Let's do it," I said, and we arranged to meet the following morning right after she got off the air, for breakfast at a place near the studio.

It was a few minutes before you realized anything was wrong. Because whatever it was wasn't all that wrong. Just wrong enough to be a major problem. Slow, was what it was. A beat behind the conversation. Not fully comprehending.

"You work in my father's office?" The question came a second time. We'd already talked about it when Stu had introduced us.

"Yes, honey, he does," Stu said patiently. It seemed an odd word to be using with an eight-year-old boy.

"Do you know how to type?"

Stu shook his head. "That's not what David does."

I smiled at him. "But I do know how to type. Do you?"

"Oh, yeah," Ricky said, grinning. "I can type as fast as a machine gun." And he held his hands out in front of him and rat-tat-tatted in a circle.

"You'll have to show me some time," I said. "I mean, how you type."

He turned to his father. "Could I?"

"Sure, you can, Ricky," Stu said.

"Now!" Ricky said, suddenly excited. "Let's go there now."

"We can't now," Stu said. "I promised your mother I'd get you home in time for school."

"I don't have school," Ricky said. "It's Saturday."

"No, Ricky," Stu said firmly. "It's Wednesday."

"Well, I don't," said Ricky, sullen now.

Stu shifted on the park bench and took a quarter from his pocket. "You see that man over there selling papers?"

Ricky looked around. "Yes, I see him."

But he didn't really, and Stu had to turn him in the right direction. "Buy a *Times* for me." Stu gave him the quarter and he was off.

"He'll get the right one," Stu said. "The guy knows who we are. We do this a couple of times a week." And when Ricky reached the newspaper stand, the man looked over and waved. Stu waved back.

I'd stumbled on them as I was hurrying through the park, trying to get back to my place before eight-thirty in case Rebecca called. I'd spent an unplanned night at Margo's, the first time in this second run, and was thinking hard about what I'd say to Rebecca if she'd tried to phone me this morning, when suddenly Stu was in front of me, looking up startled from his bench. I wasn't too thrilled about running into somebody when I looked this rumpled and unshaven, but I needn't have worried. Stu wouldn't have noticed if I'd sprouted another head. He was too busy being unhappy that I'd discovered him.

This was the guilty secret, no question about that. He said as much later, over coffee at my house. Yes, he'd have coffee, but that was all for him. And then, while I showered and shaved, he knocked off half a coffee cake and a small loaf of unsliced rye.

"So now you know," he said, pouring a second cup. "I walked out and left her with all of that. That makes me a shit, I know that, but that wasn't why I left."

"You sure you don't want some toast?"

He didn't hear the irony. Just raised his hand and shook me off. "Can't—still trying to lose a few. Smells terrific, though."

Just plain old white toast. That's all he'd left me with.

"It wasn't Ricky. It was *her.* She was the one I walked out on, because there was nothing left between us." It came out mechanically. He'd said all this before. Maybe to someone paid to listen.

But he knew the way it must look, he said. Problem kid who demanded a lot of special attention, and he'd left her with the burden of dealing with it day-to-day. What kind of man does a thing like that?

The phone rang. It was Rebecca, and I told her I'd call back later.

Walking to the office, he kept up this whole thing about guilt and the money he'd spent on special schools and how he'd often thought he should go back. I wasn't sure what kind of absolution he was looking for, so I asked about Carl Steinberg. That put him back on solid ground.

He turned to me and grinned. "Donald Scheer says he doesn't like him. But I'm starting to think he might win."

Carl Steinberg had been involved in a monumental series

of ties with Elliott Cross, and the plan had been for Elliott to beat him, and then lose to Henry Cavanaugh. But now that Donald Scheer had vetoed using Henry, there was no one standing in the wings. We were all agreed that Steinberg was nothing special, but Stu was convinced that now that we were number one, this was the time to go with someone ordinary. Coast with someone, he'd said, so the next terrific person would stick out that much more and give us a shot in the arm if we started to slip.

Okay. If there was going to be a plot line, that was as good as any.

The news that we were number one had been sent over last Tuesday along with a case of champagne. The champagne was as much to soothe hurt feelings as it was to celebrate our status, because Stu had made no secret of his displeasure with Donald Scheer's rejection of Henry Cavanaugh. That argument had gone on for two days, with Stu at first refusing to accede to the client's wishes. But finally he'd allowed himself to be overruled, if not persuaded. It was only for now, Donald Scheer had assured him. There was certainly no policy against using people from any group. It was a matter of timing, and now was not the time.

Later, after everything blew up, I often thought about Henry Cavanaugh and the close call he didn't know he'd had. But even if he'd found out we planned to use him, he'd never have understood the danger because he'd have assumed that he'd never have gone along. He'd have laughed off the possibility that he'd ever have let himself become involved. He'd be certain it was something he couldn't possibly have done. Of course that's what he'd think. What he'd never know was that it was something Elliott Cross would never have done, or Carl Steinberg, or any of the others.

"I need cigarettes," I said at the drugstore. "I'll see you upstairs." But this wasn't a day Stu wanted to be alone, even for a few minutes, and he followed me inside.

"He's learning to read a little," Stu said when we were alone in the elevator. "Not sentences yet, but words. Some words. And he knows his alphabet."

"He's a nice-looking boy," I said.

The elevator stopped and Stu turned to me. "You can't really tell at first, can you?"

I shook my head. The door slid open and we stepped out.

12

"TALK TO HIM. HE LISTENS TO YOU." THAT WAS FRANK DEAN talking, pleading really.

He was always jumpy on show days, but today it was worse than usual. He had burst in on me wild-eyed, slamming the door shut behind him. Now he was leaning over my desk pressing his knuckles white. I'd been working on an intro for Mike Prince, but I turned away from the typewriter and sat back, trying to restore an air of calm. "Open the door," I said quietly.

He looked at me as if I was crazy.

"He can't hear us. He's over at Capricorn," I said. "The point is, my door is always open. If you leave it shut, the whole office will wonder what's going on in here."

Frank turned and opened the door. "You don't seem to understand how serious this is. The Doc really means it."

"When's the last time you talked to him?"

"This morning. We had breakfast."

I looked at him. "How come you didn't panic till now?" It was almost eleven-thirty.

"I kept thinking I'd still be able to talk him out of it. He said he'd be home all morning, but I've been trying since ten o'clock and he doesn't answer his phone."

We'd been referring to Elliott Cross as The Doc since the cover story ran in *Time*. The piece had said that's what the staff called him. It hadn't been, but it was now.

"I guess he doesn't want to talk," I said.

Frank looked at me as if I came from another planet. "No kidding," he snapped. "No wonder Stu thinks you're some kind of genius."

I felt myself redden a little. "Why don't you take a quiet walk around the block," I said.

"Why don't you take a flying fuck at the moon!" And then he turned and stormed out of my office so fast he almost knocked a container of coffee out of Toby's hands. She stared after him as he hurried down the hall, and then turned back to me.

"Everything okay?" she asked.

"Artistic differences," I said.

Toby nodded and continued to her office. Frank's short fuse no longer had the power to surprise.

We had lunch at his desk. His idea. No apology, of course, just a matter-of-fact phone call ten minutes later suggesting we continue our discussion. He'd order food.

Elliott Cross had been hard to handle ever since the story ran in *Time*. He wanted out. The newspaper stories, big as they'd been, had grown routine, but the sudden splash of magazine covers had made him feel surrounded by himself, and the slick pages inside had introduced him to a man he didn't recognize. The overwhelming praise, the almost worshipful tone, the quotes from academics about how much his success had done to elevate respect for intellectual achievement. The outer Doc had seemed to handle it with the style and grace we'd all come to expect from Elliott Cross, but the inner Doc had panicked. And it was the inner Doc Frank Dean had to deal with every week.

"He says no matter what, this is his last week. He'll blow

every question in the second game if I don't guarantee that Steinberg beats him."

"Didn't you tell him you can't control Steinberg? How can you guarantee anything?"

This time Frank softened his contemptuous look with something meant to be a smile. "The man's not a moron," he said. "He knows Steinberg's getting answers."

Of course he'd know. Even though Frank had been careful to deny it, the evidence was all too clear. The nature of the game was such that if Elliott's little set of instructions called for him to get almost everything right and miss just a few strategic questions, then any opponent who kept pace with him in a dramatic series of ties would have to be getting the same kind of help.

"I can deny it all I like," Frank said, "but it doesn't take a genius to figure out what's going on. I'm telling you, he'd better lose that first match tonight, because if he doesn't, he'll damn sure lose the second, no matter what he has to do. The man's a basket case. All he wants is out." He glanced at his watch. "What time's Stu getting back?"

"He's not. He's having lunch at Capricorn. He said he'd meet me at the studio."

"Can't wait till we get to the studio. Let's get him on the phone. He's got to go along with this."

But before I placed the call, I wanted another look at the details. "Can Elliott lose without your having to change what you've set with Steinberg?"

Frank nodded. He took the chart out of his pocket. The *only* chart. The one piece of paper that wasn't filed anywhere, and that wound up being torn into tiny pieces and flushed down a toilet in the sixth floor men's room right after every show. He laid it on the desk and showed me.

"The fifth question. If Doc misses it, he loses. All Steinberg has to do is what he's already set up to do."

That was important. If Carl Steinberg got a change this late and then went on to win, he'd have even more reason to believe the Doc had been getting help. He had reason enough as it was.

I picked up the phone and put in a call to Capricorn. But Stu was in a meeting with Donald Scheer and they couldn't be interrupted. I left word for him to call me, and marked it urgent.

"Suppose Stu doesn't call?"

I shrugged. "We'll talk to him at the studio."

Frank shook his head. "Too late then. The one thing I won't do is closet myself with either one of these guys over there. You know that's out."

I did know. That was something we'd avoided right from the beginning. Everything was light and casual once we got to the studio.

"What time are they due? Seven?"

Frank nodded.

"Okay, that gives us plenty of time."

"Not really," Frank said. "Right now I can't get in touch with the Doc. I might have to go over to his place and camp out before I find him. I don't know how long that will take. He might be on one of his famous walks by the river."

There'd been a photo of that in the *Time* story. Elliott Cross through a morning mist. His eyes cast down in contemplation, his collar up against the early chill. A frozen moment that captured the spirit of the man.

"He'll phone in," I said. "He has to. That's the only way he can get what he wants."

"But suppose he calls before you hear from Stu? What do I tell him?"

I thought about that for a minute. On the one hand, it would take only a few seconds to make the kind of change Frank Dean was talking about. It could be done so quickly that despite Frank's uneasiness he could even do it at the studio if he had to. But on the other hand there was some danger in not giving Elliott Cross an early answer. It would mean he'd have the whole afternoon to stew about it. And apparently he'd been doing enough of that already.

"If he calls, give him what he wants," I said. "Do it the way you showed me. I'll take my chances with Stu."

Frank nodded. "Believe me, there's no other sensible choice."

In the real world, that was true. But Stu wouldn't think so. Nothing was either obvious or sensible until it had been stamped with his approval.

I indicated the food mess on Frank's desk and asked how much I owed him. He waved me off. "Company picnic," he said.

"Let me know when the Doc calls," I said. If he called first, Stu wouldn't get a vote. I found myself hoping that happened.

First match, third question. The Doc gets it right. Something easy, really. The category was musicals, and Mike Prince asked him the name of the musical that had been based on the Damon Runyon story, "The Idyll of Miss Sara Brown." *Guys And Dolls*, Elliott had answered quickly, flashing that famous smile of relief that showed how pleasant it was to field the easy ones.

They'd keep getting tougher as we went up the line, and we'd be back with question four right after this brief message.

I turned to Stu, but he was staring straight ahead. I was being punished with silence, which in many ways was better than the alternative. He'd gotten there late and I'd told him the change we'd made. You could see his temper climb up his face like the mercury on a *Looney Tunes* thermometer. But he hadn't said a word. And now he turned to Vince Martoni.

"Can we get tighter on Steinberg?"

"Of course," Vince said.

Stu's head snapped back in my direction. "Excuse me," he said crisply, and as I leaned back he brushed past me and out the sliding doors for a word with Murray Cashin, who always stood at the back of the house. I was being carefully frosted. No doubt about that.

Out of commercial and up on two. Mike Prince pulled back the switch on his lectern that seemed to turn on the lights in Carl Steinberg's booth. "Question four," he said to Carl, and Carl nodded. That meant the Doc had gotten his question right. Otherwise Carl would be dealing with the same question his opponent had missed.

Mike Prince held the question card up high. "John O'Hara wrote the stories on which this musical was based. Name it."

And this time it was Carl Steinberg who smiled. Easy. *"Pal Joey,"* he said.

"Right!" said Mike Prince. Applause. "Carl, we'll be back to you in a moment." And he switched off Carl Steinberg's booth and turned on the Doc's. Not really turning it on, you understand. That would have been against forty thousand union rules. But the electrician took his cues from the movements of Mike's hands on the dummy switches. "All right, Elliott," he said. "Question five."

Elliott smiled. "He doesn't miss many, does he?"

"No, he doesn't," Mike agreed. "Are you ready?"

Elliott nodded.

Mike picked up the question and hoisted it aloft. "The musical *Oklahoma* is based on another play. Name the play and the man who wrote it."

The Doc put his hand to his chin and thought about that. "Well," he said, "the play was *Green Grow the Lilacs.*"

"That's right," Mike said. "And the writer?"

"Mmm," said the Doc. "It's a name that sounds as if it could be a woman's name . . . " And his fingers worked farther up his jaw. "I do know it," he said, still struggling.

"Take a few more seconds," said Mike, and Elliott nodded. There was a very slight murmur as the crowd felt the danger that he might really be in trouble. But they'd seen him go through this before and then at the last possible moment come up with an answer.

"*Green Grow the Lilacs,*" Elliott repeated, "written by . . ."

Another long pause, finally broken by Mike Prince. "I must call for your answer."

The Doc struggled for another few seconds, then seemed to slump. "I just can't seem to think of it," he said quietly, and the crowd reacted strongly.

"You know what happens," said Mike, carefully spelling it out. "If your opponent can answer this question, the match is his. I'll leave your booth turned on so you can hear how he responds."

Elliott nodded and Mike turned back to Carl Steinberg, pulling the switch. "Carl," he said, "your opponent has missed." Carl nodded, a tiny smile escaping his efforts to maintain a decorous straight face.

"Here comes Question five," Mike went on. "If you can answer it correctly, you will be our new champion." And Mike read the question, asking first for the name of the play *Oklahoma* was based on.

Carl got it.

"And now, for the championship, the name of the writer."

Carl couldn't help breaking into an enormous grin. "It was written," he said, "by Lynn Riggs."

"That's right!" said Mike, "and Carl Steinberg, you've just won twenty-three thousand dollars!"

The band went into the winner's fanfare, but the audience was so stunned that it was a moment before the applause began. And when it did, it was instantly apparent that the swelling sounds of approval were not for the winner, but for the beaten Elliott Cross. Carl Steinberg realized it at once and as soon as both men were out of their booths, Carl pumped his hand warmly, and then stepped back to join in the applause for the finally defeated champ.

Stu's head snapped back toward Vince Martoni. "Get off

Steinberg," he barked. "Give me Elliott. That's who they're applauding."

"Take one!" said Vince, and there was that face again, a little sheepish in defeat but still smiling warmly as he nodded his thanks for the applause that was obviously his.

"Keep it coming!" yelled Stu, and the assistant director kept pumping the applause sign, but he didn't really have to. In another second the crowd was on its feet, and there's no telling how long that ovation might have gone on if it finally hadn't occurred to Elliott that the only way to stop it was to raise his hand. As the sound died down, it was clear he had to say something, and say something he did. While his words have not stayed with us with the power of Lou Gehrig's echoing farewell, they seemed mighty effective at the time, and if there was a dry eye in the house, it would have been hard to find.

Afterward, not even the sad realization that his long reign was over could stem the tide of wild congratulations that flooded into the press room from everywhere. It seemed that the enormity of his achievement could only be fully appreciated now that the string of victories had ended.

"Relieved. He says he's relieved," Lenny Basch shouted into a telephone. And then he finally managed to pull Elliott closer and shove the phone into his hand. "Is this crazy, or what?" he asked no one in particular as he reached for another phone. He had it almost to his ear when he noticed me standing near him. He clamped the phone against his chest to muffle the sound and fumbled in his jacket pocket. "Jesus, David, I didn't see you. This came while the show was on." He pulled out a crumpled telephone message and handed it to me. The word *Important* was scrawled across it, but all it contained was my name and an unfamiliar number that looked like a business phone. I started to ask him about it, but he'd already put the phone to his ear. "Who'm I talking to?" he bellowed above the noise.

I pushed my way to the little office we'd used on other occasions and dialed the number. After seven rings I was about to hang up when an operator finally answered. "Mount Sinai," she said, and that left me a little speechless because I suddenly realized I had no idea who to ask for.

It was a double room, but the other bed was empty. The room was bare; no personal effects. There'd been no time to pack.

The usual IV was set up reassuringly, dispensing those vital fluids, but she was still out cold, breathing long and deep. They'd warned me it might be hours before she came around, but I'd come up anyway, just to get a look at her.

Sleeping pills. And then panic. She'd tried to call me, but couldn't get through and finally called the hospital. They'd sent an ambulance for her and pumped her out, and somebody had left the message for me. But all I had was the number, and without details it had been twenty minutes on the phone before the emergency room and I could figure out who I was calling about.

I suppose I should have missed her at the show, but since that night in the rain we hadn't talked much at the studio. It had reached the point, I'd thought, where we hardly noticed each other. But now that I was here, I wasn't surprised that I'd been the one she called for. Only one thing could have made her do this, and that would leave me the next in line.

"Relative?" An intern had slipped in behind me. No, I told him, just a friend. He nodded and stepped closer to her, shining one of those clinical flashlights into the eye his fingers held open. "Carla!" He shouted it loud enough to be heard several buildings away, but she didn't move. He yelled it at her again, but still no response. He turned back to me. "How long's she been out like this?"

I shrugged.

He looked at his watch. "I'd say she's not going to be much different till eight, nine in the morning. Not much point in hanging around."

"Are you the doctor who admitted her?"

He shook his head. "I just came on."

"What do you think? She going to be all right?"

"You the husband? Boyfriend?"

"Neither. Just a friend."

He smiled. "Not that it matters. Yeah, she'll be all right—depending on what you call all right."

"What does that mean?"

He shrugged. *"Something* made her do it."

I stayed for a while after he left, knowing that, as he'd said, there was no real point to it. But leaving too soon would have felt like some kind of desertion.

Chalk-white skin; muscles slack in something more than sleep. She looked as if she'd come closer than the vital signs might say. What kind of pain had made her do it? And why had I seen nothing? We'd passed each other every week, and I'd smiled and kept on going. She had my attention now.

I made myself stay a half hour after I felt the first impulse to leave. But later, walking the two miles home, I felt myself pulling back already. I'd be around, of course, but this was the time to go easy.

"Have you been following me?" It came out sharply, less a question than an accusation. He stepped back and looked confused behind those wire glasses. We were in a florist shop. My order was being put together and I'd seen his reflection in the sliding case.

"Well, no—not really," said Matthew.

I'd spotted him a few blocks back, across the street, but I'd been careful not to catch his eye. Now he'd followed me inside. "What *is* it, Matthew?" I asked impatiently.

He sputtered through a couple of false starts and then said he'd seen me on the street before and thought maybe I could join him for a cup of coffee.

"I don't have time, Matthew," I said curtly. "Now tell me what you want. Why are you following me? And why are you following Mike Prince?"

More hems and haws, and then: "He's the one I want to talk to. I thought maybe you'd help me."

"I don't tell Mike Prince who to talk to."

"Prince isn't his real name, is it?"

"I don't know, Matthew."

"I mean, he's Jewish, isn't he?"

"I never asked him."

"But you're going with his sister."

"His sister's Jewish. Now step back, Matthew. I'd like to reach my wallet."

"Oh, sorry," he said and backed away. He stood too close to people. It drove me nuts.

The white-smocked woman had presented my wrapped bouquet and asked for twelve dollars. Matthew stared at my wallet while I took out a twenty, and when she went to get my change I shoved the wallet close to his face.

"Anything in there that interests you?"

He shook his head impassively.

"What does it take to embarrass you, Matthew?"

"I'm embarrassed."

"Good. Then maybe you'll stop all this skulking around."

"I want to talk to Mike Prince."

"Why?"

"There are things I want him to know."

The woman came back with my change and I put it away and picked up the flowers again.

"Matthew, I'm on my way to see a friend in the hospital, and I really don't have time for this."

"Ask him to take my call."

"I don't tell him who he should talk to. And stop following people, Matthew. It isn't nice." I started past him toward the door and then turned back. "Go back to spending the money."

"It's almost gone," he said.

Almost gone. Out on the street, that line rattled through me. How could nearly fifty thousand dollars be almost gone in less than two months? And what about money for taxes? Had some been set aside, or was that almost gone, too? Everything about you continues to give me the creeps, Matthew. And now I'm a little afraid of you.

They'd moved Carla to another room, also semiprivate, but this time there was someone in the other bed, an older woman moaning constantly.

"Gall bladder," Carla said, and when I looked toward her sympathetically Carla told me she never responded. "I'm not sure if she speaks English."

I sat on Carla's bed. "Does she ever stop moaning?"

"Sometimes. You'll get used to it."

"Soon, I hope."

The overweight, put-upon nurse shuffled back into the room. She'd found a vase for my flowers.

"Where do you want these?" she asked curtly.

"On the dresser," Carla said. There weren't a lot of choices. The nurse put them down and left.

"Are they all that sweet and friendly?"

"Hey, she's my buddy. You should meet the night nurse."

I smiled, and there was an awkward little pause. Carla shifted in bed and smoothed down the covers nervously.

"You didn't come to stare at me, did you?"

"What does that mean?"

"You know. Trying to figure out if I'll try to do it again. I won't, you know."

I nodded.

She threw her head back and forced a smile. "I'm getting out of here tomorrow."

Of course. There wasn't much reason to hold her. "Then what?"

She stared at me for a moment and the smile slowly disappeared. "Stan went back to his wife. I guess you figured that much out."

"We don't have to talk about this now."

"I was on the phone trying to call you before the pills were halfway down."

An aberration, was how she saw it. A once-in-a-lifetime thing. A cry for help. A won't-he-be-sorry-when-he-hears. A little of each.

"So Elliott finally lost." She said it brightly, forcing the smile again. "I saw it on the news. Murray says Donald Scheer's in mourning."

"Murray called?"

She nodded. "Nice guy, Murray. You'd be surprised. I mean, nice enough, I guess. He wants me to see his analyst. The new guy, how's he going to do? What's his name again?"

I told her.

"Well, good for him. Good for him."

Suddenly her brows came together and she snarled. "I hate that little turd. The thought of him embarrasses me."

I took her hand and held it, and she began to cry quietly. When she regained enough control to speak again, she asked me if I'd mind leaving, and the truth was that I didn't mind at all.

The tall white cups started showing up every day at five of twelve. Perry, the office boy, went out to get them. He was the one who'd introduced Stu to the magical substance inside.

There was this hot-dog stand on Broadway and Forty-sixth, and they were selling frozen chocolate malts that ran just fifty calories per enormous serving. There weren't many subjects on which Stu and Perry could have a conversation, but as soon as Stu saw Perry diving into one of these numbers, he sat down and listened for twenty minutes about how this place had stumbled onto the formula and now had two guys working full-time turning out the stuff. From then on there was a standing order for six a day.

Frank Dean and Toby sat in on certain days, and it was hard to know whether Stu was more pleased at being joined by converts, or upset because more eaters meant fewer cups left over. The leftover cups, of course, were his.

"Do you believe this?" he would ask anyone who cared to listen. "I mean, fifty calories, and the stuff's delicious." And he'd go back to knocking off however many were left sitting on his desk.

I told Margo about it one night at dinner. We were sitting in a mostly empty restaurant finishing the last of the wine. The restaurant was empty because it was only half past six. She had to be in bed by eight. The first time we'd done this, it had seemed eerie to be finishing dinner this early, but by now I'd begun to enjoy the extra attention the unhurried waiters could give us.

She laughed when I told her Stu sometimes ate as many as five at a sitting, and she wrote down the address of the place they came from. Three days later, she broke the story on the air. The frozen malts, their analysis had shown, contained not the advertised 50 calories per serving, but a whopping 340. "No wonder they're so delicious," said Margo to the camera. "Let the buyer beware, and see you Thursday." In earlier days she'd have used the Latin phrase, but she'd learned to trim her sails.

Stu, of course, was less furious at the bad news than he was at the messenger.

"It's not the frozen malts. Who gives a fuck about ice cream. *She's* the one I'm worried about."

He was crammed into my cubicle, his back against the shut door, hulking over my desk because there was no room for him to do anything else.

"How much are you seeing of her?"

Not that much, I told him, and that was mostly true. Maybe

once or twice a week. Not more than that because we weren't sure what we were to each other.

"I assume you keep your mouth shut. Has she tried to ask any questions?"

I wasn't enjoying this conversation. I suggested we talk about something else.

Stu frowned. "Her business is trouble. Try to remember that."

"I know what her business is," I said. "I used to be in it."

Stu nodded. "It's the pillow talk that scares me."

"Any other topic you like," I said firmly. "You pick it."

My phone rang, and he grabbed it quickly. "Yeah?"

He listened.

"He'll call back later." And he hung up. "The board's got a message for you," he said. "I was expecting a call."

Probably. He always was. Bad manners to pick up the phone in my office? It wasn't something he'd think about. He angled his head back for a minute, considering something, then decided to say it. "You know Harvey Gold?"

"Was that him on the phone?"

Stu frowned again. "Why would he be calling you?"

"I guess he wouldn't. Yes, I know him."

"He's working on something big for me. Could be absolutely fantastic."

So Harvey had finally sold himself.

"In fact," Stu went on, "I shouldn't even be talking about it. I'm telling you because I want you to know things aren't exactly standing still around here. That's why I want you to be careful."

I nodded.

"And Capricorn is talking daytime. I showed them an idea they're nuts about. We've got to find time to work on it."

"Okay," I said.

He leaned forward over the desk. "I want to be sure you take this seriously," he said. "She's a reporter. She went after this ice-cream thing because that's what she does. She goes after things."

He kept staring at me, waiting for me to answer. "What's the daytime idea?" I asked him.

He froze for a second, and then leaned back and started to describe it, but I heard none of it because I was busy remembering how Margo had known about Henry Cavanaugh. Not by name, of course, but that there was someone black we'd wanted to book who'd been turned down cold by Capricorn. I'd been surprised that she'd found out about it, and she'd laughed. "Not as miraculous as you'd imagine. We get information the same way cops solve crimes. Tips. That's all it is. People love to talk." Stu was right. There was plenty to be careful about. And I was as aware of it as he.

13

THE SALE HAD BEEN IN THE WORKS FOR MONTHS. AT FIRST, STU
had referred to it only obliquely, as that something terrific that
Harvey Gold was working on. Then, gradually, unable to keep
such monumental news to himself, he had let bits and pieces
leak to the only one he could tell things to. That was me; the
brother he never had, the son he longed for, the father confes-
sor to whom he could bare his soul.

There was a new player in the game these days; Herschel
Sachs, the lawyer who represented Columbia Pictures, Arthur
Godfrey, the Stoneham family, the Federation of Jewish Chari-
ties (no fee), and, now, Stu Leonard Productions.

"I assume you brought him, I can talk in front of him," Hank
said. His friends called him Hank. We were sitting at a table at
21, and to hear Stu tell it, this had become his second home. "No
more Toots Shor's," Stu was saying. "Toots never leaves you
alone, except when somebody more important comes in." Depending on his audience, Stu became either the casual boulevard-
ier who was known at every eatery in town, or the man of simple

tastes who never saw the inside of an elegant restaurant. Either way he made his listener understand that he never touched the food.

The table was set for two. Stu was having just celery and a glass of water. But somehow when Hank had reached into the basket of rolls there was nothing under the napkin. I was just asking the waiter for more.

"Talk away," Stu said. "He knows most of it already."

"Not bad, huh?" Hank grinned at me. "And now comes the best part of all. I think I outdid myself with this one." It had been all his doing, of course. Or Harvey Gold's. Depending on which one you were talking to.

"First, there's money. They came up to two point four."

Stu let out a yelp and reached for my martini, which he downed in one joyous gulp. Then he chased it with the contents of his freshly filled water glass (another gulp) and leaned back grinning, oblivious to the stares from nearby tables. "Jee-*sus*," he said. "That is a ton of money."

The asking price had been two million six, but Stu hadn't expected their counter to come anywhere close. This was close.

"*And,* you haven't heard the best part yet." Hank was chuckling, appreciating in advance the praise that was about to be heaped upon him as he revealed his further brilliance. "The money doesn't include 'Corky,' or 'Help Wanted.' I pulled them both out of the deal. That was the compromise. They bought 'Face to Face' and 'Steeplechase,' plus first look at anything new. That's it. Period. That's what they get for two million four."

"Hank, you're not to be trusted." Stu grinned at him, reaching across the table to shake his hand. He turned to me. "I mean, is this guy something?"

"Fantastic," I said. "Congratulations."

I'd meant it for Stu, but it was Hank who said thank-you.

"Steeplechase" was the new daytime show that had gone on the air in February (out of cycle; that's how anxious they were) and by the middle of March had jumped to number two in the daytime ratings. This second success had convinced the network that Stu Leonard Productions was more than a lucky accident, and Harvey Gold had come up with the notion of selling out for a lovely capital gain. Harvey had brought in rumpled, jowly, Harvard Law School Hank, who knew everybody in town, or if he didn't, picked up the phone and became some stranger's dearest friend within five minutes. That deep, raspy voice filled every room it entered, and that giant ego, inflated as the body it lived in, did not overestimate its owner's importance.

So we had a celebration going here, although what it had to do with me was hard to figure.

"Are you superstitious?" Stu suddenly asked me, apparently dead serious.

I shook my head.

"Some people think it's bad luck to toast in water. Does that bother you?"

I shook it again.

He turned to Hank. "I'm off booze till I drop another eight pounds." He turned back to me, talking to Hank but looking at me. "Hank, I'm going to tell you about this man. I couldn't have done it without him. Not a chance. He knows how I think; he knows how I like to operate. If there's something I need, I ask and he's already done it." He raised his glass, and Hank solemnly raised his. "So here's to David. I've never depended so much on another human being in my life, or wanted to. Here's to you, my friend." He drained the water glass again, held it on high for a dramatic second, and then lowered it slowly to the table. I swear there were tears in his eyes.

A month later we were celebrating again. His house this time; the two of us. Dinner again, and served, of course, under the all-too-familiar rules.

"May I bring you a plate for dessert?" Abbie leaned forward to ask him.

Stu looked up. "Dessert? Are you trying to kill me?"

Abbie waited a second while he composed a suitable answer. Then he straightened up. "As you wish, sir," he said and left the room.

He had asked me here to see something fantastic, something of which he was very proud. He would show me that something right after dinner, which meant right after we played our final food game with my enormous helping of Grand Marnier mousse. I took the first spoonful and watched him devour the rest.

"Now we go to the living room," Stu said grandly, pushing back from the table. The living room. Okay. Normally we'd be heading for the smaller, cozier, paneled den, with its velvet throw pillows and darkly mirrored bar.

"Now, don't make fun of me, David," he said, reaching for the rheostat that controlled the lights.

"Okay," I said, a little cautiously.

And he raised not the room lights, but a single focused spot that brought to life a painting hung at eye level on the wall not six feet from us. It was small as these things go—fifteen inches high and twenty-two inches wide, I found out later.

"Pierre Bonnard," he said in tones that were properly reverential.

I stepped closer for a better look. I'd never seen anything like it outside a museum. A soft, warm, country landscape, and beautiful indeed.

"Trees Near Vernon," he said. "1915."

He had bought it the day before for fifty-six thousand dollars, and that was the second fact I now had trouble coping with. First, here was this incredible painting hanging on the wall of an apartment lived in by someone I knew very well; and second, it had been paid for with a check that was large enough to buy a good-sized house in Scarsdale.

"After 1912 Bonnard spent most of his life at Vernon. Monet lived nearby. At Giverny. They visited back and forth. Monet would drive over with his daughter-in-law, Blanche. Or the Bonnards would drive to Giverny. Maybe to see the water lilies."

He touched the rheostat again and brought the room lights up to background level. "Let's stay in here."

There was brandy on the coffee table, and just one glass; for me. He splashed enough brandy in to cover the bottom. "This is an Armagnac I've been anxious for you to try," he said, raising the glass to taste it. "Hmm, very nice," he said, putting it down. Three glasses later I still hadn't had my first sip.

"You know what I'd give to stand right there?" he asked, pointing to the picture. "I mean directly on that spot, looking at just what he was looking at." He laughed. "Do you know what you'd see?"

"You'd see what he painted."

Stu shook his head emphatically. "No, you wouldn't, that's the point. That's the miracle. You'd see nothing special; some scruffy trees, that's all. No more worth a second look than any other trees."

"Then why would you want to stand there?"

"To see the difference, that's why. Because I know there is one. To see the difference between what's there and what he painted. That's where they have us, you know."

And he started to tell me why the artist has it all over the rest of us. He's not hemmed in by limits, the way the rest of us are. The artist paints not what he sees, but what he imagines. His painting is an image upon which he has imposed his will.

"That's where they have us," he said again. "Reality is just a starting point for them."

But not for him. For him reality was something he had to deal with every day, and reality was there to break your heart.

Reality, for example, was that Hilda Wragge was funny, but not as funny as she had to be. You couldn't take funny to the bank unless it showed up on schedule, so Hilda needed help. Left to herself, there was no telling when Hilda's sense of humor might kick in. That was reality for you; the demon that never behaved.

Take the barber thing, for instance. The thing with the balloons.

There'd been this stunt show two years ago that he'd produced for some new aerosol hair spray. They'd wanted a jackpot stunt at the end; something where the money would build as people tried and failed each week, until finally someone managed to do whatever the stunt might be. After sitting around in meetings for almost a week he'd finally come up with something that seemed perfect. The barber college thing. Lather up a balloon and give the contestant a straight razor. If he could shave off the lather without breaking the balloon, he'd be a winner. That was the graduation test at barber college. It took some skill, but if you could do it they gave you your diploma.

The day they were supposed to introduce the new jackpot stunt on the air, he went off to a corner of the studio and lathered up a balloon to try it for himself. The balloon didn't break. Even when he *tried* he couldn't break it. The only way he could finally do it was to hold the balloon with one hand and slash away like Jack the Ripper. He pulled the stunt out of the show and took a week to come up with something else. But that was reality for you. Unreliable. Nothing you could count on. Only the people who dealt in make-believe could be endlessly certain of their ability to breathe life into their fantasies.

The more Armagnac he poured into my glass, the more expansive he became. His arms moved wildly as he explained how we'd trapped ourselves again. We'd imagined a reality that didn't exist, and had sold it in the best of faith. Now we had to make it happen. We had to produce what we'd imagined. When the artist does that, the world applauds.

"Steeplechase" was a horse race quiz where the hurdles were the harder questions, and selling it had triggered a major office shuffle and a total paint job, but not the leasing of any new space because, as Stu said, who knew how long anything would last in this crazy business we're in?

So there was some doubling up, and now squeezed into Frank Dean's old office (he'd been moved to something smaller) were the two new people who'd been brought in to head the "Steeplechase" staff. Neither had had any experience, but that didn't bother Stu. Experience you can buy all day. The smart ones learn it all in a hurry.

And what had impressed him about Carter Boyd? Nothing the rest of us could see. Carter had performed capably enough as stage manager on "Face to Face," but if he possessed unusual ability, he'd never had much chance to show it. Stu's respect for Carter stemmed less from anything definable than from the way Carter's clothes seemed to alternate so easily between three-piece perfection and the kind of sweaters you'd wear to a catered picnic. And from the confident, comfortable accent of command that Carter had picked up at Exeter, maybe, or Princeton. Or maybe even at home.

So Carter was offered the job of producer of "Steeplechase" and now had half of Frank Dean's old office. ("Isn't it demeaning to ask him to share an office?" "He'll agree to anything if he wants the job." Big grin. "And besides, let him see where he fits in around here.") The other half of the office went to the new associate producer, Donald Scheer's friend Sam. Sam of the rolling gate and impeccable taste.

Policy decision. That's what I had asked for before the show went on. We'd carefully worked out the format so that one way or another, this one would work. Let's leave it alone, I insisted. Of course we will, said Stu. There was no reason to mess with it. Players buzzed in with answers in direct competition, so there was always some kind of progress. And even the tougher hurdle questions could be written to get slowly easier. It would be a simple matter to tailor the material so that it could not fail to produce answers.

Terrific. But three weeks after we were on the air we were in a meeting at the agency for the cigarette company that had bought ten spots a week.

"Where's the excitement? Where's the crackle?"

"Give it a chance," Stu said. "It's new. It's just getting started."

"It's new, but I'm getting old," said Harley Poole. He was a smiling dumpling of a man, always bizarrely dressed. Today in seersucker overalls over an open blue work shirt, with an engineer's cap that he now removed as he tipped his head forward. "Gray hairs. I never had them before."

"The nighttime show started out slow," Stu said.

Harley shrugged. "Capricorn's very patient. My guys are in a hurry. Off the nighttime hit they picked your show to introduce the new filter-tip version of their biggest brand. They've got a lot riding here."

"It'll work for them."

Harley grinned broadly. "Is that what you want me to tell them?"

Stu stared at him for a minute, then took a deep breath and slowly let it out. "Okay, let's say it's an hour from now and you're on the phone with your guys telling them how our meeting went. What would you like to be saying?"

Harley frowned at that one. He stood up, without gaining much in height, and took a step toward his window. It had started to snow. "Do you believe this? I'll be two hours getting home." He turned back to us. "That, Mr. Leonard, was a very fine question. I give high marks for that question, because, of course, I'll be making that call. And here's exactly what I'd like to be able to say.

"I'd like to be able to tell them that you were prepared to work day and night analyzing the elements that made "Face to Face" the number-one show on the air. And that you'd then take those elements, whatever they were, and lay them over "Steeplechase" so that within two weeks we'd start to see the numbers climb."

Stu grinned and stood up. "I hope you remember what you just said, because I wouldn't change a word if I were you."

Harley nodded. "I'm glad to hear that that's your plan."

Stu stuck out his hand. "Tell them I'm so confident we can produce results that I'm thinking about buying their stock."

"They'll love that," Harley said. "Especially in the amounts that you can afford these days."

Stu laughed, and Harley turned to me. "I didn't catch your name," he said.

"Wimple," I said. "I work in the mail room."

He laughed because of course we'd met several times before, and we were just these guys, you see, who understood each other.

It was less than a week after the newspapers reported the sale of Stu Leonard Productions that Matthew Sklar made his move. Through Lenny Basch. And me.

"He never told you?" Lenny seemed incredulous.

I reaffirmed the fact.

Lenny really seemed to find it hard to believe. He shook his head slowly. "You see, that's half the problem. Matthew isn't wrong about that. Stu doesn't take him seriously. I tell you, that's half the problem."

We were seated in wire-backed chairs around a rusty, once-white table in what Lenny called his garden; a tiny gravel pit outside the kitchen of his ground floor apartment-office in West Seventy-third. There was just about room enough for the two of us and the plaster elephant, maybe three feet high, rain streaked and forlorn, that leaned against the wooden fence. It was an Indian elephant, Lenny had told me. You could tell by something or other, and it had been given to him by someone whose name I was supposed to recognize. All of the elephants in his collection had come as gifts over the years; all but the first two or three. Everybody in the business knew he collected them, and he kept getting them from friends who traveled all over the world. He had over two hundred elephants now, all shapes and sizes, and they were scattered everywhere in the cluttered rooms we'd come through. Most of them were gift shop items; he wouldn't kid me about that. But one or two had real value, especially this large one in the garden. He never told me why.

What Lenny was amazed I hadn't heard was that Matthew had asked Stu to consider him as the emcee of "Steeplechase" before the show had gone on the air, and that Stu had promised to think about it.

"But you know what? He never called him back. Matthew had to read in the papers that Mike Prince was doing that one too."

I mumbled something about how Stu must have figured that, since it was going to be Mike, it would be pretty obvious to Matthew that he couldn't be considered.

"Why couldn't he call and tell him that? I mean, he promised the kid."

"Well, okay," I said lamely. "But you know how busy Stu is."

"I'll tell you something," he said. "My business is bullshit, and that excuse smells just like my business. He never took the whole thing seriously for a minute. If he had, he'd have talked it over with you. He was stringing the kid along, is all."

"I don't know anything about that," I said.

"Hey, I believe you, that's the point. You see the point I'm trying to make here?"

I looked at my watch. "Maybe you'd better tell me, Lenny, because I have to be somewhere in twenty minutes."

Lenny nodded soberly. "I understand. Look, I'm grateful you came here at all. I think maybe with your help we can get all of this straightened out. He listens to you."

"Who does?"

Lenny smiled. "I thought you were in a hurry. Now who's wasting time?"

"You mean Stu?"

Lenny nodded. "I think maybe you can make him listen to reason."

I moved my legs straight out, trying to get better settled in the uncomfortable chair. "It's too late for 'Steeplechase,' I said.

Lenny snorted and twisted his face. "What am I, some kind of moron? Don't you think I know that?"

"Then tell Matthew."

Lenny shook his head. "He's onto something else these days. That's the problem. He's got a lightning mind and he thinks of new things every second. And I'm telling you, this time I can't talk him out of it. You ready for some coffee?"

There was an aluminum pot on the table, and two chipped enamel mugs. I shook my head, and he poured some for himself. Then he reached down beside his chair for a tattered fiber envelope and tossed it on the table. "Take a look in there."

I knew I didn't want to, but whatever was in there would have to be looked at sooner or later. I reached in and pulled out five pages of crudely typed manuscript with Matthew's name at the top. "Scenario: The Index Intelligence, by Matthew Sklar."

"It's an outline," Lenny said. "He calls it a scenario. He doesn't know what that means. Neither do I. Anyway, it's an idea he has for a movie."

I looked at the pages. Words crossed out. Letters out of line. It looked like something Matthew would have typed.

"He thinks Stu should produce it. He wants fifty thousand dollars to do the screenplay. In advance."

Just as simple as that. I looked down at the pages again and dropped them on the table. "And you can't talk him out of it?"

Lenny shrugged. "I tried, believe me."

"Why's that, Lenny? Why would you want to talk him out of it?"

"Are you kidding me? I represent Stu Leonard, don't you think I know that? I mean, why should Stu pay that kind of money in advance to somebody who never wrote a line before? It's crazy. That's what I said to Matthew."

So I was here because he was afraid that face to face, Stu

might really kill him this time. Okay. Not that it mattered. The same thing was happening no matter who found out about it first.

Lenny stood up. "Look, I know you gotta go. The problem is, I can't talk that stubborn bastard out of this. Tell Stu I'll keep on trying, but I just don't like my chances." He picked up the pages and stuffed them back into the brown envelope. "Why don't you take this with you."

"I imagine Matthew has a carbon."

"Oh, yeah. Don't worry about it. Give it to Stu. Maybe he'll read it and think it's terrific."

I stood up and took the envelope. "I guess that would solve a lot of problems."

"Absolutely," Lenny said.

Human perversity being what it is, my interest in Rebecca was immediately restimulated by her sudden insistence that we break things off.

We were at my place. One of our very rare meetings there. In the beginning when such an evening had been arranged, it had been something *I* had pressed for. But over the past few months, pressure for such a rendezvous, with its obvious privacy and promise of a few relaxed hours, had shifted from me to Rebecca. She'd several times mentioned that, with Josh spending the night with his father, she might be able to join me, if not overnight, at least for several hours. But my skill at juggling simultaneous relationships had always been minimal, and now that I was seeing Margo occasionally, I felt uneasy about letting things get closer with Rebecca. But this time she'd come up with enough advance notice so that I found it difficult to make excuses. So I picked up some simple items of food and a recommended bottle of Brane-Cantenac and set myself up for as guilt-free an evening of pleasure as I could manage.

Not a chance. She was here because we had a lot to talk about.

Her ex-husband had raised the possibility of their getting back together. Partly for the sake of the boy, of course, but also because he missed the life they'd had together. Not the most flattering way he might have put it, but still she'd promised she'd give it some serious thought. She'd been doing just that, and the first thing that was obvious is that she'd have to stop seeing me.

I nodded agreement, and had every intention of being perfectly wonderful about all of this. In fact, for a brief moment, I actually felt relief. But then that perversity I mentioned before started working away at me, and before I knew it I was standing behind her, refilling her glass with one hand and with the other hand lightly pressing her shoulder. And when I put the bottle down, that hand stayed on her shoulder, and then moved down and held her warmly. And in another few seconds, we were caressing each other as tenderly as if there'd been no prior discussion at all.

But later, as she was getting dressed, she made it clear that this would be the last time. She owed it to herself to give herself every chance to put her marriage back together.

I walked downstairs with her and helped her into the panel truck.

"I'll have fond memories of this ridiculous vehicle," I said.

She smiled. "If I find anything back there that belongs to you, I'll let you know."

I nodded and bent down to kiss her through the open window. "I hope it works out."

"It may, you know."

I nodded again and she started the engine and drove away.

Lenny Basch had sense enough not to answer his phone for several days, but Stu kept right on calling and by the third day the message he left with the answering service was so vicious that the supervisor called back to say that their people were not required to take that kind of verbal abuse from anyone, and they'd been instructed to terminate the conversation if he raised his voice again. All of which touched off another tirade from Stu about the questionable ethics of an answering service that would run interference for a blackmailing scumbag like Lenny Basch. At which point the supervisor apparently terminated the conversation, because Stu suddenly pulled the receiver away from his ear and gave it a funny look before slamming it into its cradle.

But when he called me into his office two hours later, I found him actually smiling as he looked through Matthew's messy pages.

"This is almost funny," he said when he looked up and saw me.

"At ten thousand dollars a page? You have some sense of humor."

"Did you read it?"

I nodded.

"Well?"

I shrugged. "No surprises. It's exactly what I expected. It would be clumsy if it weren't incoherent."

Stu was still smiling. "So you don't think it's worth the money."

I walked to the couch and sat down. "You seem a lot calmer suddenly. What brought you back to earth?"

"I called him. He's coming in tomorrow."

"To pick up his check?"

Stu tilted his chair way back. The classic pose. He felt himself back in control. "Matthew and I are going to do a little work on this together. See if we can hammer it into shape."

"What about the money?"

"He understands that's down the line. He's agreed to wait at least a week or two."

"And then?"

Stu smiled. "Who knows? If it's coming along, I think he'll wait another week or two."

"What about Lenny?"

"He's already tried to call. Don't talk to him if he tries to reach you."

"What about Monday? He'll show up at the studio."

"Don't let him get you alone, that's all. I'd throw him out on his ass, but we have a contract. He may be in breach, but I don't know how I'd explain that to anybody."

Still smiling, he pulled his chair forward and picked up Matthew's pages again. "I'll tell you something funny," he said. "I think maybe I can make something out of this shit. There might even be some fun in this."

The meetings with Matthew Sklar were called for eight in the morning, a couple of times a week at first, then as frequently as Stu needed to make them to keep Matthew convinced of his continuing interest. Matthew always emerged from these sessions full of smiles, content that he'd basked in Stu's full attention for a flattering hour or so. How long would these meetings go on? It wasn't the kind of question Stu ever asked himself, or liked to be asked. Just a little while longer, I was sure he told himself.

The extra burden on his time became the excuse Stu needed for making a procedural change he'd wanted to make all along. After the meeting with Harley Poole, "Steeplechase" had indeed begun to display the excitement and crackle the client had asked for, but so far Stu had done all the work himself. It had been easier with "Steeplechase," because the nature of the game was such that a long-term winner often happened naturally, and even when the process needed extra help, it could be arranged by working with only one player. But now that the meetings with Matthew were eating into his time, he decided to delegate the briefing assignment. To my astonishment, Carter

Boyd accepted it as part of his job. Stu gave him the option of quitting, but also explained that one of the ways people were judged in this business was by their ability to do what had to be done.

So "Steeplechase" was now running itself, and Stu was taking special pleasure in having recruited Carter Boyd. No matter what background they came from, no matter what he'd asked them to do, there was still no one he'd ever gone after who had ever turned him down.

14

THE WESTERN TERMINUS OF THE PONY EXPRESS WAS EITHER Sacramento or Placerville, depending on which book you looked it up in, so the Pony Express question in our Old West category played it safe and asked instead for the city in Missouri where the run had started. The books agreed on that one, but Sidney Kahn and Olivia Ryan didn't. Kansas City, said Sidney incorrectly, and his reign as champion ended when Olivia came up with St. Joe.

Sidney had been our longest-running champion since Elliott Cross, and left us with winnings of $153,000. He was a young lawyer from Omaha, Nebraska, who'd been in New York for three years and had met with considerable favor from Capricorn because, Donald Scheer had said, there was something fine in the man. The country would take to him, Donald Scheer believed, because of the fascinating combination of a name that seemed to indicate ethnicity with the purely American sound of the Midwestern accent. In Sidney Kahn, we had the best of both our country's worlds. He was the melting pot personified. The phone call after his first appearance expressed the hope that we'd be seeing a lot of him.

Olivia Ryan was tall, with long red hair and freckles, and Stu's crush on her began the day Toby first put her picture on his desk. It was hopeless, of course, because Olivia was happily married to a professor of anthropology at NYU, where she was a graduate student in the same subject. Stu wondered if there might not be a problem with a married woman. Wasn't it entirely possible that if we approached Olivia to appear on the show under the usual ground rules, she could feel a spousal obligation to talk the whole thing over with her husband?

"How do we stop her?" Frank Dean had asked.

"We can't. That's what makes me uncomfortable. But if we go with her, I think you'd better try. At least she'll get some idea of how seriously we take all this."

But there'd been no need for any special effort to get Olivia to take it seriously. She'd burst into tears when Frank Dean had made his initial proposal, and when she recovered she'd turned him down so firmly that a further attempt had seemed pointless. Still, Frank had gotten her to promise to call him the next morning, and after two or three days of further telephone conversations she had finally reached the point where she understood that a week or two of ties with Sidney Kahn, with its prospect of winning maybe a thousand dollars, was not so out of the question. She had indeed discussed it with her husband, who, for an academic, had turned out to be very much a man of the world. It was he who had convinced his wife that it was a simple matter of adjusting to reality; if she didn't do it, someone else would. And, besides, there was in the Ryan family the usual pile of bills to be weighed against the usual scruples, with the added promise of secrecy finally tipping the scales.

But instead of the series of ties she'd expected, Olivia found herself a sudden winner, and the unwelcome result had left her thoroughly shaken. Afterward, there was a long private scene with Frank Dean during which she refused to join the customary group in the press room and made it very clear that she felt betrayed.

"Betrayed!" Stu snorted when this was reported to him. "Who betrayed her? Sidney missed one. How were you supposed to know?"

"I told her that," Frank said. "I have the feeling she didn't believe me."

"That's her problem," Stu said. "She should have come down here." But he smiled. If someone else had defied the rules, he'd have been furious. But Olivia Ryan could do no wrong. At least for now.

The question about the Pony Express had sent Margo to the well-stocked reference corner of her new apartment on Central Park South, and when I showed up early the next evening, she was prepared with a series of facts about the fabled enterprise. Generally, we never discussed anything that happened on the show. I wasn't even aware of whether or not she watched it. But the Pony Express had sparked her imagination. One fact especially.

"Do you know how long it lasted?"

I shook my head. I had no idea.

"I mean, here was this incredible operation that's passed into folklore. They've made movies about it. It's as much a part of the West as roundups and saloons with swinging doors."

All true, I acknowledged.

"Take a guess. How long?"

I shrugged. I really hadn't thought about it.

"Come on. Just guess."

"Okay," I said slowly. "Fifteen years. Maybe twenty years."

She grinned. "That's what I'd have said. Or thirty, maybe. Or even forty."

All possible, I agreed.

"But the answer is a year and a half."

That was, indeed, a surprise.

It had started in April 1860. A letter mailed at St. Joseph got to Sacramento (or Placerville) in eight or nine days, which was something of a miracle compared with the thirty days it had taken up to then to send mail along the safer, southern route. The Pony Express set its all-time record when it delivered Lincoln's Inaugural Address to the West Coast in an amazing seven days. But the entire enterprise was out of business by late October 1861, when the completion of the telegraph made all that dash and heavy breathing pointless.

"A year and a half," Margo repeated slowly.

We'd gone out to dinner at a place nearby; early, even though she wasn't on the show tomorrow, because she had to get to bed fairly early every night to maintain some kind of sane routine. She'd invited me to dinner at her place, but I'd countered with the suggestion of this new steak house in her area I'd heard about. I'd thought I was doing her a favor. She worked too hard to be fixing meals and cleaning up, and she refused to have anyone in to do it for her. Spending money on the apartment was okay, and on expensive furniture. But on people to clean up after you? She hadn't reached the point where that seemed right. Nobody should have to do that for anyone.

When our steaks came she said that's what she'd been planning to serve tonight, for old time's sake, and there was a wistful tone in her voice that made me wonder for a minute if maybe I should have let her do it. It had been the first time since we'd started seeing each other again that she'd suggested eating in.

"Remember those meals in Waterbury?" she asked. I nodded. "Showing the butcher just how thick we wanted him to cut the meat."

"And then being shocked by the bill."

She laughed, but didn't change her mood. This wasn't the Margo I was used to. I'd seen her a lot of ways, but never so warmly involved in the glow of pleasant memories. "Those were good days, David."

I smiled and nodded again, and we talked some more about those days. Things between us had settled into a kind of friendship that we both understood was no longer a prelude to anything else. We made love sometimes, and sometimes we didn't.

"You'll never know how hard it was to leave."

That one really surprised me. I said so.

She shook her head. "Bravado. That's all. I was scared to death of coming to New York, and I was sick about leaving you. You must have known that."

I shook my head. "You had me fooled."

She smiled. "Don't you know me well enough to know I've always been afraid to give in to my feelings? The only reason I can talk about it now is because, finally, I know it's over."

She took a sip of wine and looked at the glass as she put it down. "I've been feeling so sentimental tonight, I almost asked for sparkling burgundy."

That one got to me, but I covered it with a grin. "If you had, they'd have thrown us out."

She picked up her fork and played with her food for a minute, then put it down again. "Just before I made the decision—I mean a billion years ago, back in that peaceful Stone Age—I went through a couple of days when I couldn't decide if I should go ahead with the job in New York, or see if you'd marry me, and stay."

Well, don't think that one didn't turn me inside out. First, there was the total surprise. The last thing in the world I'd have ever suspected. Then the sheer impact of wondering how I'd have behaved back then if she'd done it. Or—no, not wondering really. Knowing full well what I would have said and how different everything else in our lives would have been.

"I don't know why I'm going into all this," she said. "I hope it doesn't upset you."

It did, but I said it didn't. It did partly because the Margo I remembered had not lived in any peaceful Stone Age. There'd been nothing peaceful about her. And if she remembered it that

way, the memories we shared were from two very different angles.

"I guess I just want you to know," she said, "that regardless
of how things are now, or how they're ever going to be, those
days mean a lot to me."

I reached for my wine just to give myself a break in the
action. When I put the glass down I picked up my knife and fork.
"Eat your food," I said firmly. "It's getting cold."

She smiled and picked up her implements again. "Just for
refusing to get sloppy with me, I'm not going to tell you how
long we were together back then."

"Okay, see if I care," I said.

"A year and a half," she said. "Maybe a little longer."

The next day she started working on a Pony Express feature
for the show. An essay wraparound, with clips from the appropriate movies and man-in-the-street interviews that had people
guessing how long it had been in existence. But the whole thing
had to be shelved because on Thursday Joe McCarthy died, and
they sent her to Washington to do a reaction story. She called
me Thursday night.

"I hate it," she said. "All I'm getting is careful PR stuff. No
one will open up. It was cirrhosis of the liver. He was an alco-
holic, but no one wants to talk about it."

But the piece she did was terrific. She took every subject's
reluctance and strung the empty mumblings together to make
the point. It was so good that when she came back they started
talking to her about doing the show every day, moving from
feature coverage to being cohost, with occasional hard news
assignments outside. They made her an offer that sounded staggering, but she had no idea what staggering really was. Did I
know anybody who could help her settle the deal? Someone had
suggested Harvey Gold. No, I told her; she didn't really need an
agent. She needed a lawyer who was familiar with these things.
Or one who could make himself familiar in a hurry. And I recommended Herschel Sachs. Hank.

———

Olivia Ryan was going to lose. She'd been involved in the customary titanic series of ties for the past two weeks and Frank
Dean and I had assumed that she'd win in dramatic fashion
either this week or next.

"Exactly the point," Stu grinned. "That's what everybody
thinks. It's time we had some surprises."

Frank Dean seemed troubled. "It's not what she expects," he
said.

Stu turned to him. "How can she expect anything? Nothing
happens more than one week ahead."

Frank nodded.

Stu's phone rang and he picked it up. "Yeah, okay, put her
on," he said. Then he covered the mouthpiece and gestured for
us both to sit down. "This'll only take a minute," he said.

Personal call. But he had no embarrassment about that.
Business calls were private, but if the call was personal, he could
talk to anyone as if he were alone in the room. It was Linda Kane.
Or Linda Kane Walsh, as the columnists called her. Or Linda
Walsh, as she referred to herself.

"What time?" he asked, leaning back with his eyes closed.
He always talked with his eyes closed on personal calls. Maybe
that's how he got his privacy. "Okay," he said, "but I'm going
to sit there with my hands in my lap."

That would mean they'd be going to an auction. Probably at
Parke-Bernet, which he had learned to pronounce confidently
with its final *t*.

Linda Kane was a stage actress who didn't work a lot these
days. She'd been married to Billy Walsh, the lyricist who'd had
several Broadway hits in the late forties, and whose death left
her sitting on all that ASCAP money. Her own successes seemed
to be harder for people to recall, but like Hilda Wragge, whose
friend she was, she was better known just for being herself.
Hilda had introduced her to Stu, and he'd been enchanted at

once. What impressed him about Linda was the ease and style
with which she'd learned to handle all that money. She moved
in circles where the gloss was high and quiet.

"Why don't we have something afterward," he said. "Maybe
the Algonquin." Then she said something that made him laugh,
and he said good-bye.

He put down the receiver and turned to Frank without skipping a beat. "What she expects doesn't matter."

It came faster than Frank had expected. She, of course, was
Olivia Ryan. No polite transitions for Stu. Just right back to
where he'd dropped the marker.

Frank cleared his throat and said he understood. Stu turned
to me. "Tell Toby I want to see who she's got sitting in the files.
Somebody terrific. Maybe we'll let this next one run forever."

But Frank Dean's uneasiness had been well founded. This
was, indeed, not what Olivia Ryan had expected, and if anything
she was even more unhappy about it than he'd feared. After a
day to think it over and, presumably, to discuss it with the
professor, she told him bluntly that she would not agree to miss
any questions.

"Then she's out there on her own," Stu said. "We don't give
her any answers."

"That could be a little embarrassing," Frank said. "She may
miss something awfully easy."

"Not very smart, you're telling me?"

Frank bristled. "As smart as they come. As smart as anyone
we've had, except maybe Matthew. But how the fuck do I know
what she knows!"

Stu shrugged. "I say she's going to lose. If she gives us only
one way that can happen, then that's the way. We've had people
miss easy questions before. Tell Toby we'll meet in my office at
twelve-thirty to pick someone who might really be able to stay
on till hell freezes over. I want to see every application she's got.
Tell her to send out for sandwiches if you like. Whatever you
want. Nothing for me."

Of course.

Olivia Ryan stuck to her guns, but not even her refusal to do what he wanted changed Stu's attitude toward her. "Why should she collaborate in her own defeat?" Stu asked, somewhat more generously than he had when Matthew Sklar had balked in a similar situation. There was no doubt of how he felt about Olivia, and husband or not he might well have made a move in her direction had not his own stricture about not getting involved with contestants kept him firmly in line. "That's the one I could go for," he said quietly when her big close-up opened the show the next Monday night.

Toby had pushed hard for the new challenger to be this contractor from Greenwich she'd found, whose only drawback was that he walked with an enormous rocking limp, the legacy of childhood polio. Stu had finally decided the limp was okay; it could become his trademark. "Does he use a cane?" Stu had asked.

"He can't get around without one," Toby had told him, and that had clinched it.

Now he was introduced. "A contractor from Greenwich, Connecticut," came the announcer's voice over music. "Let's welcome Michael Paresi!"

Applause. Music up and out.

Light conversation with Mike Prince about how they both had the same first name. Then a little background on the housing development Michael was just completing. Then shake hands with Olivia and into your booths. It took Michael Paresi a bit longer than usual, but he got there and settled down, and we were under way.

It was all over in four questions. She had gotten her easy number-two question, correctly naming Balboa as the explorer who had claimed the Pacific for Spain. Kid stuff, but we all breathed easier when she got it. Her number-four question asked her to name the Navy flier who had died in March, and who, in the 1920s, had become the first man to fly over both the north and south poles. She'd taken a while with that one and finally, to my extreme embarrassment, mumbled something about Wiley Post. That, of course, was wrong, Wiley Post having been the pilot who died with Will Rogers when their plane went down in Alaska in 1935. Where she'd even dredged up the name was beyond me. And why she'd be more familiar with it than with the name of Admiral Richard E. Byrd, whose obit had only recently appeared in every major publication, was even more of a mystery.

Not the ending we'd hoped for, but not as messy as it might have been.

"My God, I haven't heard the name Wiley Post in twenty years," Donald Scheer said afterward.

"She must have been two years old the year he crashed," Murray Cashin said. "If she was born at all."

But we were never to find out what had brought Wiley Post to Olivia's mind, because there was never a chance to ask her. She was out the door the second the show was over.

Murray Cashin mumbled something about how it might have been nice if she'd stayed around to hand over the mantle of victory, but Stu, as always, defended her. "It takes a special kind of class to just go quietly," he said.

"Tomorrow's Adults" was the name Elliott Cross had chosen for his column. It ran in the *Post* twice a week. The *Mirror* had actually offered a few bucks more, but appearing in the liberal *New York Post* had meant a lot to the Doc.

Stu knew there was a problem the first time Matthew failed to show up for a writing session one morning at eight, and then couldn't be reached for two days. Finally there was a message from Matthew, hand-delivered, that he was selling his story, all of it, to the *Daily News* for fifty thousand dollars, and there was no point in trying to stop him.

Stu was in motion as soon as he read it, grabbing me on his

way out of the office, commandeering a cab by practically throwing his body in front of it, and then giving the driver the address of Lenny Basch.

"Somehow, he's the one who knows what's going on."

Lenny didn't answer the doorbell, but Stu was certain that he was really inside, cowering, knowing full well who was out there. "We'll wait," Stu said. "We'll go in with the next delivery boy. Or tackle him when he tries to come out."

An hour went by, with Stu ringing the doorbell long and hard every minute or two. Nobody stirred inside.

"Let's go back to the office," I tried to persuade him, but of course he wouldn't listen. Then suddenly we saw Lenny appear around the corner, heading home with a couple of bags of groceries. He froze for a second when he spotted us, then dropped the bags and did a running one-eighty.

Stu was after him with more speed than I would have thought possible, and grabbed him within a block. He had him in a headlock when I pulled up, and I was terrified of what he might do.

"Easy, Stu," I said in as calm a voice as I could manage.

"Don't worry," he said, puffing hard. "I just want to make sure he doesn't go anywhere."

The last was addressed more to Lenny than me, and I thought it was a fair assumption that Lenny had got the idea.

"You can let him go," I said.

Stu looked down at him. "Can I, Lenny?"

But Stu's grip was too tight for Lenny to be able to talk.

"Let him go. I've got him," I said, having grabbed him by the belt. Stu did, and Lenny stood up slowly, his hand to his throat, his eyes still showing fear.

"Let's go to your place," Stu said, and without waiting for an answer he grabbed him by the arm and started dragging him back down the street. We stopped when we reached the grocery bags on the sidewalk, and Stu told him to pick them up. When we got to Lenny's door, Stu took the packages while Lenny fumbled for his key and clumsily let us in. As soon as we were inside, Stu shoved him onto the couch and dropped the grocery bags to the floor.

"Jesus, Stu, there are eggs in there," Lenny whined.

Stu walked closer and stood over him. "Tell me about Matthew," he said. "And don't make me pull it out of you piece by piece. Tell me all of it. I'll know if I don't get it all, and I wouldn't hold anything back if I were you."

Lenny didn't. He was thoroughly frightened this time.

Matthew had gone nuts when he'd seen the first of Elliott's columns in the *Post.* Why Elliott Cross and not him? he'd complained to Lenny. Matthew had some ideas for a column of his own, and if that white-bread doctor could get himself a column, why couldn't Lenny line one up for him? Anyway, Lenny promised to try, but meanwhile Matthew called Elliott Cross to ask him to put in a good word for him at the *Post,* and that's when he found out that Elliott was now a client of Lenny's, and that it had been Lenny who had set the deal with the *Post.*

Stu was shocked. "You mean that now you represent Elliott Cross?"

"Just for this one thing," Lenny said. "He wouldn't give me more than that."

Stu shook his head slowly. "I honest to God don't believe what I see when I look at you," he said. "Just when I think I understand how low you are, you sink a few feet lower."

"What's the problem?" Lenny asked. "I had this idea for a column. I called around and got someone interested. Why shouldn't I get a commission?"

"Because you had to know what this would do to Matthew."

"I didn't think he'd find out I had anything to do with it. How did I know he'd call the Doc?"

Suddenly all the air seemed to go out of Stu. Even his clothes seemed to go limp as he slumped into one of the threadbare armchairs. "But why should you care?" he said in a voice that was barely audible. "What's the difference if Matthew gets money for a bullshit screenplay, or for selling some phony story to the newspapers? You get your slice either way."

Not even now did Stu allow his attitude to slip. Matthew's story was phony, he remembered to insist. Matthew could claim whatever he liked, but no one had ever given him answers.

"It isn't like that, Stu," Lenny said. "What kind of person do you think I am?"

Stu stared straight ahead for just a minute, his body slack, most of it hanging over the chair that, like every chair, was much too small to hold him. Looking at him I wondered if he'd finally begun to realize that there was only one way all of this could ever end.

But then the body tone seemed to return and he almost literally pulled himself together. "Find him, Lenny," he said. "Camp out on his doorstep if you have to, but find him and get him to my office."

Lenny nodded.

"I'm not just talking, you understand. I want you to bring him in."

"I will, Stu. You can count on it."

Stu got up. "That's good," he said, "because that's what I'm doing. Don't make me mad again, Lenny."

In the cab on the way back, Stu's slowly spreading smile was the sign that the old certainties had started to return. The one thing in which he had endless confidence was his own ability to handle Matthew Sklar. "Not because I'm so damn smart," he explained, "but because when you get right down to it, there's no way he can destroy us without destroying himself. That makes it tough for him to run around blowing whistles. No matter how much he wants to, no matter how much he may need the money, no matter how jealous he is of Elliott Cross."

And for a while that seemed to be right. Lenny did what he was supposed to do, found Matthew and brought him in. And Stu went into whatever hypnotic little number it was that mostly worked with Matthew and got the early-morning screenplay meetings started up again. And I found myself hoping that the article of faith Stu clung to would hold through all of this, that everyone involved could be counted on to behave in his own best interest.

If we could depend on that, we'd be fine.

15

IT WAS THE BEST OF TIMES; IT WAS SOON TO BE THE WORST OF times. On the horizon, the taller danger signals could be clearly seen, more visible every day to anyone who knew where to look. It was the summer of our great success, and the winter of the permanent knot in my stomach.

We were riding higher than even Stu's optimistic soul could ever have foreseen. The nighttime show was mostly number one, with only an occasional dip to second place that always triggered a phone call from Donald Scheer. Hadn't the questions been a little bland last week? Hadn't the losing players been uninteresting? We must watch the fine tuning, he would warn in solemn tones; whatever rises falls again. But then the next week's numbers would bounce us back on top and there'd be smiles and glowing tributes, and an extra tot of rum for the crew.

And the daytime show, in its quieter way, was doing very well. No press conferences or headlines, but every week it took its time period and rated no worse than third in the overall standings. The network was constantly urging us, through Harvey Gold, to come up with something new. Anything. We couldn't miss. "They think you guys are geniuses," Harvey kept insisting. He'd left his job at William Morris by now, and with the still-pale Conrad never far behind, had formed the Harvey Gold Agency, the name of which, he liked to explain, had been chosen because he was a man with an enormous ego, working in a business that rewarded those who displayed it.

We spent at least part of every day tinkering with new ideas, rejecting almost everything because much was expected of us now, but eager to find something workable because, as Harvey kept reminding us, the package price on the next one would be considerably north of terrific. Since my royalty was figured on the package price, that suited me just fine.

By August we had a format for a music game that looked pretty good, and the network grabbed it as quickly as Harvey Gold had said they would. They gagged on the asking price, but finally settled on a figure that was close enough, sending a smiling Stu to his desk for the afternoon with a yellow pad and an adding machine, planning his autumn budget for antiques. Antiques were the latest thing, ever since Linda Kane Walsh had opened his eyes to the beauty of Newport desks and their various wooden cousins, and to the incredible prices that a small group of knowledgeable, well-heeled, mostly well-bred bidders were willing to shell out for these irreplaceable treasures.

Things were great, and when a co-op came on the market in the building next to Stu's, he was after me to put in a bid. The board had a reputation for being less than thrilled with anyone brown-eyed and swarthy, but Stu had gone to high school with one of the members and there was a chance he could get them to make an exception. It was a gem of an apartment, and I had myself convinced that the only way barriers came down was when someone stormed them. But a little work on my own yellow pad brought me up against the irreducible cash minimum I'd need to swing it, and when Stu offered to lend me whatever it took, the realities were back there staring at me once again. How could I make such an enormous commitment in the face of an impending disaster whose only mystery was the date of its arrival?

It was the best of times, but all I could see was the growing danger in a secret that each week was shared by one and sometimes two new people—contestants who'd been persuaded to sign on with the usual assurances. So each week I found myself standing in the control room at the back of the studio, listening to the ticking of my private bomb. How could this constantly expanding circle of insiders remain forever silent? How could this intricate mesh of illusion fail to snag on something unexpected?

The only relief was that now there was someone I allowed myself to talk to. Carla. She had left the Capricorn agency because, it turned out, her beloved Stan had right from the beginning been housed under the same corporate roof. He worked there as a copywriter. That's where they'd met, although she'd been careful not to mention that fact before. Cover, you know. I wasn't to know who he was. I might do something to embarrass us all, and maybe I would have. But the point was that once he'd declared their relationship over, the continuing daily contact had begun to be a strain on her vital organs. After a couple of weeks of hunting, she finally found a copywriting job of her own at another agency and wound up making a lot more money.

My need to talk to someone was overwhelming, and Carla's no longer being involved in our activities in even the most peripheral way suddenly seemed to provide that someone. It meant loading her up with my guilty secret, but the simple fact was that there was no one else available; she was the only candidate. Once I'd started talking, it had all come tumbling out in one marathon debriefing session that lasted half the night. She hadn't been all that surprised. Remember, she'd met Ginger Malloy before he'd turned into a genius. What she hadn't expected was the extent of it. Anyway, the relief of at last having an outlet was even greater than I'd imagined, and every new turn of events, no matter how inconsequential, had now routinely become a part of our normal conversation.

"It isn't my birthday." We were at her place. Her new place on Forty-sixth Street that was half the size of her spacious, high-ceilinged old apartment on Riverside Drive. I'd tried to talk her out of it, but this place had the appeal of being three times as expensive. A white envelope had suddenly been placed in front of me, with my name italicked on the front in the India-ink calligraphy Carla was so good at.

"Open it," she said.

I picked it up and looked at it for a moment, not having any idea what this was supposed to be.

"I swear it won't explode."

I smiled and opened it, and slid out three crisp hundred-dollar bills with a card that had the one word, *Thanks*.

"Thanks," she said redundantly, and for a moment there I came about as close to breaking down as I have since the day I started pretending to be an adult.

This wasn't money I'd ever expected to see again. I'd never really considered it a loan, although that's what we'd called it just to make her feel more comfortable.

"That doesn't make us even," she said, "but it makes me feel a lot better."

It made the money part even. That's how much it had been, to my surprise. I'd expected it to be more.

"Now, how about something to drink?"

I didn't really care, but I nodded because it relieved me of the need to speak.

She went to get the ice without having to leave the room. That was the charm of the place, she'd said. You could do everything except use the bathroom without having to leave the room.

"You'd better put those bills away," she called from the

wall-less kitchen just a few feet away. "You know how forgetful you are."

I'd been holding them in my hand, but now I walked to the chair where I'd hung my jacket and slipped the money into my wallet.

Carla had swallowed all those pills last fall not merely because Stan had left her, but because he'd left her with a little something to remember him by. He'd known nothing about that part of it because Carla, of course, hadn't wanted him to feel trapped. So she'd just taken the pills. Afterward, when she'd decided there was only one solution, I'd gotten the name of a problem-solver from Lenny Basch, who I knew would know such things, and we'd set out for Trenton early one Saturday morning. Why so far away? Because this guy was a humanitarian, Lenny had assured me. Safe, effective, and he didn't shove you out the door. I'd like him.

I'd offered to share the driving, but I should have known better. "It's boring being the passenger," she'd shouted over the wind as we roared through New Jersey in that green MG for which she'd still never bought a top.

"It's not boring at all," I shouted back. "Slow down and let me be bored!"

She laughed. She thought I was kidding. Several centuries later, after one brief stop for lunch ("Maybe I'm not supposed to eat," she'd frowned), we found the house on a quiet street where the leaves were in their final celebration of brilliant color, and I pulled into the driveway as he'd instructed me to on the telephone yesterday. Straight back to the rear of the house. The garage door was open as he'd promised it would be, and I pulled directly in, as he'd asked me to. He must have been watching at the window and seen us, because he was there at once to pull the overhead door shut behind us and help Carla out of the car. He was a tall man, with a face like a basset hound. But he looked kind, and that was what mattered.

Afterward, he brewed a pot of tea over which he slipped a

quilted cozy after he'd poured us each a cup. No one else seemed to be home on this Saturday afternoon, although there were signs that a wife and children lived here. Privacy, I guess. More for him than for us. I gave him the three hundred dollars in a plain white envelope, and he thanked me without looking inside. Rather a classy touch, I thought. He insisted we stay for a while. As long as we liked, he said; his wife wouldn't be back for a couple of hours. Oh, and we were to put the top up on the way back, and of course, Carla wasn't to drive.

We couldn't do much about the nonexistent top, but we'd brought a blanket and Carla curled up in that and frowned up at me as I struggled with the gear shift pattern. The doctor raised the garage door and wished us a pleasant trip, and Carla instructed me to press down to get into reverse. I did, jumped the car and stalled it, and then started over and got things under control. She was crying softly by the time we hit the main road.

"That enough ice?" She handed me the drink and I nodded.

"You didn't have to do that, you know." I meant the money.

"I do know," she said softly. "And I love you for that. But it's part of the therapy. Like changing jobs and getting out of that apartment. Now life starts over."

I took her hand and leaned forward to kiss the top of her head. We did a lot of hand holding these days, but that was all. It wasn't something we talked about, but it didn't take a lot of imagination for me to understand that affection was what Carla needed right now. If there was ever again to be more than that, it would have to wait until time had done its magic. Affection was just fine from my end too. My bruises weren't as visible, and probably not as deep, but in the middle of the night I knew exactly where they were.

"Now," she said, sitting up, "what do you mean, you're going to kill him?" She took a sip of her drink and turned to me.

I looked at her. "Is that what I said?"

She nodded emphatically. "Those were the exact words."

I laughed because of course I'd calmed down a lot since that
phone call last night at almost one o'clock. And, of course, I'd
been treated to the customary effusive apologies as soon as I'd
gotten into the office this morning. It had been one of those
things that had gotten out of hand because I'd been unable to
strike back at the moment it happened. We'd been about to start
a run-through of the new music show, and when Stu picked up
his script and found that it had been stapled instead of paper-
clipped, he'd launched into a wild fury. He did five fuming
minutes on how he never worked with a script by folding back
the pages; he always took the fucking thing apart. And you can't
pull out staples without making a mess and breaking fingernails,
and who authorized this, anyway? I remembered that at one
point that afternoon, Nicole had said we're out of paper clips,
can I staple these together, and I'd said yes, so I told that to Stu.
He'd glared at me for a second, then barked, "Next time check
it with me," and turned and stormed away. And I'd stood there
with smoke coming out of my ears because this was fucking
ridiculous and I wanted to tear his head off, but we had a studio
full of people standing by to do a run-through. It wasn't just this
time that had my stomach boiling. This was just one more of an
endless series of similar incidents, the most recent of which had
seen me foolish enough to answer some simple questions that
had been asked on the phone by someone from the BBC who
was in town and thinking of recommending a British production
of "Face to Face." I should never have spoken to him, Stu had
explained, because I had no way of knowing what plans *he* might
already have made. Next time such a thing occurred, please refer
the call to him. Okay. Let me know when there's something I can
handle. Obviously it wasn't to be the monumental staple or
paper-clip decision. But maybe one of these days something
would come along that was just my size.

I'd spent the rest of the run-through with my blood pressure
steadily rising, and the second we were finished I stormed out
of there without a word to anyone. That's when I'd called Carla.
Awakened her, of course.

I picked up my drink and sipped it, then put it down and laughed at how ridiculous all of that must have sounded. "I must be losing my sense of proportion."

"Stan always used to say . . ."

She stopped when I turned to her.

"Oh, I can talk about him now. That's my self-improvement project for the month. He existed; we had an affair—he even had a name. *Has* a name. And I can say it."

"Yes," I said. "I heard you."

"Anyway," she said, "Stan was very big on the idea that sometimes the things that bug us most are the things that are least important."

I didn't trust myself to comment, so I just nodded.

She smiled. "I gather you don't want to pursue that."

I took another sip of my drink and held the glass up. "What is this I'm drinking?"

"Jack Daniels. Would you rather have something else?"

"No, I was just curious. I can't tell one kind of booze from another."

"Scotch tastes smoky."

"Not to me it doesn't. But thanks for reminding me."

She might have reached the point where she could mention his name without getting hysterical, but I wasn't sure I could. Besides, the only time she ever sounded ridiculous was when she talked about Stan.

She shifted on the couch. "Let me ask you something," she said.

I gave permission.

"He doesn't make a major decision without talking it over with you, isn't that right?"

We were back to Stu. "I don't know. Partly right, I suppose."

"So obviously he respects your opinion."

I thought about that. "It's rarely my *opinion* he wants. It's my endorsement."

"Okay, even so. The man thinks you're brilliant. Why let little things drive you up the wall?"

Okay, I said, so let's not talk about Stu. You're right, he's
a little thing. Or if he's not, then staples are, and so's the BBC.
Let's talk about some of the big things that are driving me up
the wall these days. And I told her we now had another one.
Another contestant who, like Olivia Ryan, had gone into business for himself. Only he'd done it without warning us. He'd
been rehearsed to miss a question on medicine, but instead
he'd answered it correctly, throwing Stu and me into another
of those silent control room panics. Monday night he'll go on
without any answers, and who knows what will happen? But
beyond that, here was someone else who'd told us we no
longer controlled him. That was one thing that was driving me
up that famous wall. And then there was Matthew, who had
once again stopped his morning bullshit sessions and had
dropped out of sight. His wife had told Lenny Basch that
maybe he'd gone to Miami Beach, she wasn't sure, but meanwhile, she'd complained, here she was with this taxicab that
was just sitting there twelve hours a day, and she didn't know
whether to hire a guy to handle the day shift, or try to get a
hack license herself. No, she hadn't heard from him and she
didn't really know what he was doing there, or even if that's
where he'd really gone, but she thought maybe it had something to do with gambling.

I stayed for another couple of hours, enjoying the freedom
of simply talking my head off. My feet were on the coffee table
and I was leaning back and being blissfully indiscreet. I could
count on Carla to be quiet. I knew I could. We were lucky to have
each other. I almost said that as I was leaving.

Carla said it was the close quarters that did it, and she may have
been right. It had clearly been a contributing cause in her own
case, and she figured that made her an expert on the power of
good old propinquity. Say what you want about not fishing off
the company pier, office temptations are hard to resist because

of all that daily closeness. Who are you supposed to flip for? Some stranger, or someone you see every day?

The first any of us knew about it was when Donald Scheer called Stu in an uncharacteristic rage and demanded that Sam be fired.

"What for?" I asked a still-astonished Stu.

It seemed that Sam had been seen by a Capricorn account exec sitting in a dimly lit corner of a small checkered-tablecloth restaurant not far from the studio, holding hands with Carter Boyd.

Okay. Yes, I guess I was surprised. But only about Carter, and only because I'd never really thought about it. "Carter Boyd isn't married," I said. "He can fuck anybody he likes."

"But he can't fuck anybody *Donald Scheer* likes."

I thought about that for a minute. Stu picked up the brass Buddha on his desk and stared at it, almost as if he were asking for some kind of intervention. Then he put it down again.

"Why just Sam?" I asked. "Why not Carter too?"

"Carter's up to me, the way he sees it. I hired Carter. But Sam is someone *he* recommended for a job. That makes it worse, you see."

Oh, I saw all right. I saw what Stu did. And it obviously had nothing to do with anything that made any sense. I walked over to the couch and sat down.

"What does Gautama have to say?" I asked.

Stu grinned. "He thinks it's bullshit. But it confirms what he said right along. The origin of suffering is desire."

I couldn't really argue with that. I sat there and played with the phrase for a minute, turning it around in my head to see if it made sense backward, but it didn't really seem to. Too bad; it would have been interesting. "Exactly how much suffering are we going to have around here?"

Stu brought his eyebrows together and looked at me. "Don't be cryptic," he said. "Leave that for The Enlightened One."

"Are you going to can him?"

Stu tilted his chair back and thought about it for another minute. "Which one? Don't forget, he left Carter up to me."

I started to say something, but he stopped me. "The answer is no. I'm not going to fire either one of them."

There was something in the measured, earnest way he said it that had clearly been meant to draw applause, but I have this stubborn streak that sometimes makes it hard for me to cheer in the expected places. Such victories are small, but they seem to mean a lot to me.

"I'll have to talk to them both, of course," he said.

"Separately, I hope."

He threw a look at me. "You want to do it?"

I shook my head.

"The point is, they've got to learn to be discreet. You know I'm never going to hear the end of this. Donald Scheer isn't happy when he doesn't get his own way."

"Neither am I," I said. "But I've learned to adjust."

There was a knock on the door that was so unexpected it startled me.

"Yes!" Stu bellowed.

The door opened and in walked Sam, so perfectly on cue that I wondered exactly what he was doing here. But Stu seemed as surprised to see him as I was.

"Have you seen this?" Sam asked. He was holding up a copy of the *Post.*

Stu shook his head.

"Page four," Sam said, dropping the paper on Stu's desk. Stu waited till he left the room before picking it up.

Considering the topic we'd just been discussing, I half-expected it to be a gossip item, but the more I thought about it the less likely that seemed. Neither principal's name meant a thing in the gossip world. Something in Elliott Cross's column maybe? But why would Sam be calling our attention to a tip on raising tomorrow's adults? Stu read the item quickly and tossed the paper to me when he was done.

Background: Several other nighttime quizzes had gone on the air since ours, but only one had been successful; a show called "King of the Hill." They currently had a champion running who'd been on about ten weeks and was clearly the smartest man on earth. Unless, of course, he was winning his victories the same way our guys did.

The news story was a challenge flung by Cory Lane, the producer of "King of the Hill," to Elliott Cross. It was an invitation for Elliott to come on the show and do battle with Arnold Zimmer, their meat packer from Kansas City; the man who just last week had in dazzling succession correctly named the number-one best-selling single for 1956, the dogma promulgated in the papal bull issued by Pope Pius IX in 1854, and the only two men ever to win baseball's triple crown *twice.* In order, that would be Elvis Presley's "Don't Be Cruel," the Immaculate Conception, and Ted Williams and Rogers Hornsby. No wonder they were so damn proud of him.

The idea was for a challenge round that would extend over two weeks and settle once and for all the question of who was the greatest quiz contestant who ever lived. Notice it was Elliott Cross they wanted. We'd had others win more money and stay on longer, but the Doc was the one who'd made the impact.

Stu waited till I finished reading it. "Do you believe this fucking imbecile?" he asked.

I smiled. "Do you think our guy can beat him?"

He grinned as he thought about it. "He could if they played on our show."

But that clearly wasn't the plan.

There were phone calls back and forth for the rest of the day, including several from a sweaty Elliott Cross, who wasn't quite sure how to handle this, and seemed to resent the fact that the story had broken in what he now referred to as his paper. Murray Cashin called to say that he and Donald Scheer thought it might not be a bad idea. The ratings were still holding up, but the time

211

for a shot in the arm was before you needed it. Uncle Joe thought it might be terrific when he called, as he often did, to ask when the hell they were going to see me. Alyse, he said, thought that Elliott's accepting the challenge would be the perfect way to demonstrate once and for all that the show was on the up-and-up. Even Mike Prince had an insane moment when it seemed like a marvelous idea, but a glacial stare from Stu quickly brought him to his senses.

After two solid hours on the phone, explaining over and over to an endless series of reporters why Elliott Cross would not agree to such a contest, Stu finally slumped in his chair and said no more newspaper calls; refer them all to Lenny Basch. And then he called Lenny and told him what to say.

"Jesus," he said, putting the phone down for what he hoped was the last time today, "can you believe this?" He pushed himself back from the desk and slowly gathered the strength to stand and stretch that enormous frame. Stretch it out he did, his hands actually touching the ceiling. Then slowly he lowered his arms, as slowly as if they were being controlled by mechanical means. When they were finally all the way down he hunched his shoulders once, apparently pulling himself together, and then stood tall for a second before maneuvering himself out from behind the desk.

"One of these days I'm going to get a chance to do something terrible to this Cory Lane." He looked at me. "I mean something really ghastly. In the first place, what kind of name is that? That's a name for a lobby card, not a living human being. But I tell you, one day I'll get a shot at this little turd . . . " He clenched his fists in frustration.

One more phone call. Stu picked it up, and then cupped his hand over the mouthpiece. "You're not going to believe who this is," he whispered hoarsely. He took his hand away. "Okay, put him on." Pause. Then, "Hello, Mr. Lane, how are you?"

He looked at me and shrugged, then shut his eyes not the way he did on private calls, but more in pain. "Okay," he said finally, "Cory, it is."

He listened again, then agreed that, yes, it might have been better if Cory had discussed it with us privately first, but he could understand how his enthusiasm might have run away with him. Yes, we had made up our minds, and no, there would not be any challenge round, as he'd just finished telling every reporter in the contiguous United States. No, he would not reconsider; this was really very definite. Of course he didn't resent Cory's having issued the challenge; he had every right to do so. Then a terse good-bye, a slam of the phone down into its cradle, and a "FUCK!" so loud I expected to see some plaster fall.

By the next day we were back to the normal bullshit. There was an ex-singer we were after to host the new music show, which was going on the air in October, and his agent was on the phone insisting that his man be allowed to sing on the show at least once every day, and Stu was livid because the deal had been set and nobody had said a word about that before. And this was a *game* show we were talking about, not a USO appearance.

"I thought we had a deal," Stu bellowed into the phone. "Don't tell me what's good for the show. That's what I tell you. Listen, he's a washed-up boy singer who used to wear brown-and-white shoes and vocalize when somebody nodded in his direction. Tell him all the big bands went away. If he doesn't do this show, he spends his weekends at the Log Cabin in Armonk, singing to three pimply couples."

Then there was Mike Prince, who had a problem with his fan mail, and spent an hour trying to convince Stu he needed some-body full-time to answer the letters and send out autographed pictures. Stu told him he'd think about it. Then Toby came in with the questions for Monday's show, and Stu flung them back at her, screaming they were much too hard. What she didn't know was that we'd be dealing with a renegade contestant who wasn't getting answers and who might have trouble with his own telephone number. And, of course, Murray Cashin called three times because he was sure Stu didn't understand how important it was to Donald Scheer to get Sam out of there. And late in the day, Elliott Cross met Frank Dean for a drink, because Frank was the only man he could talk to, and the Doc was worried sick that his refusal to accept the challenge might put him in a terrible light.

"Let's say it does," Frank Dean said to him wearily. "You got any better ideas?"

16

THE FIRST EXPLOSION WASN'T OURS. IT HAPPENED IN THE MINE field next door.

It was April 1958. Another fall and winter had gone by. Months are never uneventful, but these had contained nothing too different from the events that might have been expected. The leaves did their autumn tricks again, and Christmas was held on time, but there were very few surprises. One, I suppose, was the dismal fate of the music show, which Stu had thought would be our third straight hit. It went on in October, and was dead by the first of the year. But everything else continued flying as high as ever, and on the surface we were in marvelous shape. Oddly enough, that surface didn't change even after the explosion, but those of us who were aware of what had been bubbling underneath now had still more reason to be nervous. Here's what happened.

A player on "Fame and Fortune," a daytime game produced by another company, had been waiting in a dressing room for his turn to go on and, finding himself alone, calmly began to search through the purse of a woman who was then onstage. It was unclear whether or not he knew what he was looking for, but what he found was some slips of paper that contained answers to the puzzles she was at that very moment being asked to solve. He hollered foul, either because his sense of decency had been outraged or because nobody had offered any answers to him.

The story made the front page of every paper in town, and two days later he was down at the district attorney's office telling it again. The day after that the show was yanked off the air.

The impact at our office was considerable, as you might expect, with reactions running from deep gloom (Frank Dean and me), to shocked disbelief (almost everyone else), to a kind of smug self-satisfaction (Stu). There was no way, said Stu, that such a thing could ever happen to us. There were several reasons, all having to do with our basically sounder approach, and he started to enumerate those reasons. Halfway through his explanation my neck began to feel too big for my collar and I had the feeling that if I remained there listening to any more of this there was a genuine possibility that I might explode. That didn't seem desirable, so I spun around suddenly and walked out of his office without saying a word. I kept on going right through the reception room and straight out the main door, not even looking back to answer the question Nicole shouted after me about whether or not I'd be gone for the day.

It was Buster Keaton in something with trains, but I'd have been sitting there no matter what it was. Where do you go when there's no habit of walking into bars? The museum had always been my refuge.

I'd walked the almost-mile from the office without any desti- nation consciously in mind, more to wander than to get any- where in particular, but then there it was, with its name tilted ninety degrees from readable, running skyward up the side of the building in what must once have seemed an act of modern defiance.

The old friends on the wall were my old masters. If once they had caused a stir in the art world into which they'd been born, no sense of it remained for me. *Guernica, The Sleeping Gypsy, The Piano Lesson;* they were as familiar, as comforting, as fondly remembered as the warm surroundings of some favored adolescent retreat. What I took from them had more to do with reassurance, my own continuing need for finding things as they'd always been, than with any feeling for the place they held in the scheme of things.

I'd come here many times for many reasons. To try to expand my perceptions; to try to pick up attractive, cultured women; to pass an empty hour between appointments; to eat the chicken salad that came on a plate with half a canned peach; to see films like *Man's Hope* that could be seen nowhere else but in that small, nearly always empty theater.

The building was warm and safe. Its doors filtered out abrasive people. It was schoolroom, lounge, and sanctuary.

I'd walked in today on automatic pilot and drifted along my usual route through the permanent collection. Gradually the panic, the fears that had been stirred up by the "Fame and Fortune" disaster, seemed to subside. No facts had changed, but simply being away from the office, being here, seemed to have a soothing effect. In a few short minutes I became a part of these surroundings, relaxed to the point where old habits started to take over and I actually found myself casting my eyes around in search of someone female who might not be repelled by a comment on how much I'd always loved Matisse. There seemed to be one or two possible targets, but my normal inhibitions were reinforced today by a feeling that I was probably better off alone.

So I'd drifted down to the basement theater, and now I was watching Buster Keaton for no better reason than he was the one who was playing today. There he is on top of the caboose, looking backward as the train speeds toward a tunnel. Turn around, Buster, look out! But he's busy knotting the end of a rope as the train starts into the tunnel; he sees nothing. Then at the last possible instant he casually lies flat to lower the rope, having no idea that he'd ever been in danger. He passes safely into the tunnel, and the two guys a few rows in front of me laugh hard in appreciation. Oh, those silent comics! I smile because it is kind of funny, but I've never laughed out loud at anything I couldn't hear.

The picture ended, followed by the usual splash of flashing dots, and as the dim side lights came on I stood up and stretched. I reached for my loosened tie and in a practiced move slid it back into place without buttoning my collar.

I stepped out into the hall thinking about what activity might be next, and there in front of me was a young attractive woman with a beige coat over her arm, looking hard at the movie poster. If I was going to start a conversation, it had to be right away. There is the briefest moment within which such things remain spontaneous and are therefore unthreatening, even friendly. When the moment's lost, any approach becomes an offensive leer. I didn't skip a beat.

"You'd love the movie," I said. "But that was the last show today."

She looked at me and smiled. "I was afraid of that," she said.

Tan skirt with a white blouse not quite tucked all the way in, blonde-brown hair that had probably started the day neatly combed, and a kind of knowing smile that might mean nothing at all.

"Since you can't get to see it today, I'd be happy to tell you all about it over a cup of coffee."

The smile disappeared as she suddenly went tense. "Oh, no," she said. "I couldn't really do that." And she turned quickly in something of a panic and walked away, her heels clicking rapidly on the uncarpeted floor.

There may be other things as deflating as that kind of swift rejection, but I'd have trouble naming them. I turned to the poster to give myself a quiet minute in which to pull my shattered psyche together, and then I headed upstairs to spend a few minutes in the photography section, looking again at the clouds that Stieglitz called equivalents.

I stopped in the bookstore on the way out, because Carla loved art books and I thought I might find something to bring to her. I flipped through a couple of things, and then decided I wasn't really in the mood. I was about to start out when I felt a tap on my shoulder and heard someone female say, "Excuse me." I turned quickly and locked eyes with the same blondish-brownish-haired woman I'd seen outside the theater. I jumped back because the contact had seemed almost physical.

"I'm sorry," I said awkwardly. "I mean, I hope you don't think I'm following you."

That same smile again. What made it interesting, I think, was that it wasn't really quite straight.

"Of course not," she said. "I saw you here when I came into the bookstore. I just wanted to tell you that I'm really sorry if I seemed rude before. I mean, what I should have told you is that I'm married."

She had put on her beige coat, and now that it was no longer over her arm I could see the wedding ring.

"Oh," I said. "I see."

"Anyway," she said, "I think I could have handled it better."

I nodded for a second, not really sure where I wanted to take this conversation. "You were fine," I said. "I just hope you don't think I go around trying to make contact with every strange woman I see."

She laughed. "I don't know what you do," she said. "But whatever it is, I'm sure it's never offensive."

I thought that over briefly. "I think I'll take that as a compliment," I said. "Listen, now that I know you're married, can't we have coffee anyway? I mean, married people drink coffee, don't they?"

A raised eyebrow appeared above the knowing smile. "They do," she said. "And when they do, it sometimes gets them in trouble."

I shook my head. "No, it's alcohol that gets you in trouble. And failing to brush your teeth twice a day."

She laughed again. "I'm sure coffee would be very pleasant," she said, "but I really have to get home."

I shrugged. "Okay," I said. "So be it." But I wasn't ready to let this go. There was something about this conversation that I was enjoying. "I'm about to get a cab," I said. "Can I drop you somewhere?"

She looked at me hard and then cocked her head, adding an interesting angle to the raised eyebrow and the knowing smile. "I don't think that would be a good idea," she said.

I shrugged and finally gave up. "I'm out of all my innocent suggestions," I said. "The only other things I can think of would probably get me arrested."

She laughed again, but this time as if she meant it. "I tell you what," she said. "I'm walking west, toward the subway. If it isn't out of your way, why don't you walk along?"

It was unexpected enough to produce a bit of a tingle, and I quickly said I'd love to. We walked out of there full of conversation about the wonders of the museum, and in the five minutes it took to get to the subway I managed to find out that her name was Valerie Reed and that she and a partner had a small business designing ski clothing under the label Chamonix. If I'd asked for the telephone number she might have asked me not to call. So I trusted to the fact that I'd be able to find it in the book.

It was close to twelve that night when I stopped at the newsstand on my corner and bought all the morning papers so I could torture myself again with the follow-up stories on "Fame and Fortune." Standing there waiting for my change, I suddenly slumped, as if somebody'd let the air out. The day seemed to have started about a month ago, and I was very ready to have it end.

I'd walked all over town after I'd left Valerie Reed. I'd wandered into a bookstore and done some browsing because there was no place to go till dinnertime, and I hadn't been ready to go home. There was something about Mrs. Reed that kept pulling my mind away from whatever book I had in my hands and back to her. That slightly unkempt look, not messy, but decidedly imperfect, was somehow tantalizing. She would be someone whose blouses would resist her best efforts to keep them from gapping, and who would sometimes have lipstick flecks on her teeth. I could see her with a zipper jammed; not open, but just a little short of closed. And her hair, I imagined, would always appear as if a weather event had occurred since she'd combed it.

Around seven-thirty, I'd finally slipped into a deli on Sixth Avenue for a pastrami on rye, and then, still too jumpy to go home, I'd called Carla and asked if I could bring her some food from what was clearly the finest establishment on the eastern seaboard. She said she was tired and that she'd eaten already, but I told her I'd be over anyway.

She'd sat on the couch in a lounging robe, hugging an enormous pillow as I brought her up to date on the disturbing fate of "Fame and Fortune," and how there, but for the grace of God . . . et cetera. By eleven she was fighting back yawns and having trouble keeping her eyelids up, so I'd finally taken pity on her and left.

It had been a very long day, and as the elevator door slid open at my floor, sleep had finally become a welcome idea. I stuck the newspapers under my arm and started reaching for my keys, when in the back of my head I saw again that smile of Valerie Reed's, with its hint of knowing things it shouldn't. It was a smile that made *me* smile as I recalled it, and I was lost in a reverie composed of equal parts fatigue and pleasure until I was suddenly snapped back to the present by the enormous note that someone had taped to my door. "Don't be alarmed," the message read. "I am inside. Probably asleep. Wake me." It wasn't signed, but the handwriting was clearly Stu's.

He was sprawled on my couch, stretched out in a dark, luxurious sleep that resisted my efforts to shake him out of it. He seemed marvelously relaxed and comfortable, each breath coming in a long, deep rhythm, and when I shook him a second time, much harder, the only result was a hitch in his breathing, followed by a quick return to normal. He was out cold.

I took off my jacket and tie and went into the bathroom for the usual purpose. I washed and then brushed my teeth, and when I turned around to hang up the towel, he was suddenly behind me, the unexpected hulk of him scaring me half to death.

"Jesus," I said. "Next time sound your horn."

He looked at me. "What time is it?"

"I don't know," I said irritably. "Look at your watch." I'd taken mine off and left it on my dresser.

He raised his arm to look, and then dropped it again. "Quarter after twelve. I've been here since ten o'clock."

"How the fuck did you get in?"

He grinned. "You forget who the janitor is in this charming old building of yours."

Ginger Malloy. I'd forgotten that they were old friends.

I took a deep breath and tried to get my pulse to slow down just a little. "You want me to make some coffee?"

He shook his head.

"Okay," I said, "no coffee. But let's move it to the other room, okay?"

"Oh," he said, apparently unaware that his huge frame had been blocking the hallway. He turned and went back to the living room. I followed him and sat down while he stood in front of the couch and stretched. "I gather you're not too happy to see me."

"I'm having trouble believing that you felt free to shoot your way in."

He looked at me and grinned. "That's not very hospitable."

But it wasn't striking me funny. "Never again, Stu. Understand? I don't like it."

He saw I meant it. "Okay," he said, lowering himself onto the couch. "It won't happen again. You have my promise. You got a piece of paper for me to sign, I'll give it to you in writing. But now let's talk about why I came."

And that suddenly made me nervous. It could have been for any reason. I'd been out of touch since early afternoon and in the climate of the last few days, no disaster was impossible.

"Okay," I said. "You'd better tell me."

He looked at me and grinned. "How'd you like to do another show?"

I had no idea what he was talking about, but at least I was relieved at the direction the conversation was taking. Any news that didn't involve Matthew Sklar couldn't be all bad.

"What show?"

Still grinning, he looked down and shook his head slowly in admiration. "That nervy pistol, Harvey Gold. You won't believe what he did this afternoon."

"I can't believe anything if you don't tell me."

He looked up at me. "That's what I'm doing. You in some kind of a hurry?"

"I'm tired, Stu. I want to go to bed. This wasn't a meeting I had on my schedule."

He stared at me for a minute, obviously not happy with my attitude. But then he grinned again. "You're not going to fucking believe what they want us to do."

"Who?" I asked him, not quite following this. "Harvey Gold?"

He shook his head. No, Capricorn. It seemed that Harvey Gold had called Donald Scheer this afternoon and suggested that Capricorn buy the rights to "Fame and Fortune," which could probably be picked up for a buck eighty-five, now that the show was worthless. Then they'd turn the format over to us and have us produce a nighttime version. We represent integrity, Harvey Gold had told them. Donald Scheer had liked that. He was ready to go for it if we were willing.

"I told him I wanted to talk to you," Stu said.

I nodded dully, numbed by what I was hearing.

Stu grinned. "The format isn't half bad," he said. "Of course, we'd have to punch it up for nighttime, but I think we could make it work. It would make up for losing the music show."

There would be no way to make him understand the revulsion I was feeling. "Let's talk about it in the morning," I said quietly.

He looked at me strangely, aware that I was repelled by the idea, but totally unaware of why.

By the next morning, it had passed. Murray Cashin called to say that he and Donald had talked it over again last night and decided that once a show had a bad name, it would be imprudent to try to revive it. We'll pass on this one, Murray said. Please tell Harvey thanks, but no thanks.

Harvey had shrugged. One day we'd all learn to listen to him. He didn't understand all this sensitivity. This was a deal that could have brought in some lovely dollars, and money was how we kept score in the business.

I let a week go by before I looked up Chamonix. There were two of them, a dry-cleaning establishment and one that just said Chamonix, Inc. Inc. turned out to be right, but Mrs. Reed wasn't in when I called and I didn't want to leave a message, so I said I'd try again. I tried the following day, and every day for a week with the same result, until I finally got the idea that Mrs. Reed wasn't taking calls from anyone because she was that anxious not to get anything started with me.

But three weeks later she called me. She hoped she wasn't bothering me, she said, and she was sure I was pestered with this kind of call all the time, but she had a friend who was dying to go on a quiz show and could I tell her who this friend should call. I did, and then kept the conversation going with a brilliant question about how she'd been, which she answered pleasantly enough for me to take the next step and ask her out to lunch. That would be nice, she said, and we set a time a sufficient number of days ahead so that neither of us would look too anxious.

17

THE PLANE TOUCHED DOWN IN LAS VEGAS ALMOST AN HOUR LATE. Alyse had said to meet her at the hotel, so I grabbed a cab and told the driver the Desert Inn.

We were having some of that famous desert heat, the driver said as he opened the door for me. A hundred and ten yesterday, and it should go higher today. But what did I care? he laughed. It would be a perfect seventy-two inside the casino.

As we pulled out of the airport, the enormous billboards thrust their famous names at me. Belafonte at the Flamingo. Martin and Lewis at the Sahara. Frank Sinatra. Alan King. The Will Mastin Trio, starring Sammy Davis, Jr., through Labor Day at the Sands. The driver handed me a card. "Try the lobster at The Captain's Table," he said. "Tell them Harold sent you." I took the card and said I was going to close my eyes for a minute.

The call had come in the middle of the night. Alyse had been amazingly calm as she told me what had happened. Joe had gone to bed early and awakened around one o'clock with what he was sure was heartburn. But an hour later it had gotten sufficiently worse for Alyse to call the desk and have them find a doctor. The doctor took a quick look and sent for an ambulance. Joe was awake through all of this, and busy telling everyone it was just the Lyonnaise potatoes he'd had for dinner. But at the hospital, they called it a myocardial infarction; a heart attack.

Alyse ran to me as soon as I came through the revolving door, with the kind of frantic look on her face that indicated either that things had gotten worse or that she wasn't handling this well. She threw her arms around me and kissed me for the first time since the wedding.

"God, am I glad to see you," she said.

"How's he doing?"

She pulled away and looked at me, and I saw the dark lines around her eyes that show up when sleep doesn't. "I wish I knew. They keep telling me he's doing as well as can be expected, but I don't know what that means. He looks awful. We've got to get him out of there." She was trying hard to sound calm, but she couldn't hide the undercurrent of hysteria.

She'd made up her mind about what had to be done. She wanted me to make arrangements to fly him home. She'd been talking to her father, and he'd insisted that was what we had to do. Get him into Sinai, where his own doctor can take care of him. What do they know about medicine in a place like Las Vegas?

We were still standing in the lobby and this didn't seem the perfect moment to try to have a rational discussion. "Let me just check in," I said calmly. "Then we'll go over and see him."

She nodded and went to make a phone call while I turned to the desk and did my paperwork.

"I asked the nurse to tell him your plane got in," she said going up in the elevator. "He's been asking for you." She put her hand on my arm and I could feel the tension in her fingers. "We've got to get him home, David. I'm afraid of what might happen if we leave him here."

She came into the room with me and waited while my bags

were put in place and I washed up quickly. Then we took a cab to the hospital, just a couple of miles west of the Strip.

Joe grinned as I walked in. "I guess I must be dying or you wouldn't be here." He was in a double room, paired with a man who looked to be in his eighties and who at the moment was snoring loudly.

"I came for the seafood buffet," I said. It was one of the hotel features Joe had mentioned when he'd described his vacation plans to me. Every year, Joe shut down the drugstore for the last two weeks in August, and this year he and Alyse had planned a trip through the West; Seattle, San Francisco, Los Angeles, and finally four days in Vegas.

He looked pale and ten years older, but he was sitting up and full of optimism about how quickly he'd be back on his feet. He had all kinds of instructions for me to pass along to his landlord at the drugstore about canceling deliveries of ice cream and such, and posting a notice on the window that the store would reopen by September 15.

"That's impossible," Alyse said quickly. "You'll be in the hospital longer than that. Four to six weeks, my father says. Then months at home."

Joe smiled. "Her father, the doctor," he said.

"Dentist," said Alyse, "but that's not the point. He had two friends with the same thing. He's been through all of this."

Joe nodded. Four to six weeks was right. He knew that. The doctor had already told him. But the drugstore would reopen. That was one of the things he wanted to talk to me about. Maybe I could hire someone when I got back. Some kid right out of pharmacy school. "If not September fifteenth," Joe said, "then as soon as possible. I need my doors open."

Alyse sat on the edge of the bed and looked at him. "David agrees that we should fly you home."

I was startled, but tried not to show it. Joe looked at me and frowned. "I don't know. The doctors here say I'm doing fine. Maybe I'm better off here."

"That's not something we have to decide tonight," I said quickly. "Let's see what they say tomorrow, then I'll call Sid."

Joe smiled. Sid Weinberg had been his doctor for over twenty years. Whatever Sid said would be fine with him.

The door opened and a youngish, red-haired doctor with steel-rimmed glasses came in and chatted his way lightly through the usual routine of tapping, poking, and nodding wisely at the patient's chart. "Coming along nicely," he finally said, and then he suggested that Alyse and I walk out with him. Just as we reached the door, the old man in the other bed woke up with a coughing fit and kicked off his covers, exposing his ancient genitals. I pulled the drape around his bed as we left.

The informal conference in the corridor produced nothing that could not have been said in front of Joe. There seemed to be some minor heart damage, yes, the earnest redhead admitted with a thoughtful nod, but nothing that should prevent a good recovery. A few weeks in the hospital and he should be able to go home. Assuming, of course, that there were no further set-backs. Alyse started to say something, but I cut her off quickly and steered her out of there.

"I want him on his way home *tomorrow*," Alyse said firmly in the cab on the way back to the hotel. I didn't answer for a minute, trying to figure out how to handle this. I was still steamed over the way she'd misquoted me to Joe, but there didn't seem to be any point in fighting about it. I looked at my watch, which was still on New York time. Eleven-thirty. Doctors were used to late calls. "I'll call Dr. Weinberg when I get back to the room."

"I want to be there," she said.

Alyse sat stiffly on the edge of the bed while I placed the call. Sid Weinberg listened and asked some questions, including the name of the hospital and the name of the doctor. Sid said he'd get into it tomorrow.

"Tell him we're bringing Joe home," Alyse said insistently.

I looked at her for a minute, and then passed along what

Alyse thought we should do. Not so fast, said Sid. Traveling wasn't exactly recommended for cardiac patients. Besides, we might be in a desert, but it wasn't the Sahara. Then he laughed. Or was it? Wasn't there a Sahara there? Where were we staying, anyway? He took the number and then said wait till tomorrow. He'll have talked to the doctor and the people at the hospital by then. When I hung up Alyse looked at me coldly and said I should have let her talk to him. I wasn't sure how to respond to that, so I suggested food.

The answer was a chilly no, so I went down to the coffee shop alone and had cold roast beef and potato salad, mostly because it was the best-written item on the unusually chatty menu. Whatever decision was going to be made about Joe would be made by Joe, with the advice of his doctor. And Sid Weinberg had seemed pretty clear about not wanting him moved. Unless something changed, Alyse would have to go along with that. I'd make arrangements to stay here a few more days, or as long as I had to. That would present some problems, but leaving too soon was out of the question. Especially with Alyse not making the best of sense. I looked at my watch again to see if it was too late to put in a call to Stu. It wasn't, but it only took me a minute to decide I didn't really want to.

I sat over my coffee for a few more minutes, then signed the check with the kind of confident flourish that reflected the brief power I held by being resident here. I left the coffee shop for a stroll around the hotel, and for the first time since I'd been inside this place I began to relax and feel its presence all around me. The glaring, expensive men's and women's shops lining the walkway past the coffee shop, their windows crammed with colorful tops and bottoms that looked like beach umbrellas. The shameless windows of the jewelry stores, stuffed with diamond-crusted watches and spiny porcupines of gold fashioned into rings and pins and sinkers hung from heavy chains. Then the endless bustle of the lobby, with people moving in every direction, as full of purpose as if they were making trains. And finally, the center of it all; the one big reason for all these bedrooms having been lashed together out here in the middle of absolutely nowhere; the enormous, pulsing, strangely efficient fantasy room I suddenly found myself standing in. Ladies and gentlemen, the casino.

The fascination was immediate and total. Silver-armed slot machines with plump women feeding coins from paper cups. Rows of green-topped tables, stool height, edged with players sitting passively, sliding cards under chips with quiet, practiced detachment, tossing in busted hands with only the mildest expressions of disgust. And at the crap tables, livelier frames of players trying to urge magic into the arms and fingers that controlled the dice, and roaring approval when they thought they'd succeeded.

I circled the casino several times, stopping for brief, educational minutes at the various events, and then a sudden roar from the dice table just behind me turned me around. Stickmen were working furiously stacking compound piles of chips and distributing them to happy players around the table's rim, and at the focus of this joyful commotion was a short, round, Oriental man, with a cigar stump clenched in the middle of his grin. He waited, accepting pats on the back while the chips were being passed around, and then picked up the dice again.

"That's six passes so far," the man next to me confided. "He just may go forever."

The shooter cocked his head and rattled the dice close to his ear, as if trying to hear the secret tumblers clicking into place. Then in one smooth sweeping move he tossed them the length of the table, just barely bouncing them off the end.

"Ten hard; ten the point," the stickman announced as two fives jumped up. All around the table, chips came down and were quickly placed around the layout in response to instructions that ranged from shouts to subtle finger moves. Then the stickman pushed the dice back toward the shooter.

"All right, lots of numbers," someone urged, and he started

rolling them. Six. Five. Five again. Two. Eight. He must have rolled a dozen paying numbers before the dice finally settled on six and four.

"Ten, it came easy," the stickman intoned. And again official hands moved chips all over the table.

I stood there and watched in fascination as he held the dice for six more long and apparently profitable passes before he finally sevened out. There was a brief groan of disappointment, but then a ripple of applause. "Good hand," the stickman said in admiration, pulling in the losing chips.

The now deposed shooter grinned his thanks and turned away, bumping into me accidentally as he moved. "Sorry," he mumbled automatically. He started to walk past me, and then looked back. "I hope you won a bundle," he said.

"Not a dime," I said. "I wasn't betting." He seemed surprised, but then he grinned again.

"That makes two of us," he said.

That made it my turn to be surprised. He hadn't been betting? Was that possible?

"Did you see me placing any chips?" he asked.

I hadn't, but I was new to all of this, and I'd just assumed that he'd been making his bets in some sophisticated way that wasn't apparent to us neophytes, the way people bought Rembrandts at fancy auctions.

"I tell you what," he said finally. "Since you and I were the only ones who didn't win a nickel, I'll buy you a drink." I nodded, and we went to the cocktail lounge; or really the bar, I guess. Somebody loud and female was singing in the room they called the lounge.

His name was Tommy Nakamura, and he was a Nisei, he said; Japanese-American. The Japanese part you could tell from the name, he explained, as opposed to Chinese or Korean. Oriental names that were multisyllabled were always Japanese. The American part I didn't need help with. It was obvious from the way he talked. A kind of slow, drawling, confident pattern of speech that wouldn't have been out of place in a John Wayne movie.

"What was I doing with the dice, you're wondering?"

Yes, that was exactly what I was wondering.

He shrugged. "I come here every night when I'm in town. I play blackjack at the dollar table, just to watch the human beings. I'll win or lose maybe twenty, thirty dollars, so it isn't really gambling. Gambling is something I don't do anymore."

He took a sip of his gin and tonic. "Last night there were three loud Texans in here shooting crap. I went over to watch because these guys really kill me. Mostly they were losing, but they didn't seem to mind as long as they got to flash those pinky rings. One of these guys gets the dice and turns to me. 'My man,' he says, 'you look lucky. Roll these fuckers for me.'

"I look lucky," Tommy Nakamura snorted. "Inscrutable Oriental, right? Maybe the Jap will bring us luck. Or the Chink, or whatever he is. Well, anyway, I haven't shot crap in a very long time, so I figured what the hell."

He took another sip, held the glass away from his lips for a second, then drank the rest of it down.

"I threw two craps and then missed a six point, but that didn't discourage these guys. They were convinced that somewhere in this chubby Oriental hulk, Lady Luck was hiding. They had me throwing every time they got the dice. I lost a lot more for them than I won, but people remember what they want to remember. Anyway, I had a good time. What's your name?"

I told him, and he asked me what I did. When he heard my answer, his eyes went wide. "No kidding," he said. "I watch it every Monday night." And he was filled with a million questions about how we picked our people, and did we have any idea what kind of things they knew before they went on, so we could tailor the questions? Well, maybe a little, I told him, but you never could be sure what anyone might know. He asked about Elliott Cross, still the one everyone remembered, even though it had been a year and a half since he'd been on. Wonderful man, I told him.

"What do you mean, people remember what they want to remember?" I finally asked.

"Oh, yes." He smiled. "Well, tonight a guy came in who'd been at the table last night. He stopped where I was playing blackjack and started talking. Then he asked if I'd roll the dice for him, seeing as how I'd been so lucky last night. You hear what I'm saying? He thought I'd had some kind of big streak. It never happened, but he thought it had. Why? Because in his head he remembered the lucky Jap."

Two more drinks came down in front of us and Tommy Nakamura picked his up and took a sip. He drank it like a man who was always thirsty, as if the alcohol didn't count.

"So what happens?" He grinned. "The lucky Jap comes through. That guy I won for will stand there now and lose every cent of it back, plus another ton. But the story he'll tell tomorrow will be about that one big roll, and how he knew the chubby little Jap was lucky."

Tommy Nakamura shook his head and smiled indulgently. Then he picked up his glass, drained it, and looked around for the cocktail waitress. He caught her eye, nodded, and in a moment there was another one in front of him.

Three more went down quickly with no apparent effect as he told me about himself. He had just opened a Mercedes dealership in Santa Monica in partnership with this Jewish guy who used to be his accountant. Was I Jewish? I nodded, not quite sure what it was that always seemed to give me away. Tommy owned two thirds of the enterprise and ran everything except the business side, whatever that meant, and sales had been curving steadily upward ever since they'd opened their doors in July.

He continued talking in a steady stream, needing no helpful prompts to keep the conversation flowing, and I had the feeling that he'd have been just as voluble without the booze. He was one of those people who loved to talk, and in his case that was fine because he did it well. I can't describe what it was, but there was something in the quiet drawl that came out of that round face that had me paying close attention. Which was just as well, because the story suddenly got a lot more interesting as he began revealing more about himself than I'd expected to hear. More, really, than at first I found it easy to believe.

In the same matter-of-fact, pleasant drawl that had delivered the details of his business interests, he now went on to say that he'd recently been paroled after having served three years of a five-to-twenty prison sentence for armed robbery, and that during those three years he'd finally decided to put an end to what had been a lifetime of criminal activity. This prison resolve had nothing to do with any moral reawakening; it was a simple matter of facing what he now perceived as reality.

He had been the best he knew at his trade, which had been mostly robbing banks. He had planned every detail of every job with the kind of meticulous care that had been consciously designed to produce maximum results with zero risk. Not minimum risk, but *zero* risk. Minimum risk meant you weren't likely to get caught. Zero risk meant just what it said, and for almost twenty-five years it had been a goal he'd thought he'd achieved. But then something went wrong; someone failed to follow some very explicit orders.

Everyone he'd recruited for this one particular job had received his standard instructions: Take only vault money, no money from the tellers' windows. Tellers' money might be marked; it wasn't worth the risk. But one confederate had gotten greedy and cleaned out a teller's drawer, and two days later the man was picked up when he paid for a steak dinner with a traceable hundred-dollar bill. There followed the usual deal with the DA's office where, in return for the customary light sentence, he turned in all the others, and suddenly Tommy Nakamura found his very smart ass in the slammer, where he was forced to face the fact that there was no such thing as zero risk.

But he'd been lucky, Tommy said, because when the time

came to start his life over there were people he could turn to. Legitimate people who'd always been fascinated by the little they knew about the way he'd lived, and who were now willing to help him with cosignatures on bank loans and real estate leases, and recommendations in the right places that ultimately helped him secure the auto franchise he wanted.

Tommy smiled. "You know what it's like to walk into a bank you once thought about knocking off and ask for a sizable loan?"

I didn't. In fact, it occurred to me that I would be unlikely ever to enter a bank for either purpose. My business in banks tended to be the middle-class kind that involved a lot of standing in line.

As he talked, I looked at Tommy Nakamura and began to notice things about him that I was surprised I hadn't seen before. His size and his commanding overall appearance had made such a strong initial impression that it took a while to get around to details that on someone else would have been instantly startling. His hair, for example, was long and shiny and tied in back in a pony tail. Around his neck he wore a coral choker and three gold necklaces, all on display at the open throat of his pleated guayabera. And his fingernails were the longest I'd ever seen, extending at least an inch past the tips of his fingers. They were buffed and polished to a splendid shine, but their menacing curve gave them the look of the hooked talons of some enormous bird of prey, strong enough to grab a screaming rabbit.

He was a regular here in Vegas, coming maybe two or three times a month. He still had contacts here in town, and although his current activities provided no need for him to use them, he saw no reason to give up his old friends; except, of course, for the two or three his parole officer insisted he strike from his list. He had once been an enthusiastic gambler, but there too, he'd finally come to face the realities. There was no such thing as playing it smart. No matter how much you knew, how glibly you could quote the odds, if you played consistently you had to lose.

Did I know why? He didn't wait for an answer. Because they had all the money.

Oh, yes, there were the odds of course, and the house had those in its favor, just the way all the books said it did. But while the odds were a factor, they weren't the biggest reason. The biggest reason was simple: The money overwhelms you.

"If you and I decide to shoot a private game of crap," he said, "and you start with a hundred dollars, and I start with a hundred thousand, who do you think comes out the winner?" Once again, he didn't wait for an answer. "Your pathetic little hundred may double itself, triple itself, even go ten times. But sooner or later I'll take it away. All I have to do is keep you playing." He indicated the room around us. "That's what this is all about. The carpeting, the marble, the crystal chandeliers; the free flights out here for the high rollers, with the free rooms and the comped meals. All of it's designed for just one thing: to keep you playing. And if that's what's good for them, how can it be good for you?"

Unless somebody's died, no telephone call should ever begin with, "Did I wake you?"

It was five-fifteen in the morning, and my marathon conversation with Tommy Nakamura had gone on till past three o'clock. "Do you know what time it is here?"

"Early, I know." The voice on the phone was Valerie Reed's. "I'm calling from the airport."

There was another pause as I tried to get my head organized enough to process simple thoughts. Then "What airport?" I asked in a tone that had just enough edge in it to show I wasn't pleased.

"Listen," she said lightly, "you can go back to sleep in a minute. I've got something I think you'll be glad to hear."

I was obviously supposed to ask her what that was, but I wasn't feeling cooperative.

"I'm about to get on a plane," she said. "I'm coming out. Today."

That did it. That cleared my head like a whiff of smelling salts.

"I was going to surprise you, but then I suddenly thought, how do I know who you've got in your room?"

"Never mind that," I said. "What do you mean, you're coming out?"

"Relax," she said quickly. "Nothing dramatic. I made some phone calls yesterday to some of the shops out there. The Sportswear Shop right where you're staying, among others. They want to see what I have."

I laughed. "And you're getting away with that? I mean, how many sweaters can they buy?"

"Not many, but it's showcase time. That's the point, you see. It isn't how much they buy that matters; it's the importance of having Chamonix seen in the right stores."

Among her minor imperfections, Valerie had a slightly bent *r*. Nothing definite enough to be able to imitate in print, but nonetheless there, especially in words like "right." Right stores. I don't know if it was the familiar sound that made me smile, or the idea that these promenade stores could in any way be considered right.

"These are the right stores?"

"Don't knock it. He thinks it's a good idea."

He, as you may already have guessed, was *Mr.* Reed. Wesley Hammond Reed, the now-sixty-two-year-old lawyer Valerie had married eight years ago, when she was twenty-four. She'd been his private secretary, then several other things, and finally, to the surprise of everyone who knew them, his wife.

"How's your uncle?"

The question snapped reality back into place. How was Joe this morning? Had Sid Weinberg talked to the hospital yet? Then I remembered it was only five-fifteen. I told her he'd seemed as well as could be expected, and then I got back to the point of her call.

"I can't believe you figured out an excuse to get away."

"I'm terribly resourceful."

"What time are you getting here?"

"Around two-fifteen. Try to be in your room."

I laughed. "That shouldn't be too difficult." And I told her what time I'd gotten to bed. That made it her turn to laugh. We talked for another minute, and then she told me to go back to sleep.

I put the phone down and turned off the light with the idea of doing just that, but it didn't seem to be in the cards. I had just begun to feel a little drowsy when I found my attention drawn to the thin vertical line of light that started to appear at the point where the heavy drape halves overlapped. The dawning day was mostly being held outside, but there was this thin line that defied man's best attempt to keep it from intruding. I got out of bed to try to make the line disappear, but when I lay down again I could see that my efforts hadn't seemed to make much difference.

Valerie Reed and I had wasted very little time since the lunch she'd finally allowed us to have. There'd been a second lunch that same week, with a lot of urgent hand holding, and then several daytime visits to my apartment that had Ginger's eyes popping as he forced himself to choke back the questions he knew I would never answer.

We'd both been clear from the start that this was a romance that wasn't going anywhere. In fact, there was a great deal of question as to whether it was really a romance at all. Whatever it was, we were both having a marvelous time as we found in each other undemanding affection and the kind of mutual response that rarely occurs outside of erotic dreams. She was happily married, she kept saying, and I had no reason to doubt her, or to try to convince her otherwise. Our arrangement was perfect for me, which surprised me a little, because it wasn't my usual style. I'd fantasized my share of irresponsible, mindless affairs, but in practice I'd always tended toward candy and flowers. But this was working fine.

My eyes refused to stay closed and I finally allowed them to drift toward the glowing clock on the night table, which, to my surprise, now read six-thirty-five. Adding on three hours to make it New York time, that made it the perfect time to put in a call to Stu.

"Jesus," he said, "what's happening? I was on the phone with Hank, but I hung up when I heard it was you. When are you getting back?"

Not sure, I told him. It might be several days.

"Several days! That's impossible," he said. "Don't they have doctors out there? What good are *you* going to do?"

I'd be back as soon as I could, I said.

"Listen," he said. "That crazy bastard's drinking again. He won't listen to anyone but you."

That would be Shadow he was talking about. Shadow, who didn't seem to have a last name, was bullied by human voices, and was the only man in the world who understood how our giant three-tiered horizontal wheel was supposed to go together. We had yet another new show scheduled to start its daytime run on the last Monday in August, and our fate was in the hands of this brilliant, skinny lush who even on a good day had trouble holding his screwdriver steady.

"You've got to get back here. That monstrosity keeps tearing itself apart!" The wheel, he meant. Or the three wheels, really. Never mind why, but they were supposed to counter-rotate very fast on their common vertical axis and then all three stop on a dime. A couple of times they had, but mostly there'd been grinding sounds and the stripping of gears, with people frantically pulling electrical connections to get the machine to stop, and then Shadow climbing inside that skeleton of grimy, acrid metal and making adjustments that no one but him understood—if he did.

"We have two weeks! That's *all,*" Stu bellowed. "Two weeks to make this idiot fucking Erector Set behave. *I need you here!*"

I promised to be back as soon as I could, and to call Shadow right away, which I did. I could almost smell his pungent breath on the phone, but at least he was there and working. "There" was a display house on Park Avenue just below 125th Street. They'd built stuff for carnivals, for Barnum & Bailey, for industrial shows, but never before had they worked on a schedule this tight. They needed a lot of reminding about deadlines, and that was the subject I now raised with Shadow, who swore he'd been on the job all along and hadn't touched even a drop. It was obvious that neither was true, but I was more concerned with the future than the past. Okay, I said, I believe you. And then I played on his sympathies a little more heavily than good taste would normally allow, making the point several times over that it was important for me to stay out here in Vegas because my uncle was the only family I had left, and I could allow myself to stay with him only if I could be sure that he, Shadow, was doing his job without my being there to look over his shoulder. I could be absolutely sure, he said, and an emotional catch in his voice indicated that at least he meant the promise while he was making it. Yes, he vowed, he'd get it working. He'd live in the shop if he had to. And no, he wouldn't be at all upset if I called him a couple of times a day, as long as I kept everybody else away from him. It was the others who drove him crazy. As soon as I hung up, I called Western Union and dictated a telegram to Stu: TALKED TO SHADOW AND EVERYTHING'S FINE. DO NOT, REPEAT NOT, CALL HIM NO MATTER WHAT. IT MAKES HIM JUMPY, AND WE ALL KNOW WHAT HAPPENS THEN. I SWEAR, I'LL CALL HIM TWICE A DAY.

I hung up and went in to brush my teeth, which were surprisingly fuzzy considering how few hours it had been since they'd last been scrubbed. It was now about eight-fifteen, and I put in a call to Sid Weinberg. He might not have had a chance to call the hospital yet, but it seemed like a good idea to make contact.

He was there and he had indeed talked to Joe's doctor, who'd impressed him as a perfectly sensible young man who knew as much about treating cardiac cases as anyone did.

"There's no way Joe can be moved," Sid Weinberg said. "The result could be catastrophic. The hospital won't even release him unless he and Alyse sign all kinds of legal waivers. That's how dangerous it is. He's to stay right where he is."

I'd assumed right along that's what he'd say. Now, I told him, all I have to do is make Alyse understand.

"Do you want me to call her?"

Definitely a good idea. "If you wouldn't mind," I said.

"Of course not," he said brusquely. "She's at the same hotel, right?"

"Yes. Listen," I said quickly. "What does this doctor out here think about Joe?"

Sid Weinberg laughed. "He thinks he's very nice, for a New Yorker."

"Some of my best friends are New Yorkers," I said.

Sid laughed again, then suddenly turned sober. "He thinks it looks pretty good. You understand, it's odds we're talking about here. It's maybe five to one that he'll be fine. But when you pick up a revolver to play Russian roulette, it's five to one you won't blow your brains out. You want to play?"

I told him I understood.

"Now, what's her name again? His wife?"

"Alyse," I said.

"Of course. He should have gotten married before my memory went. Okay, I'll call her right away."

I thought again about trying to get back to sleep, but it seemed impossible, so I went the other way and showered to get myself fully awake. I was in the middle of shaving when the phone rang. Alyse. Angry.

"Did you call my father?"

It took a moment for me to be sure I heard her correctly. Then another moment to reject the automatic response of Why would I call your father? and respond with a simple no.

"I don't believe you."

There was a shrill tone that added a further note of insanity to what she was saying. I shifted the phone to my right ear and wiped off the lather with the bath towel I'd dragged with me from the bathroom. I moved the phone back to its usual spot before I answered. "Alyse, I don't even remember your father's name. I couldn't talk to him if I wanted to."

She took a minute to think about that, or to think about something, because there was this long pause on the line. Then she said sharply, "I've decided to leave Joe right here where he is. In the hospital right here. I've decided we shouldn't move him."

"All right," I said slowly, a little surprised at the way it was coming out.

"Can you stay here for a while? I mean in Vegas?"

"Of course," I said quickly, grateful that the matter seemed settled. Her father had obviously had something to do with it. Apparently he'd advised her to go along with Sid Weinberg's decision. And she'd concluded that I'd called him first and made some kind of heavy argument. Nothing paranoid about old Alyse.

"I'm about ready for breakfast," I said in a carefully pleasant tone. "Care to join me?"

"Can't," she said. "I have to get to the hospital."

"I'll skip breakfast, then, and go over with you."

"No," she said. "Visiting hours aren't till two o'clock. They let me come anytime."

Wife, see. Has me outranked. "All right, then, I'll see you later."

"Try to get there at two o'clock," she said. "You know how much he likes to see you."

Two o'clock. "Okay," I said. "I'll see you then."

It didn't seem the right moment to mention that two o'clock might be a problem.

18

I REMEMBER SOMETHING FROM ROUSSEAU'S *CONFESSIONS*, BACK when I was skipping through the classics for the dirty parts. He was on this journey with a group of people that included a young married couple. He found the wife terribly attractive, and through some kind of solution that seems available only to the French, actually managed several liaisons with her while her husband remained oblivious in a nearby *relais* room.

Anyway, the part I remember is that while Rousseau was mildly disapproving of the fact that a married woman would give herself in such a fashion, he found that her amorous skills were such as to justify her behavior, since the charming woman was simply expressing herself in the manner that suited her best.

If I am ever called upon to defend Valerie Reed, I will use a similar argument.

I have never believed that effectiveness in this sort of thing had anything to do with technique or imagination. But whatever its source, its presence is unmistakable. And like everything lovely, it is impossible to define.

It is also overwhelming. It mutes the sounds of ticking clocks and buries all sense of outside matters. Which is why it was almost an hour before the guilt set in.

"Put that down!" Valerie Reed frowned at me as I reached across her for my watch. Three-thirty. Not really surprising, but getting late.

I put the watch down and lay back, having quickly checked it against the glowing alarm clock next to the telephone. They were in rough agreement. "I think it's time you went and sold some wool to Mr. Sportswear."

"Dressed like this?"

"Maybe some lipstick."

She moved on top of me and leaned forward with her forearms on my chest. "Are you trying to get rid of me?"

"Not very successfully, it seems."

She stared at me for a minute, suddenly looking very serious. "You're nothing I had in mind, you know."

I did know. Here we were frolicking as freely as a couple of wood nymphs. Two civilized people who knew all the accepted conventions, who'd been trained to make cocktail conversation without pawing and rubbing each other, but who were never more than a layer away from this kind of joyous freedom. I'd been the seeker, of course. Simply because I'd been unattached and free to fantasize about every woman who came in view. But Valerie had sought none of this. Not at this point in her life. It's what she'd tried to avoid when she'd practically run away from me that day in the museum. But it had happened anyway.

"Are we having dinner tonight?"

I nodded. "Dinner, yes. But not tonight, exactly. I have to be back there at a little after eight."

"Two visits in the same day?"

"That's what I'm here for, remember? To see as much of him as I can."

She sat up and shook her hair into some kind of decent order. She'd comb it again in a minute, but then five minutes later it would look pretty much the way it did now. "Where will I meet you? The dining room downstairs?"

"I don't think so. We might run into Alyse. I don't know what her plans are. I don't even know how I'm going to manage to get away from her. Anyway, there's a place called The Captain's Table where they tell me the lobster is terrific. I'll meet you there at six."

"How do I get there?"

"Ask any taxi driver."

She turned and looked at me and smiled. "What a marvelous hour," she said quietly. "I'm glad I'm staying overnight. We've never been able to do that. I know it's silly, but I like the idea of waking up next to you."

"Easy does it," I said quietly.

She stood up and headed toward the bathroom. "Yes, I know. Easy, easy, easy. Why should it ever be anything but easy?" She shut the door lightly behind her.

I got out of bed and went to the chair that had my jacket draped across the back. I reached into the righthand pocket and pulled out the folded check; my check for a thousand dollars, made out to the Desert Inn, but with a line drawn through it and now back in my possession. "Oh, yes," the pinstriped supervisor in the cashier's area had told the pockmarked teller who'd asked him the question. "He's a friend of Tommy's," and he'd disappeared to look for the check in another room while the teller counted my chips. When he reappeared having found it, he showed the check to the teller, who nodded to indicate that my chips more than covered it. Pin stripes had then drawn the line through it and handed it back, and the teller had opened the cash drawer and counted out another $320.

I folded the check again and slipped it back into the jacket pocket with a silly grin on my face, as pleased with myself as if I'd done something terrific. It had been an amazing morning.

"I'll be out in a minute," Valerie yelled from the bathroom, but I was familiar with the length of her minutes and I yelled back for her to try to hurry. I glanced at my watch and then reached into the other pocket of my jacket to take another look at the telephone messages. There were four of them that I'd picked up about two o'clock, just before I came back to my room. Three were from Stu and there was one I hadn't expected, from Carla. I'd stuffed them away and gone upstairs to place a quick call to Joe at the hospital to tell him that something terribly important had come up and I'd be stuck making phone calls for an hour or so, but I'd try to get to the hospital by three.

I looked at my watch again. I'd be lucky to be there by four.

I thought about calling Stu, but that could be a conversation that might go on longer than I wanted it to, so instead I put in a call to see how Shadow was doing.

I'd have been better off not knowing. The owner of the place said he'd gone home sick after lunch, which was his way of saying they'd found him in the john asleep over a bottle of wine.

"Listen," I said, with as much growl as I could muster. "We have a show going on in two weeks. If we miss our date because your company didn't deliver, you'll be looking at a lawsuit that will keep you busy for the rest of your life. If I were you, I'd pick him up wherever he lives in a cab tomorrow morning and stay within six inches of that pathetic little bastard every minute of the day. And I'd do the same the next day, and the day after that. Till this job is finished. And then if this thing actually comes off on time, I'd write two thank-you notes: one to him, and one to me. I'll talk to you in the morning." And I slammed the phone down before he had a chance to answer.

The pony-tailed young girl in the gift shop was taking forever with the wrapping, and doing it as clumsily as if Scotch tape had been invented an hour ago. But I wanted this package wrapped, even badly; even if I had to wait.

"Could I be paying while you're doing this?" I asked.

She looked up from her tangle. "What? Oh, yes. Up front. Here's the slip."

I dashed up front and paid, then went back and hurried her through the final steps. Then I tore out of there and into a cab. Five minutes later I breezed into Joe's room past the bed of his sleeping roommate and handed Joe the crudely wrapped package. "See if you're strong enough to open that," I said.

He took it delightedly, and as he started to undo it I leaned over to kiss Alyse. She glanced at her watch as she offered me her cheek.

"Oh, great!" Joe said, holding up the checkers set. "Perfect. Now I can walk out of this place a rich man."

"Pretty cocky," I said.

"You in the mood to get beaten?"

"You must be joking," I said, sitting on the edge of the bed. "I'd be amazed if you even remembered how to set them up."

"Quarter a game," Joe said, "and you go first."

We'd been doing this, Joe and I, ever since I could remember. At first, when I'd been eight or nine, there was no way I could win a game. But gradually I'd watched the way he played, and I'd learned to stay away from the one-man sacrifices that led to double jumps. By the time I was twelve I could hold him even. He'd win his share, but so would I. I'd had no idea how good either one of us was until I started playing my friends and realized that no one could beat me. When I was sixteen, I entered a city-wide tournament and got to the quarterfinals, which really wasn't bad considering the park-bench competition.

"I play the winner," Alyse said as she picked up a magazine.

Joe looked at her a little strangely. "I didn't know you played."

Alyse laughed. "Of course I play. It's a children's game."

"Children play it," Joe said patiently, "but unless you've played a lot, I don't think you'll have much fun against David or me."

Alyse laughed again. "It'll be fine," she said.

Joe won the first game, a lengthy affair. But then instead of asking Alyse if she wanted her turn, he simply set up the checkers again. If she noticed, she was wise enough to say nothing. Halfway through the next game she put the magazine down, stood up, and stretched.

"I think I'll go downstairs and get a cup of coffee," she said. "Since David got here late, I'm sure he'd like a few minutes alone with you." And she left.

We played totally absorbed, the way we always had. No problems existed outside the frame of the checkerboard. Whole afternoons had gone by this way, with the two of us focused on nothing else. Evenings too.

"You're still at it?" Alyse asked as she came back into the room.

I looked at my watch. Six o'clock. "I thought visiting hours were over at five-thirty," I said.

"They are," said Joe. "I guess we didn't hear the announcement."

"It doesn't matter," said Alyse. "I had the doctor arrange it so I could eat with you," she said to Joe.

Joe smiled and nodded, and I stood up. "I'll be back around eight o'clock," I said.

Joe indicated the board. "You don't want to finish this game?"

"I concede," I said. "That makes it fifty cents I owe you."

"*Owe* me, nothing. You'll pay me now." It was a longstanding private joke. Whoever was behind promised to pay up later; whoever was ahead insisted on having his money now.

"Oh, Joe, don't be that way," Alyse said. "He can pay you later." She'd missed the tone. Maybe anyone would have.

I reached into my pocket and took out two quarters. "No," I said, "what's fair is fair. I expect to be winning them back, with interest."

Joe put them on the night table. "In that case, I'd better keep them handy."

I left and had trouble getting a cab. There were none hanging around this long after visiting hours. But the desk nurse saw my problem and called one for me.

Dinner with Valerie was hurried but pleasant, and we were both happy with the idea that I'd be free to join her again at nine o'clock. Her plane didn't leave till eleven the next morning.

I got back to the hospital just a little after eight, and when Joe didn't suggest resuming the checker game, neither did I. We talked for the hour, rather pleasantly. Alyse seemed calmer than she'd been since I'd arrived in Vegas.

We shared a cab back to the hotel, told each other how tired we were, and went to our separate rooms. I called down to the desk again to check for messages. Stu had called twice more, but it was obviously too late to call him back. I called Valerie.

"Would you mind coming here to my room?" she asked.

"Of course not."

"It's just that he might call. Oh, he won't, I know. But in case he did, it might be wise for me to be where I'm supposed to be."

"I'll be there in five minutes," I said.

"Knock three times." I could hear the smile in her voice. "That kind of thing appeals to me."

I did, and she said who was it? and I said the Count of Monte Cristo, which seemed a lot funnier at the time, and we began our one time together when, at least at the start, there was no need to think about time. Morning seemed an eternity away, distant enough to be nothing worth thinking about. There was even time to talk, and it seemed a glorious luxury as we chattered in the dark and learned more about each other than we'd ever known before.

We awoke at eight and ordered room service, which I charged to my room.

"Room 715?" the bellman asked, staring at what I'd written.

"That's right," I said.

"But this is 1202."

"I know," I said. "It's all right."

He looked from one of us to the other, a little more bewildered than I'd have expected a hotel employee to be, then finished setting things up and left.

After we finished, I tossed my napkin on the table and stood up and allowed as how it was time for me to get back to my room and do morning things if I were going to get her to the airport by ten-thirty.

"Go as you are," she said.

I looked down at my outfit and grinned. My pants were okay, but my shirt looked as if I'd slept in it. Which hadn't been the case. "The grooming police would arrest me. Besides, I have to take a shower. If I didn't, somebody would find out."

"Shower here."

"And crawl back into yesterday's underwear?"

"Just for an hour or so. After I leave, you can do the job right."

I looked over at my underwear and socks on the room's only chair. I'd gotten dressed quickly to look respectable for the room-service man and hadn't much wanted to get back into them. But why not, really? They hadn't seemed disgusting last night when I'd taken them off. How much could have happened overnight?

"It's even silly to take the time to shower," she said, standing behind me now, her hand lightly on my shoulder.

I turned and patted her hand. "Essential," I said. "How else will I know I'm awake?"

I got up quickly, picked up my things from the chair, and went into the bathroom. I'd just gotten the water adjusted when the glass door opened and she was in there beside me.

"Now it isn't so silly," she said.

We were late, of course, because watching clocks was not one of Valerie's great skills, while diverting my attention was. It was two minutes past eleven when we raced out onto the apron just as they were starting to pull the rolling stairway away from the plane. The cabin door had already been shut, but we managed to persuade them to shove the stairway back into place and open up again. She turned to kiss me, then turned again and quickly disappeared inside. I mumbled some kind of thank-you to the overalled guy who'd helped us, then climbed down the steps. I turned when I hit the apron to see if she'd found a window to wave from, but I couldn't see her. I moved farther away as the propellers sputtered and the engines coughed to life. All the window seats would be gone, of course, but I kept hoping that she'd be resourceful enough to figure out a way to get in a final wave no matter what. I waited till the plane started moving toward the runway, and then I finally gave up and headed back to the terminal building.

I was going to get over this quickly, I knew. Probably as soon as I found my way into another shower and a change of clothes. But for the moment she was hard to shake.

I walked slowly through the terminal building, absently stroking the unfamiliar stubble at my chin. It had been harder to say good-bye than I'd expected.

I walked past the newsstand and out the swinging doors into the desert glare. A cabbie caught my eye and I nodded and started toward him, but then I suddenly stopped short as something hit me like the classic ton of bricks.

"Taxi?" the cabbie asked.

I shook my head. "In a minute," I said, and then I turned and ran back into the building. The newsstand. Something had caught my eye but hadn't really registered till now. I glanced quickly at the headlines on yesterday's *New York Times*. Nothing there. But right next to it was something fresher, this morning's *Los Angeles Times* just off the plane from the coast; and there it was, the story I'd seen and walked right past. My insides did involuntary flips as I reached into my pocket for some change and bought the paper. I folded it casually under my arm and walked to a bench near the entrance to read it sitting down.

———

Bright red stains spread through the shaving cream. I put the razor down and fumbled through my toilet kit, but couldn't find a styptic pencil. It wasn't just a nick; it was one of those things where the razor had actually slipped, and without some help from a styptic pencil it was going to be a while before the cut stopped bleeding.

I tore off the standard tiny square of toilet paper, put it in place, and watched the red spread quickly from the center to the edges. Capillary action was what that was. The tiny passages in the paper just drawing that fluid along as if it were soda being sucked up through a straw. That would be capillary action, Mr. Brodsky, I said to my general science teacher, and he said absolutely right, and it was just another example of how things we learned here in Laboratory helped to explain the things that occurred in everyday life.

I replaced the tissue with some I'd folded over several times and stared at myself in the mirror while the new square reddened, too. Hacked away at yourself pretty good there, kiddo. Do we want to talk about that? No, we don't. Not even for a minute. Let's just forget the heady bullshit here and stick with the good old law of parsimony, which calls for applying the simplest possible explanation. Shaving at one in the afternoon instead of the customary eight o'clock, so the beard's unusually thick. Brand-new blade, unfamiliar bathroom. Could have happened to anyone.

The phone rang again with a sound that went right through me. It was Stu, of course. He was out of breath.

"Just got back," he said. He'd been in a marathon meeting with Hank Sachs till now, almost four o'clock, their time.

"Does Hank know the truth?" I asked him.

"Hank knows that Matthew Sklar is lying through his teeth."

I took a minute digesting that one. "How can your lawyer help you if he doesn't know the truth?"

There was a pause. "When are you coming back," he asked

in a blue-steel voice. And then I understood: We weren't going to talk about this on the phone. The lines might be tapped, you see.

"As soon as I can," I said. "Give me another day to make sure Joe is settled."

"How is he?" Stu asked, remembering that he should be interested.

"Coming along."

"Then you can leave. Get a plane out tonight."

"I can't tonight," I said quietly. "Joe's going to hear about all of this. I've got to talk to him."

"What are you, his father?"

"Cut it out, Stu."

There was another pause while he worked on some other kind of approach. "I need your help back here. There are a million things that have to be decided."

"Of course. But give me a break. I didn't know about any of this till a couple of hours ago."

"You could've found out yesterday if you'd returned my calls."

True enough. But if I had, I'd have missed the kind of terrific day that no one should ever miss.

"Okay," he said briskly, "one more day. But then get back here." I said I would, and hung up.

I kept changing the blood-soaked squares of toilet paper until finally the bleeding stopped and there was only an ugly red line that I could expect to have for several days.

I was suddenly anxious to know how much coverage the story had gotten. I called down to the newsstand and was told today's New York papers wouldn't be in till tomorrow morning. What about TV? I clicked on the set and was relieved to find that normal programming was purring along. But what else had I really expected? It wasn't exactly as if someone had dropped a bomb on Washington.

I picked up the *L.A. Times* and read the story again. Quiz

contestant Matthew Sklar had filed a complaint with the New York District Attorney's Office alleging that he had been given answers throughout his many appearances on the television quiz show, "Face to Face." Then a rehash of the accusations that had been made against the other show, "Fame and Fortune," and a promise from the DA's office to look into both matters further and to set up a special unit to investigate, if such action seemed to be warranted.

Not an enormous story, really. Front page, but not the lead story. I wasn't sure what I'd expected, but it was something bigger and blacker. Of course, this was the Los Angeles paper. I'd have to wait a day to see how they were handling it in New York.

Meanwhile, what to tell Joe? He had a television set in his room, but I had no idea what he'd seen. Had it been on the morning news? Yes, probably. All of this had happened some time yesterday. But how big had they played it?

I'd have to talk it over with Joe. I'd have to tell him there was nothing to the story. The man's a pathological liar. Such people can't be controlled. And Joe would believe me, of course. He'd believe anything I said.

It was because I'd been absorbed, I know, in that imagined conversation with Joe that the sudden ring of the telephone blasted me back to the present with a piercing sound louder, more threatening than any this same phone had ever made before. Phones don't do that, of course. A given phone in a given room will ring at the same decibel level each time it receives a standard impulse from a standard source. I know that. But this time this ringing phone had set my heart banging so hard I had to let it ring again, more normally, before I could pick it up.

"David?"

It was Margo. A crisp Margo. All business. Her one word made that clear.

"Yes," I said.

"This is Margo."

I smiled at that. And just for a minute, damn near said Margo *who?* "Yes, I know," I said.

"I can't hear you. Speak up, David."

"I'm here," I said louder.

"I suppose you know why I'm calling."

I shifted in my seat, not really sure what to answer. "I think it would save time if you just tell me."

"All right," she said, and did. It was Matthew Sklar, of course. She'd just spent three hours with him in her office. He'd be her guest tomorrow morning, live, for fifteen minutes. "That's more time than we give the secretary of state," she said.

"The secretary needs better PR."

"The point is," she went on, "this is a very big story. And an ugly one. And I'm sorry it has to be you. But the least I could do was let you know it was coming."

"Is this where I say thank you?"

She slid past that and just went on. "I'm trying to get Stu Leonard for a statement, but so far he's not returning calls. Do you know where he is?"

"Is this for attribution?"

"Everything is, David. I'm not paying for this call, the company is."

"Then why don't I call you back."

There was a pause on the line, and finally she said, "Okay. We'll make this private time. Where'd you find him, David?"

It was clear she meant Matthew, not Stu. "Never mind that; the question is where'd *you* find him? Why's he doing your show? Does he love getting up that early?"

She'd found him, it turned out, some time ago. She'd been watching the show one night at a small dinner party, the night both Elliott Cross and Matthew had missed the same question about Benjamin Harrison. Half the room had found it hard to believe that guys this smart would have trouble naming the president who'd served between Grover Cleveland's terms. *Think that's bad?* someone had asked. *You should have seen the mess with Beaumarchais.* And they'd told her about that, and the next day she'd gone to the network screening room and watched a kinescope.

"So I called Matthew," she said, "and met him for a drink."

"Then? While he was still on?"

"Yes. Of course."

"Why didn't you tell me?"

"There was nothing to tell. I asked him if he'd had any kind of help, and he said no. I didn't believe him, but I dropped it. I don't know if I was thinking of lawsuits, or you."

"Lawsuits," I said.

"Don't be so sure. Halfway through that drink I was hoping he'd deny it." But she'd made the contact. And yesterday, when the story broke, he called her. She was the only reporter in town he knew.

"Congratulations."

That seemed to soften her. "Oh, David, you know I hate that you're involved."

"Tell me something," I said. "How would you have handled this if you and I were still together?"

She didn't hesitate. "I don't do if questions," she said crisply. "I have enough trouble with the here and now."

It was almost three when I got to the hospital room, and it was Alyse who asked the first question. It was as if she couldn't wait. What's this all about, anyway? Hadn't I always told her such things didn't happen?

They didn't, I explained patiently; she'd have to take my word for that. But she wouldn't drop it. If there was nothing to the story, why would they put it on the TV news? And for a crazy moment I found myself wondering how she could know that Margo was planning to blast it open tomorrow morning. But then I reminded myself that she was talking about the smaller item that had run today. If that one caught her eye, wait till she sees the rocket display tomorrow.

"Leave David alone," Joe said wearily. "He didn't come here to talk about this." And with the final observation that it all seemed mighty strange to her, she excused herself to go to the bathroom and Joe reached for the checkers set.

We played till Alyse came back, and then I left. It was quarter of nine when I got back to the hotel, and I thought about calling Carla back. She wouldn't care if I woke her. But there were too many things that made it hard for me to talk to her right now.

I stepped into the casino and walked around aimlessly for a while, tempted to play as I recalled my remarkable comeback of this morning, but not really able to think about anything else but the walls that were finally tumbling down. I went back to my room before nine-thirty and crawled into bed and shut it all out with sleep.

But I was up before the alarm went off and clicked on the TV. It was six A.M., and the East had seen it already. This last hour was a live repeat for the Western time zones, and Matthew seemed almost comfortable as he went through it for his second time. Margo had trouble holding the spot to fifteen minutes. For me, it was like watching a personal horror film where every word was true.

I went back to sleep when it was over, hiding behind the heavy Vegas drapes that kept the sunshine out, and slept till the phone awakened me with the news that Joe had died. A second heart attack. It was Alyse, screaming hysterically that I should have done what she'd wanted me to all along; arranged to fly him home. "Now you'll have to," she wailed. "Now he'll be going home."

I met her at the hospital and helped her make the arrangements, which I'd expected to be complicated but turned out to be simple because it was the kind of thing that had to be dealt with all the time. Afterward, an orderly led me back to what had been Joe's room and I gathered his personal effects in a bag for Alyse. I left the checkers set.

Walking out of the room all I could think was why, as long as he'd had to die, it couldn't have been before he'd heard.

19

THE DRESSMAKER'S DUMMY STOOD IN THE CORNER OF THE
interrogation room, gray with a greenish cast picked up from the
dull green walls. It was headless, with a cloth torso and a wire
skirt, and seemed to come from another century. Stu had said
it was where they hid the microphone. He was convinced there
were microphones everywhere. Every morning when he entered
the small, unmarked hotel suite of offices we'd rented, he un-
screwed all the telephone mouthpieces looking for bugs, and
then got down on his hands and knees for a final check before
he'd start a conversation. The dressmaker's dummy was hiding
something. What else would it be doing here?

The clerk who had brought me to this room twenty minutes
ago had promised that Mr. Lefkowitz would be with me right
away. By now I was beginning to wonder if the delay wasn't part
of the process, a ploy designed to let the gray chill of the place
establish itself as the background for the questioning to follow.

There was an old wooden desk at the end of the room, with
a schoolteacher's straight-backed chair. Behind the desk, cen-

tered in the narrow wall, was a translucent window, its glass reinforced with octagons of chicken wire. To the right of the window was a plain wooden clothes tree with a brown artist's smock hanging limp from one of its branches. The walls were bare. It was an office that might have come from a stage production of some grim institutional drama. Except for the dressmaker's dummy.

The investigation had started a couple of weeks ago, with every edition of every paper filled with stories about who had been seen and who was scheduled to be seen by Ira Lefkowitz, the assistant district attorney assigned to investigate the complaints and then recommend whether or not the matter should be referred to a grand jury. There were daily photographs of former contestants entering and leaving. "The bastards," Hank Sachs had said when they ran Elliott Cross's frowning picture. "They could have led him out the back way." Maybe. But why would they want to?

We spent a lot of time talking to lawyers these days; mostly ours. We'd gone through several rather quickly, all recommended by Herschel Sachs. Then finally Hank came up with Leo Montenegro, who he said would be perfect for two important reasons: First, he was active in Republican party politics, and Ira Lefkowitz was the only Jewish lawyer in New York who was a registered Republican. ("What about Senator Javits?" I'd asked him, but he'd ignored the question.) And second, the man had himself once served as an assistant district attorney. That, of course, would mean he'd be on friendly terms with the guys who were running the investigation. He made it sound as if the selection of this particular man had been the result of some brilliant winnowing process, and I can remember we were all as impressed as he'd meant us to be. But that was because none of us had been aware at the time that almost every criminal lawyer in Manhattan had at one time or other worked in the DA's office.

"Who represents *you?*" Tommy Nakamura had asked the night he called.

I'd explained rather proudly about our new lawyer and all his impressive political and strategic connections. And that he was representing all of us.

"Who's paying his bill?" Tommy asked.

Stu was, of course.

"Then that's who he represents. Get yourself a lawyer of your own."

I told him there didn't seem to be a need.

Tommy sighed. "There are two kinds of people who get into trouble. The people who know what to do, and the people who don't."

There wasn't much doubt about which class he put me in. The fact was, he'd put me there that morning in Las Vegas when I couldn't get a check cashed without mentioning his name. That morning had become the cornerstone of our new friendship. I'd become his friend not by doing him a favor, but by asking one.

"I'll be in New York on Thursday," he'd said. "Can you put me up?"

The question startled me. "Yes, of course."

"Just overnight. We need to have some conversation."

And we did, for most of the night, as Tommy tried to persuade me that the only way I'd be protected was if I had someone looking out for no one's interests but my own. Of course, our discussion was complicated by the fact that I was stoutly insisting that the accusations against us were totally untrue. That made my end of the conversation a little hard to handle. Finally, as daylight started to work its way into the living room, he presented one final argument.

"I hear what you're telling me, and I have no reason to doubt even one little word of it," he said slowly in that western drawl that seemed so incongruous coming out of the very opposite of a western face. "But even if every bit of it is just exactly as you say, you better get yourself a lawyer. Because when you're playing a game you don't understand, you need someone on your side who knows all the rules.

"And if—and don't be offended if I explore the possibility—if you're involved in covering up, for whatever reason . . . " He let the thought trail off and stood up and stretched.

"Bedtime," he said. "Is this the couch I sleep on?"

"Take the bedroom," I said. "I'll sleep out here."

He grinned. "You forget, I've been in prison; I've been in internment camps. This is comfortable for me. Find me a blanket and go to bed."

He said it definitely enough to leave no room for argument. I found a blanket and a pillow.

"Listen," he'd said quietly. "Let me tell you something about cover-ups. The Mafia knows how to run them, because they're tough enough. And even the ones who aren't are more afraid of their own side than they are of the cops. But nice law-abiding guys like you can't handle it. I don't say you're trying to," he added quickly, "but if you are, I'm saying you got a problem. All you'll do is make the DA mad, and before you know it he'll have all of you in front of a grand jury, under oath, committing perjury. Except there'll be one guy who'll be too scared to risk putting his white-collar ass in jail, and then every one of you is up to your eyeballs in more trouble than you want to handle.

"So far there's no crime, you know. I had two lawyers check it very carefully. There's no law anywhere that says you can't give answers to contestants. It might not be nice, but it isn't illegal. But that's only so far. Now if the bunch of you get together and conspire to withhold information, that could be illegal. And perjury's plenty illegal. Five years' worth in lots of states, including this one."

"So far nobody's under oath," I said.

"That's just the point. So far is what we're talking about. And so far it may be bad, but it isn't out of hand. Embarrass the DA too much and it will be.

"Embarrassment's what it's all about up to now," he said. "The DA doesn't want to be embarrassed, and neither do you.

But he's got a job to do, so don't push him any further. And don't worry so much about being embarrassed. The problem here is legal, not PR. Why don't I use the bathroom first?"

I nodded, and that had been the last we'd said about it. He'd left by the time I got up the next morning, having straightened up the couch so carefully there was no trace of his having been there.

The advice had been right, of course. No laws broken; why start breaking them now?

Good, simple advice, but impossible to follow. And that was why I was waiting right now for my interview with an assistant district attorney.

Impossible to follow for two reasons. First, the admission would destroy us. If we admitted the whole thing had been a giant hoax, there was a ton of righteous wrath out there, ready to smash us all.

But the second reason was even stronger. Frank Dean was the one who felt it most deeply.

Never! he had said. He had given his word. With the breaking of the first news stories, every contestant he had ever spoken to had called in a panic, seeking Frank Dean's reassurance that he would never forget his commitment. He had sworn to each of them separately that no matter what happened he would never reveal the fact that he had given them answers. Never, he had now promised again. Never. The obligation was absolute. These people were terrified of losing respect, losing status, losing friends, losing jobs. Two were lawyers who feared disbarment. All had painted themselves into corners that had now become cells of private terror.

The doorknob clicked, the sharp metallic sound snapping my back into place, upright. I sat rigidly, waiting for someone to enter. There was muffled conversation on the other side, then silence. Then finally the door swung into the room, giving me my first glimpse of short, slight, steel-rimmed Ira Lefkowitz. He smiled a brief greeting, a mechanical smile that had nothing behind it, and immediately looked down at the yellow sheets on his clipboard. "David Beach?" he asked. A conversation-starter, really. He knew who I was.

I nodded and he stuck out his hand stiffly. "Ira Lefkowitz. Thank you for coming down."

The thanks was a bow toward the fiction that all this was strictly voluntary. There was no grand jury, you see, so of course there were no subpoenas. But they would appreciate our coming down to answer questions, was the message they'd conveyed through our brand-new lawyer. Of course, we didn't have to cooperate, this new attorney had advised us; but that might look bad in the papers. Then Leo Montenegro, our latest savior, our Republican lawyer, our man with lines to the DA's office, had shrugged. In the weeks, months, years to come, I became painfully familiar with that special shrug. It was the gesture most frequently used to summarize our legal position.

Ira Lefkowitz had stationed himself behind the desk and asked me to pull my chair into position opposite him. That had me facing away from the dressmaker's dummy and seemed to destroy the theory of the hidden microphone. Unless, of course, the dressmaker's dummy had no meaning at all and someone devoid of imagination had simply taped a bug under the desk.

"The boring stuff first," he said, taking a surprisingly elaborate silver filigree ballpoint pen from his jacket. Full name, address, date of birth, telephone number, educational background, title on the show and within the company, and length of time employed by Stu Leonard Productions. And, oh, yes, marital status. He was left-handed and wrote a cramped, falling-backward script with his wrist arched high in an awkward wrap-around. He put the pen on the desk when he was finished.

"Somebody told me you'd gone to Yale," he said, looking down at his notes.

I shook my head.

"Doesn't matter," he said. He pushed his notes a few inches away and tapped the desk for a moment, trying to decide where to begin. Then he cleared his throat carefully and picked up the pen again, just to have something to hold. "Before we start," he said slowly, "you should know there's been a new development. We now have a second contestant who appeared on your program who tells us that he or she was given material help; that is, questions and answers."

That went right through me, just as he'd known it would. A second accusing contestant, Leo Montenegro had advised us, would be the confirmation they'd be looking for. Leo, as he'd insisted we call him, had asked if there could be such a second contestant. Impossible, Stu had assured him.

He or she, Ira Lefkowitz had carefully said. He or she usually translates to she, but not this time, I didn't think. Because if there *was* a second contestant I was fairly certain of who it would be. It had to be Ginger Malloy.

Ginger had been my biggest fear right from the beginning. If he'd been down here for an interview, it wouldn't have taken the clumsiest interrogator more than eight seconds to figure out that this amiable but ignorant man couldn't possibly have answered even one question without a large portion of what they seemed to refer to around here as material help.

My fears about Ginger had been compounded by the fact that he had disappeared as soon as the investigation had begun. Simply dropped out of sight without a word to me or anyone else in the building, replaced by a new janitor who introduced himself in the hall one day. If there really was a second contestant who'd given them their confirmation, I had a large mind-bet on Ginger.

"I want you to know all the facts," Ira Lefkowitz went on, "because it means we now have everything we need to take this to the grand jury. I still hope that won't be necessary. And it may not be if you people will at last begin to cooperate."

It was all nice and polite, but the message was loud and clear.

"I'm here," I said.

He nodded. "Yes, I know. And I hope you're here to be helpful."

266

"Okay," I said.

He looked straight at me, sternly, continuing the warning. And the look had just the effect he meant it to have. He was the law, and he knew I'd come here to defy him. If I persisted, I did so at my peril. I was every bit as frightened as he meant me to be.

"I'm a nurturer," Carla said, zipping around a taxi and pulling in at the curb.

"No, you're not. You drive too fast. You drive an open car. Nurturers drive ambulances."

She slipped out of her side of the car in a tight, practiced move that kept her door from being sheered off by a passing bus. "Ambulances weave in and out of traffic and scare people half to death. They're big and threatening. My cozy little car holds just two people."

I got out and looked around. It looked like a loading zone to me. "You sure you want to park here?"

She locked the door. "We'll only be a minute."

Why lock the door of an open car? I had no idea. She came around and put her arm through mine. "I love Saturday, don't you?"

I nodded.

"No work and the stores are open. If you don't think that's paradise, go back where you came from, buddy."

We were heading toward Saks, which had advertised a preseason sale on comforters that had reminded Carla that by the end of last winter she had developed an unreasonable fear of her electric blanket.

"Buy something," she urged as we cleared the revolving door. "A tie, a wallet. It's therapeutic."

"I feel fine," I said.

"I know. But why not feel *better?*"

You can't argue with that, so I just smiled.

I'd moved in with Carla two weeks after all this had started.

There'd been one night when we'd talked till late, and then after all those months of disciplined friendship we'd gone to bed together.

I'd buried myself in Carla. She knew my fears, my shame, my horror at my own behavior. I needed to be with her constantly. And while it would have made more sense for her to move into my larger apartment, I was the one who needed refuge.

There was no one else I wanted to see. Days were spent alone with Stu in that depressing hotel office suite now that the network, with Capricorn's backing, had removed us from the show. It was all for the best, Donald Scheer had explained at one of those brown-lettuce luncheons in the Capricorn dining room. It would just be for the few weeks it would take to put this thing to rest, and then we'd all be back. We understood completely, Stu had reassured him from the tiny adjacent kitchen, popping stale rolls while he searched for the instant coffee.

The hotel suite had been the first offices we'd looked at, and Stu had taken them on the spot. The suite was furnished, the phones were in, and it was convenient. Besides, it was only to be for a week or two. So that's where we spent our days now. All day. Every day, Monday through Friday. Going down to the newsstand for every edition of every paper. Surrounded by it every minute of every day. At night, I wanted to see no one but Carla.

Valerie Reed had called, and I'd made excuses. Of course it was all untrue, I'd earnestly assured her the very afternoon I'd gotten back from lying my head off to Ira Lefkowitz. I promised I'd call her as soon as things eased up.

Margo I'd spoken to only once, to turn down her invitation to appear on a segment she was arranging to discuss the accusations. Elliott Cross would be on, she told me, and someone from the network. Stu had turned her down, and she wanted to know if I'd appear. That was the show where Elliott Cross, looking straight at the camera, swore to everyone watching that no one had ever given him answers; that if anyone had ever tried he would instantly have reported such an attempt to the proper authorities; that those who knew him would be well aware that no other course would have been possible for him. "I do not believe in deception," he had said with the simple eloquence that had always been his hallmark. There'd been a silence after that. And finally Margo had said she'd found it deeply moving, and then led into a commercial.

Carla held the patchwork quilt at arm's length, and then slowly put it down. "I can't let you do it. It's too expensive."

"That's partly why I want to. Half the fun is buying you something expensive."

She shook her head. "Some other time. This time I'd feel as if I had you cornered."

"Okay," I said. "Forget it. Then next week, when it's inconvenient, I'll have to come back here on my own, try to remember what it was you liked, and wind up buying some ugly serape. But that's okay. That's better than having you feel as if you pushed me into it."

She looked at me and smiled, and when the saleswoman came over I whipped out my checkbook and started writing, only to be told that they would accept checks only on merchandise that was being sent. Carla wanted to take it with us, so the paperwork got changed as she charged it to her account and I gave her the check made out to the store, which she'd then send in after they billed her. Complicated, but when you're a deadbeat who can't get people to accept his checks, you have to settle for whatever works. For a minute, it took the edge off the presentation, but only for a minute.

We were heading for the Berkshires, to see what was left of the foliage display and then bundle overnight in an old inn some friend at work had recommended. That decision had been made yesterday, after the DA had announced that the quiz-show accusations would indeed be turned over to the grand jury, that witnesses would be subpoenaed, and that it would then be up to the grand jury to decide what action was appropriate. In other words, Leo Montenegro had explained, whether or not there'd be indictments.

"I want to sleep with it tonight," Carla shouted over the wind as we flew up the Taconic. She meant the quilt, of course. There'd been plenty of comforters, including the ones on sale, but once we'd seen the bright colors of the handmade patchwork quilt, nothing else was possible. I nodded. Conversation was difficult with the wind banging at us in the open car.

Dinner was so comfortable that neither of us would admit how bad the food was. After dinner, we moved to the wicker furniture at the living-room end and sat in front of the fire sipping brandy. We stayed there until another couple sat down on the couch at right angles to ours and started what they thought was a pleasant conversation. But conversations with strangers could never be pleasant for me just then because they always led to the one question I couldn't handle; the one about what I did. So I started yawning and we excused ourselves and went up to bed even though it was only nine-thirty. We stripped the tan comforter off the bed and replaced it with our patchwork quilt. It was under that beautiful quilt that I suddenly found myself filled with more than I'd ever expected to feel for another human being.

20

IN THE BEGINNING, THERE'D STILL BEEN ENOUGH WORK TO KEEP us busy. And while that didn't cure anything, at least it provided something else to think about.

There'd been the new show to get launched, with its devilish banging wheels that tore themselves apart every morning in rehearsal, and then, miraculously, clicked smoothly into place every day on the air. There was a backup system, of course, but we never had to use it. "It's the red light," Stu had insisted. "I swear to God, it knows when it's on." Nobody had a better explanation.

The new show had been successful right from the beginning, but Stu and I were gone after the second week. Part of our banishment; the network part. Toby was left in charge, finally promoted to producer. Twice a week she was summoned to the hotel suite that everyone but Stu called Elba, to go over material. Then the visits became less frequent as the show problems lost their urgency, completely overwhelmed by the awful realities of what had now escalated into a grand jury investigation.

Frank Dean had testified, swearing under oath that he had never given questions or answers to anyone. I might or might not be called, Leo Montenegro wasn't sure. Stu probably would *not* be, since he could be considered the target of this investigation. Contestants, of course, had testified; an endless procession of decent, frightened, cornered human beings, caught at something most of them hadn't really wanted to do in the first place, and now seeing themselves with too much to lose if they admitted the truth. Except, of course, for Matthew Sklar. And that second contestant Ira Lefkowitz had warned us about, who turned out to be not Ginger Malloy at all, but Olivia Ryan.

Olivia Ryan called a press conference the day she finished in the grand jury room to summarize her testimony and to announce that prior to every appearance on the show, she had sent herself registered letters which would now establish the fact that Frank Dean had given her answers. Why was she admitting to this? Simply to serve the truth. Had she always planned to do this? No. Then why had she sent herself the questions and answers by registered mail? Just so she'd have them in case it ever became necessary to substantiate her story.

This second revelation had been enough for Capricorn to discover the fact that "Face to Face" was suffering from declining ratings that now made it advisable for them to drop the show. There was no connection, they insisted, between their decision and the current investigation. Nothing, after all, had yet been proven. It was simply a matter of dropping a part of their advertising campaign that was no longer delivering viewers.

The legal scoreboard now showed one contestant who said Stu Leonard had given him help, and one who accused Frank Dean. Would there be others, Leo Montenegro asked? Stu shrugged. The famous shrug. We were telling Leo Montenegro the truth by now. There could be, but it wasn't likely. Why's that? Well, because the others had begged Frank Dean not to admit what had happened. But suppose they're overcome by the greater fear of legal consequences? They won't be, Stu said. But they *could* be, our lawyer insisted. Frank Dean had better go back in and change his testimony. He was under oath, and he was in jeopardy.

But Frank Dean wouldn't hear of it. As long as there was even one contestant left who was still dependent on his holding to his end of the bargain, he would never admit to anything. Never.

And he didn't. And on the last Tuesday in January, 1959, he was indicted for perjury.

There was a birthday party in Larchmont that night, and I was to meet Carla there. The party was for her boss, the man they called the creative head of the agency. He was turning forty and seemed to think that was terribly funny, so his wife was throwing this party to help him shake hands with middle age.

Carla had gone ahead, to help blow up balloons. I had given serious thought to calling her there and begging off, but then it seemed as if forcing myself to function might do more good than retreating to a corner and sucking my thumb.

Frank Dean had dropped into the office late that afternoon. He had been at home when he'd gotten the news from Leo Montenegro. Yes, his wife was fine. Then he spent a couple of private minutes talking with Stu, during which he repeated again that nothing on earth could get him to change his mind. It was almost seven when he left, and I walked him to the corner. Neither of us said a word.

I stopped at a newsstand outside Grand Central and quickly picked up the afternoon papers. I'd already had a glance at the headlines, at every kiosk on the way. Front page. Lead story.

I bought my ticket, checked the schedule, and saw that if I hurried I could make an earlier train than the one I'd planned on. I rushed through the gate and boarded the rear car just seconds before they shut the doors. The car was jammed, not a seat to be had, and as I turned to walk toward the front, it suddenly hit me full in the face. Spread in front of me like a tableau in some stark, surreal movie was this sea of threatening headlines, this simple result of people reading their evening papers that had arranged itself into a terrifying display. Row after row of PRODUCER INDICTED! Car after car of the endless rows moving past me as I worked my way forward in search of a seat. So perfect was each paper's position that it seemed as if it had all been rehearsed; as if each commuter had checked with some director ("Like this?") and gotten an approving nod.

I found a seat toward the front of the train, slumped down in my overcoat, and took a minute to catch my breath. Then I opened the *New York Post,* looking for some other story; anything to take my mind away from it. I flipped the pages idly, turning them over unable to focus on anything. Finally, toward the back, there was a drawing that caught my eye; a sketch of how the new flag would look, now that Alaska had entered the Union. Seven rows of seven stars each. A lumpish, boring square would replace that elegant rectangle about which I suddenly found myself unreasonably sentimental.

I got off at 125th Street. It had started to drizzle; a light winter mist. There were no cabs at the corner, so I started south on Park, wondering why nobody mugged me. There were two kids talking in a doorway, and I crossed the street to avoid walking past them. It was almost a relief to have something else to worry about.

I walked past the scenery shop that had built our three-wheeled monstrosity, then over to Lex and down, looking for a cab at first, then just walking home.

Home, of course, was Carla's place now, but I stopped off at my apartment on the way, just because I was passing by. The mailbox was stuffed with junk, so I cleaned that out and threw most of it away when I got upstairs. The telephone started ringing while I was looking through a notice from my accountant, but I didn't answer. Whoever it was was persistent. Eight, ten rings. But it finally stopped.

Still sitting in my wet overcoat I decided I'd better call Carla. She'd left me the number, just in case. She was always doing careful things like that. It didn't go with the way she whipped her car through traffic. I fished in several pockets before I found the neatly typed yellow card. FOR EMERGENCY USE ONLY: and then the number.

A young kid answered, too young to be identifiable as either a boy or a girl, and then, after a moment's confusion about what or who *I* was, he or she went off to get Carla.

"I had a feeling you'd call," she said.

"You don't mind?"

"Of course not. I tried to get you. You must have just gotten in."

"I'm not in. I'm at my place. What's wrong?"

"Nothing. Just some people here are asking questions. About the story in the paper. I thought it might be awkward for you to come here."

"I thought so, too. I'll see you later, okay?"

"Okay. David?"

There was a pause as she kept herself from asking the forbidden question. I took her off the hook.

"I'm okay," I said.

"That's good. I know it's dumb. I know you're no more okay now than you were before you said it, but it makes me feel better. It's like telling people to drive carefully. Do you know how many accidents that prevents?"

"Thousands."

"I won't be terribly late."

"Be careful on the road. This could get slippery."

"Okay."

It was probably just the steam heat working its way through the damp overcoat, but I started to feel the return of some vital glow I hadn't even known was missing. "Do we need anything from my place? I mean, as long as I'm here."

There'd been party sounds in the background, but now she

cupped the phone and shut out everything. "There's only one thing I need from your place," she whispered, and then she hung up.

Stu grabbed the phone on the first ring. He always did at Elba. "Yeah, he is," he said, and then he put it on hold and signaled for me to pick up the extension. It was Toby.

"Listen," she said, "I need to talk to you when you're alone. Call me back when you can."

"Okay," I said.

"But don't hang up yet," she said quickly. "You have to tell me something, anything at all, just so he hears there was a reason I called you. Why don't you give me Shadow's home phone number."

"I don't have the number with me," I said carefully enough for Stu to hear. "But it should be on my Rolodex."

"Okay, that should do it," she said. "Call me back as soon as you can." And she hung up.

"What does she need?" Stu asked.

I told him, and he nodded and went back to the roundup story on the quiz investigations that was in the current *Newsweek*.

An hour later he was gone, heading downtown for a strategy meeting with Leo Montenegro. As if strategy was our problem now. I called Toby back.

"There's something I have to show you," she said excitedly. "Can you meet me here?"

"At the office? Can't do that. Off-limits. You want to meet somewhere for lunch?"

"I need more privacy than that." She paused for a second. "Can you come to my place around six o'clock? It's important."

I thought about that for a moment, and then told her I'd be there. I called Carla to tell her I wouldn't be home till late, and then felt a little strange when she didn't ask me why. I had this feeling I should be giving her a reason.

"Thank you for coming," Toby said when I arrived. Whatever this was, it was obvious that it was strictly business. There'd been only that one time for us, and it was something we both treated as if it had never happened.

"Would you like something to drink?"

I shook my head.

She led me to the couch and sat me down facing six of the company's business envelopes spread out on the coffee table. They were all addressed to her, and they were numbered in pencil in the lower righthand corner, one through six.

"I give up," I said. "What's it all about?"

"Okay," she said, sitting down next to me. "Notice they were all sent registered mail."

I did notice after she said it, and now I was beginning to understand.

"I sent those to myself," she said. "And then I opened three of them and sealed them up again. See if you can tell which ones."

"You want me to open them?"

She nodded. "But examine them carefully before you do."

I turned the envelopes over and looked at them one at a time. On all of them, the circular date stamp overlapped the line where the flap was sealed to the body of the envelope; and on all of them the halves of the circles lined up perfectly. I opened them up one at a time, by peeling the flap back from the envelope as carefully as possible. There were newspaper clippings inside all of the envelopes, but Toby asked me not to look at them. I had no idea which envelopes had been tampered with.

"No idea at all," Toby repeated triumphantly.

"Absolutely none."

"Envelopes one, two, and six were not opened after I received them. Three, four, and five *were*. Look at the date stamps, and then look at the dates on the clippings inside."

The date stamped on all the envelopes was two days ago. Envelopes three, four, and five all contained clippings from this morning's *New York Times,* clippings that could have been inserted only *after* the envelopes had gone through the mail.

"Neat trick," I said admiringly. "How did you do it?"

"I'll tell you how in a minute," she said, unable to keep the excitement out of her voice. "But first, do you see the point?"

I did indeed. Olivia Ryan had supposedly proved her contention with registered letters. She said she had put questions and answers in an envelope the day before each program on which those questions were asked. She had then sent each envelope to herself by registered mail and left the accumulated envelopes unopened. The envelopes had been opened by the district attorney's office, which verified the fact that the seals had never before been broken. All of which meant that Olivia Ryan must have had foreknowledge of the questions.

"But not necessarily," Toby said. "If I could do it, so could she."

What Toby had done was simple, once she explained it. She had shut three of the envelopes not by using moisture, but by tacking the flaps down with just a touch of rubber cement. That had been all that was needed to hold the flaps in place. All six envelopes then received the postmaster's registry stamp and went through the mail. When Toby got them back, it was easy enough to pop up the flaps on the three that had been lightly cemented, wipe off the dried remnants of rubber cement, fill the envelopes with today's newspaper clippings, and then, since they'd never been properly sealed before, seal them normally by licking them shut, with the two halves of the circular registry date right back in perfect alignment. She was very proud of herself.

"Not so fast," I said. "In the first place, I'm not exactly a crime lab. *I* couldn't tell the difference, but how do we know what kind of tests they submitted those envelopes to?"

"They don't do magic," she said. "What could they look for? There was no rubber cement, because all of it was wiped off. And doing it my way, the envelope itself had really been sealed only once; *after* I got it back. I just don't believe they have a test in this world that could have picked out my envelopes."

The funny thing was, I thought she was probably right. Even if there was some theoretical lab test that might pick up the trace of rubber cement, I found myself doubting that anyone had done it. It suddenly seemed quite possible that the sanctity of registered letters was just one of those things we'd all been accepting all these years. If Toby had figured out a way to beat it, then Olivia Ryan could have.

She *could* have. But what kind of sense would any of that have made?

"Even if it's true that the letters could have been faked, why would she have done it? What reason would she have to create false evidence that would make it seem as if Frank had been giving her answers?"

"Who knows?" Toby said. "But the point is, that's exactly what she did."

"It is?"

She looked at me a little strangely. "Well, isn't it? Either Frank was giving her answers, or he wasn't."

I let that sink in for just a moment, and then, of course, it sank in *all* the way. Amazing as it seemed, Toby, née Astrid Knudsen, still believed that Stu and Frank and I were telling the world, including her, the truth. Despite everything she knew about Stu; despite having heard Matthew Sklar's accusations, and Olivia Ryan's, she still believed that we were innocent.

"Yes," I said lamely. "I guess it is."

"Will you tell Stu about this? He'll listen if you tell him. You know how impatient he gets with me."

"Okay," I said. "I'll tell him." And I did. And I thought he'd go right through the ceiling, he was so excited. I mean, this was terrific stuff. He wanted to set up a press conference right away, to challenge the district attorney's office to set up a test to determine which of several envelopes we'd provide had been tampered with. We'd get someone in public life with an impeccable reputation to verify which envelopes were which. We'd make fools of all of them.

But Leo Montenegro wasn't nearly as impressed. In the first place, he reminded us, there was a basic fact here; one that we knew, and that the DA's office wasn't likely to forget: that Olivia Ryan's envelopes were in fact genuine for the simple reason that Olivia Ryan was telling the truth. And furthermore, he went on, a press conference would accomplish nothing more than to bring down the further wrath of the DA's office. A red flag at a bull, was the familiar but accurate phrase he used. Listen, he said, thank Toby for playing with her envelopes, and tell her to start writing detective stories.

Stu brought up the subject often after that, with new reasons for wanting to raise it again with Leo. I don't really know if he ever did.

Was it worse or better for me, knowing that I had it coming? I used to wonder about that. Frank Dean and Stu claimed to see no moral problem in what we had done. We'd been dealing in entertainment. If people were fooled, it was because they wanted to be. The analogy with magic shows came up again and again. Was the magician really sawing the woman in half? Would the world consider him more honorable if, in fact, he were? The heights attained by these fanciful rationales peaked one afternoon when Frank Dean contended, in earnest tones, that what we had done was really no different from what was done every day in Westerns. They didn't use real bullets, did they?

Their pain, Frank's and Stu's, came from what they saw as the unfairness of the attacks against us. Mine from quite the opposite. I had felt guilty from the first, and typically, getting caught had turned guilt into shame. It's wonderful how getting caught can sharpen the conscience. For a while, I even found myself feeling guilty about *that*. But then I decided to leave myself alone. Or try to, anyway.

Ira Lefkowitz called for a meeting with Leo Montenegro. It's not too late, the DA's office said. Come in now, all of you, and admit the truth. Let Frank Dean go back into the grand jury room and recant; there'd be a recommendation for the indictment to be dropped.

We caucused in Leo's office and talked forever. What would happen to the contestants? Probably nothing, Leo said. But what guarantees would we have? Leo shrugged, and Frank Dean, who hadn't said a word, suddenly turned very red and stormed out of the overstuffed leather office. I followed him and finally caught up with him on the street. He didn't want to talk, but I stayed with him. This might be his last chance, I reminded him. He could be looking at a jail sentence. But he shook his head and walked away. *Never,* was what he'd promised.

Tommy Nakamura would not take no for an answer. No decisions have to be made now, he'd said. Just come out and look around. So Carla and I flew out one Friday morning in April and were met at the airport by a smiling Tommy and his wife, Anita, who drove the Mercedes convertible.

"I never drive," Tommy said. "I hate to drive. My wife and children spoil me; I never have to."

The house was in Pacific Palisades, and the guest room had a view of the ocean. Tommy had insisted we stay with him. It was only for the weekend. Tomorrow he'd take me to the showroom. That was the point of the visit.

We did that in the morning, and it was quite impressive. Business was brisk, and picking up every month, Tommy said. He showed me the sales charts, and the jagged lines looked like an optimist's dream.

"We need a salesman, and you need a new life," he said over the sandwiches his runner brought in. "Make your own hours. While you're getting paid here, make a new career for yourself in your own business, if you want to. Or stay and grow with me. Any way you want it."

I nodded, listening, not wanting to commit. That afternoon

I borrowed the car to drive Carla out to the edge of the ocean, to watch the sunset. We watched it with the top down and I wanted to pull her head to my shoulder, but I had the feeling it wasn't that kind of day.

"Well, what do you think?" I asked her on the way back.

"I hated it," she said.

I'd meant about the job, but she was dealing with the sunset.

"I mean, it's backward, is the problem. The sun's supposed to rise up out of the ocean, not sink down into it. It's like living in a mirror."

"I thought it looked pretty good," I said.

She turned to me. "Are we talking about today? Or are we discussing forever?"

"Why don't we start with today?"

"Today was fine. But that's all you can put me down for. Just today."

"I take it that means you don't want to move to California."

"I don't like palm trees, brown hills, or free car washes with every tank of gas. And when I look across an ocean, I like to imagine Europe, not Japan. Japan attacked us."

"That was a long time ago. They apologized."

"Maybe, but I still don't like it here."

"How do you know? You just got here. What are you so pissed about?"

She turned front again and stared at the road. There was no more talk about it.

She was quiet through dinner at the steak house in Malibu that we went to with Tommy and Anita. There wasn't another word about any of it until late that night, in bed, after we'd made love as quietly as possible, remembering that our room was next door to their twelve-year-old son's.

"I don't want to stop you from doing anything," she whispered. "But my life's right where I am. I love my job. I love that dirty, abrasive city. I even love my dumb apartment. But you have to do whatever you think makes sense for you."

"I won't leave you," I said.

"Bad reason," she said.

I shook my head.

She sat halfway up and looked at me. "Turn it down because you won't be happy selling cars."

"What's wrong with selling cars?"

"Nothing, for people who love it."

"What about the fact that there's no way I can work these days?"

"You can do something. There's always something."

I shook my head again. "You don't seem to understand. There's no way *any* of us can work in this business. Maybe forever."

My voice had gotten louder and she put her hand to her lips.

"You can do something. There's always something. But don't do this."

I pulled her toward me and kissed her forehead. "Okay," I said. "But stay with me."

She nodded, and then began to cry a little.

I had an urge to suggest making things permanent between us, but I try not to make important decisions when my pulse is racing. I waited till we got back to New York, and with the urge still very strong I asked her if she'd marry me after all the problems settled down. She said now or never, so we did it as soon as we could arrange the paperwork.

21

NEW YORK WAS BULLSHIT, STU SAID. *THIS* WAS THE TOWN. YOU could feel it all around you. The power waves that pulsed from the Capitol Building and the White House; the serene sense of history that rose from deep inside this white marble pantheon here beside the tidal basin.

"My God, what a man," he said, stirring himself almost to tears.

The Jefferson Memorial was the one spot he tried to visit whenever he came to Washington. "I used to know the Declaration by heart," he said as we walked out. "I had to recite it once, in fourth grade. You can't believe how much I loved doing that."

He revered Thomas Jefferson, he said. He'd once made it a point to learn everything he could about the man, but now all he remembered was the basic encyclopedia stuff; third president, Louisiana Purchase, things like that. He turned to me. "How much would you give to be able to recall every fact you've ever learned?"

"Ten dollars," I said.

He smiled patiently. "I was thinking more in terms of pieces of your soul."

Stu was heavily into the soul these days. The brass Buddha, for example, had been sent for from the office we hadn't been to for over a year, and now rested on the window ledge near his desk in the Elba suite. Sometimes when I'd come in at odd hours I'd find him seated in semidarkness, staring at the small statue, settled into a tranquil pose I'm sure he meant as meditation. When we were alone, his conversation was often flavored with vague references to the lessons of the Buddha, and at these moments I found myself faintly uncomfortable as I imagined the genuine followers who would disapprove of this invented, garbled version of what were, for them, sacred teachings. Stu would have seen no disrespect; he was taking those few things he'd learned, those basic encyclopedia facts that anyone can memorize in five minutes, and using them to make adjustments to the soul he'd so recently discovered.

The waiting cab started up when the driver saw us. Cruising cabs would be hard to find, the driver had warned us, so Stu had worked out an arrangement.

Stu reached out grandly and held the door open for me. As senior man in age and rank, he would normally be the one to receive such treatment, but having just left the monument to our nation's leading democrat, Stu was filled with egalitarian fervor.

"Drive around for a while," Stu said to the driver. "Let's watch the city light up."

It was true that he loved this town. His face had been reborn on the drive in from the airport yesterday, as the familiar buildings came into sight. He'd insisted that we stay at the Hay-Adams because it was just across the park from the White House. And today, as soon as we'd finished with the lawyers, he'd gone off on a tour of the Capitol Building as if he'd been a carefree grade-school teacher.

"He doesn't seem very worried," I'd said to Leo Montenegro.

"That's because his mind's made up," Leo said. "It's easier when you've decided what you're going to do."

Here's where things stood.

The grand jury in New York had finished up in June, with no further indictments. No criminal offense had been found, except for perjury; and while they suspected rather a lot of it, the only case they could make was the one against Frank Dean. So, damaged as that left us, at least nothing had gotten worse. It's amazing what sometimes passes for good news. There'd actually been some minor celebrating at Elba.

But the celebrations ended quickly. No sooner had the grand jury results been announced than the House Subcommittee on Legislative Oversight decided to look into the matter; if no laws had been broken, then it seemed evident to them that the country needed some new legislation. So hearings were scheduled, subpoenas went out, and Leo Montenegro arranged for us to meet in Washington with Todd Ericson, a former White House adviser in the Truman administration. "Toddy knows his way around," Leo had said.

Toddy was hired (or put on retainer, to give them their lingo) and went off to meet with Harold Kovacs, the subcommittee's chief counsel. He came back looking grim and shaking his head. There were five of us seated around his gleaming conference table: Leo Montenegro, Hank Sachs, Stu, me, and, of course, the well-connected Toddy himself, who got our attention by leaning back and taking an eternity to light his pipe.

They have a chart, he finally said. It's something the DA's office put together in New York. It's very clear, he said, and very thorough. It follows the appearance of every contestant on every episode of "Face to Face." And following this chart, he said, one sees in graphic detail how interconnected everything was. If Matthew Sklar was given questions and answers, then the same had to be true of Elliott Cross. And if it were true of Elliott Cross, then it would have to be true of the person who beat him. And so on, and on.

But, said Toddy, they are saying that they have no desire to humiliate contestants. Here's what they're willing to do. (He took a pause to get us leaning forward.) If Frank Dean, Stu Leonard, and Elliott Cross will come in and testify truthfully and fully, no other contestants need be named. And they'll recommend to the New York DA that Frank Dean's indictment be dropped.

And, asked Stu, what's the alternative? What happens if we do not agree to testify along the lines they find acceptable?

Todd Ericson stroked his chin and looked up to the ceiling before surrendering to the gesture that seemed to sum things up as perfectly in Washington as it had in New York: the familiar shrug.

That meeting had taken place two weeks ago, and in the meantime we had all met among ourselves and argued and agonized. At first it had not been possible to budge Frank Dean, but gradually he began to see that the choice we were faced with was no choice at all. Either we accepted this best arrangement that our well-respected Washington lawyer had been able to work out, this *deal,* as Frank Dean had contemptuously referred to it, or things would go from terrible to something worse. And the attempt to shield contestants would result in everyone's being named.

Now we were back in Washington again, with a couple more days of pain to be gotten through. Matthew Sklar and Olivia Ryan had testified today, with no surprises in what they had to say. The surprises would begin tomorrow morning, when Elliott Cross was scheduled. Then Stu in the afternoon, and Frank Dean some time tomorrow. Frank wouldn't come to Washington until the very last second. He didn't love this town as much as Stu did.

Our cab pulled up in front of the Hay-Adams, and Stu reached into his breast pocket to get his wallet. He handed the driver a fifty and, while he waited for his change, opened the folded sheet of paper he'd taken from the same inside pocket.

"I've been carrying this with me ever since the first stories broke," he said quietly. "For over a year I've had the feeling that almost any day I might have a reason to show it to you. But now I won't be needing it anymore."

He handed the sheet to me and I opened it up and angled it to catch the light from the street lamp. It was the handwritten paragraph he'd had me sign that first day we'd met. *I hereby agree that both while I am an employee of Stuart Leonard Productions, and after such employment terminates, I will fully respect the privacy and confidentiality of anything I might have learned here.*

He turned to me and smiled. "Now it doesn't mean shit."

The screaming kid in the dining room whose voice I'd first heard all the way out in the lobby turned out to be Ricky, Stu Leonard's son, who had just knocked over a glass of milk. A frazzled young woman was using a large napkin to wipe off his pants as the other guests continued to read their morning papers, carefully paying no attention. Stu sat patiently, making no attempt to calm the boy down.

I came over to the table and said good morning, and Stu said, "You remember Ricky, of course?" and I said yes, but the truth was I would never have recognized him. It had been three years since that day in the park, and the boy had grown enormously.

"And this is his friend Felicia," he said above the noise, indicating the young woman, who looked at me quickly and then turned her attention back to the still loudly crying Ricky.

"He spilled some milk," Stu explained unnecessarily, "and it seems to have him quite upset."

The boy finally calmed down and resumed his seat, and the dining room settled back to its normal quiet.

In his continuing enthusiasm for this capital city, Stu had called New York last night and arranged with Felicia, who was Ricky's companion these days, for the two of them to fly down to Washington early this morning. The plan was to get in some light sightseeing this morning, attend the subcommittee session at which he was scheduled to testify this afternoon, and then take a bus tour tomorrow.

I wanted to be sure I understood. "You mean you want Ricky in the room when you testify?"

Stu nodded. "He might as well hear it firsthand." He turned to the boy. "Would you like another glass of milk?" Ricky nodded. Stu gestured to the waiter and turned back to the boy.

"Remember where we're going this morning?" he asked him. She didn't wait for an answer. "We're going to see where the President lives, right, Ricky?" Ricky nodded enthusiastically, and no matter how much or how little he understood, it was obvious that he was glad to be here with his father.

"Felicia's trained to work with slow-learning children," Stu explained. "She's very good with him."

"Not always," she said, still looking a little disorganized. "I can't always control him."

"I can't always control myself," Stu said expansively, and Felicia smiled. "You do very well," he said to her gently, and she brushed a wisp of hair back into place with her fingers and nodded her thanks.

"Here's what I figured," Stu said, turning to me. "The trick is to salvage whatever good you can find. Make the best of it instead of the worst. I can't stop what's going on here, but what I can do is turn it into Ricky's introduction to his country's capital. When are you going back?"

The question was unexpected. "I don't know. Tonight, if I find out for sure they're not going to call me."

"They don't want you," Stu said. "Toddy checked that out again early this morning. Just Elliott Cross, then me, then Frank. They don't want to turn this into a circus." He laughed. He laughed because they'd already done that yesterday. That had been his comment as we'd watched the opening session. They'd begun by darkening the hearing room and showing the kinescope of the moment when Elliott Cross had defeated Matthew Sklar. Not exactly a noble moment now that the audience knew all the facts. They'd let it run right through the wild applause that had accompanied the triumphant Elliott's exit from his booth, and they'd stopped it just as he'd reached out to shake Matthew's hand.

"They love it," Stu had said contemptuously.

"Unnecessary," Todd Ericson had commented, shaking his head in disapproval.

The waiter brought the glass of milk and set it in front of Ricky.

"They don't want you," Stu said again, "and they don't want Mike Prince. They don't want to go out of their way to damage anybody's reputation. Except Elliott's, you see, and mine, and Frank's. We're dealing with saints here. A marvelous bunch of guys. Some of them I'd really like, Toddy says, if I met them under other circumstances. Anyway, there's not a reason in the world why you can't be out of here tonight."

Ricky had picked up the milk and Felicia was urging him to use both hands.

"So what happens to all of us now?" Stu asked.

A reasonable question. I wasn't sure.

"Do we stay together, or what?"

I didn't feel quite ready for this conversation. I said I hadn't decided what I'd do.

"You'll still be getting some royalty money. Why don't you do as you please?"

"As soon as I can figure out what that is."

"That's the nice thing about money," Stu said. "It gives you a little time."

I nodded, still not really wanting to have this talk. But I had to say something, so I mentioned that I might take some time to research an idea I had for a book.

Stu nodded back. "Where you going to work? You'll need an office."

I said the library was probably as good a place as any.

"You can still use the hotel office," he said, and I thanked him for that. "I mean, it's there. Why not help yourself? Did I tell you about the play Hank Sachs wants me to read?"

No, he hadn't.

It was a comedy by this TV sketch writer who'd written for all the variety shows and who Hank thought was pretty good. A first play, of course, but if it weren't, there'd be no way an unknown producer could get a shot at it. But Hank saw it as being commercial and wanted Stu to think about trying to produce it. "Read it next week," Stu urged. "If you like it, we can work on it together."

I nodded, but I knew it was something I wouldn't be doing.

We finished breakfast and the three of them left on their sightseeing tour. I took the small elevator up to my room and clicked on the television set to watch the morning's hearings. It wasn't yet nine o'clock, and as the set warmed up I heard Margo's voice a few seconds before the picture blossomed onto the screen. She was seated beside Madame Khrushchev, who had accompanied the premier on his trip to Washington for talks with Ike.

The pace of the interview was slow as it labored its way back and forth through the interpreter, but Madame Khrushchev was saying that the premier had enjoyed his helicopter ride over this beautiful capital city, and he hoped he'd be able to see much more of it before he left for home.

Margo was here in town. She might not have been assigned here just for us, but when our visit coincided with the equally publicized visit of the premier of the Soviet Union her presence here became essential. She, of course, was covering both stories, and with the skill I continued to admire even after having watched her pound away at what we'd done in an irregular series of interviews, roundtable discussions, and occasional revelations. She had handled it all meticulously, evenhandedly, and with a mask of calm that covered what was clearly outrage. I'd seen her do the hearings story yesterday, and it would have been painful enough if it had come from a stranger. She thanked Madame Khrushchev and turned to the camera and signed off.

I called home and got Carla just before she left for the office. I told her I'd be flying back some time tonight and turned down her offer to pick me up at the airport. I wouldn't be good company tonight; better to let me get home on my own. In fact, I told her, tonight was one of those nights when all smart copywriters would be fast asleep by the time their husbands got home.

Why wait around and fly back late? Because I needed the day alone. For one thing, there was the compulsion to stay in this capital that everyone seemed to admire and put myself through the ordeal of watching Elliott Cross and Stu. The hearings were being televised locally and knowing that, I couldn't leave without seeing them.

The station break ended and the hearings came on suddenly, with the kind of last-minute bustle and rustling of papers that the movies never get quite right. The session was gaveled to order, and Elliott Cross was called.

He moved down to the witness table and adjusted the microphone. In response to the first question, he told them his name and gave his occupation as pediatrician, and that's when I damn near turned the set off. I hadn't realized how painful this was going to be, and they hadn't even started yet. But then I kicked myself back into place with a lecture about how it wasn't me who was getting murdered up there, so stop feeling sorry for yourself.

He spoke quietly and answered every question just as he'd promised the subcommittee he would, truthfully and fully. And this time I was the one who saw his grace because I knew what this was doing to him. Whatever happened to Stu, to me, would be nothing compared with the total destruction he now faced. He was the one whose face had filled the screen. He was the one they'd admired.

At the noon recess I sent down for a sandwich and coffee,

and then couldn't touch either. And I was suddenly struck by something I hadn't realized before about the scene this morning in the dining room.

The basic difference in food habits between fat people and thin people is the way they respond when they're under pressure. When the tension mounts, the overweight stuff their faces, while the thin ones can't even look at food. Stu Leonard was clearly one of your heavyweights, but this morning, for the only time since I'd known him, he'd sat at a table within easy reach of food and hadn't touched a morsel.

At two o'clock the hearings resumed, and after some mumbled subcommittee business, Stu came on. I suddenly tightened as I watched him take the oath and start to answer questions. I forced myself to watch for maybe fifteen minutes and then turned off the set and packed, and got myself onto an earlier plane.

I testified in the plane on the way home. I shut my eyes and tried to nap, and there I was in some kind of paneled room with a dressmaker's dummy standing in the corner.

"Now, about this Uncle Joe," somebody said from an unfocused table in front of me.

"No more," I said, and he nodded and made the correction on his pad.

"But you crashed through his plate-glass window."

"I did," I said.

He shook his head sadly and took off his glasses. "You could spend your whole life trying to pay for a thing like that."

"It was very upsetting."

"But you were insured?"

I shook my head. "No, sir."

He thought about that for a moment, then put his glasses back on and looked down again at his notes. "There's more here, but I can't make any sense of it."

"No, sir, I suppose not."

He looked at me strangely for a minute. "Are you telling us the truth?"

"Yes, sir," I said respectfully.

There were three of them up there now, and the one in the middle took a moment to check with the others before turning back to me. He seemed ready to summarize.

"So what did you learn from all this?" he asked.

The answer seemed clear. "I learned that it's easier than it looks to shave the lather off an inflated balloon with a straight razor. There's really nothing to it."

He wrote that down carefully, then put his pen down and clasped his hands on top of the desk. When he spoke again, it was slowly and sternly.

"You're breaking my heart, do you know that?"

"Yes, sir. I understand."

He stared at me again, his head shaking slowly.

"Didn't you know something was wrong when the people you liked were lying, and the people you hated were telling the truth?"

I had no answer for that.